Warren Freeman

An Evil Wind

Warren Freeman is a practicing attorney &
writer. He and his wife, Melinda, live in
the Abel community in Cleburne County,
Alabama.

An
Evil
Wind

Warren Freeman

Published by Warren Freeman Publishing

LIBRARY OF CONGRESS CATALOGING-IN-PUBLICATION DATA

Freeman, Warren.
An Evil Wind: a novel/ Warren Freeman.
p. cm.
I. Title
TXu 1-859-507   2012

ISBN 978-09899433-0-7

Printed in the United States of America

September 2013

First Edition

ONE

Crossing the border had become easy. They said as much. "A smile, the right papers, good American English, and in five minutes you can watch the sunset in the richest nation in the world."

They said.

He had never been to America, and Marco was excited about the chance to go. A change to be sure from driving a tow motor at The Factory, and an even greater change from several years ago of hoeing corn in the hot afternoon sun after Catholic School all day.

Some of the men from The Factory that loaded the trucks had made the trip, those knowledgeable boys who seemed to always know something about everything.

"You will love the U.S.," they said.

"It's easy to take a load of mota across," one of them called out over the engine noise, as he maneuvered his tow motor to the edge of the loading dock, then onto the truck, dropping the flat holding the huge bale of cotton packed with pressure-sealed marijuana.

"The chuppa is inside; wrapped and

1

sealed tight," another said, using another slang word for the product, as he and another group readied the next bale, then looked after the tow motor as it dropped its load.

"The American dogs cannot smell it." Another said with a hint of pride.

"Hold up," an older heavy-set man called out. As the last one was loaded, he climbed onto the forks of the tow motor, his clipboard in hand, pointing with his pencil as he counted the double stacked 700 pound bales loaded into the seventeen foot truck. "Thirteen," he said, as he climbed down, making notations on his bill of lading.

"When I was young," he said to Marco's father--Miguel, who stood on the loading dock, wearing a worried look that hung from his face like a shroud, watching the loading, looking back and forth between workers, Senior Begal (the man in charge of operations) and his son. "I used to do it all the time: take a load to San Anton, get something to eat, head back. You got nothing to worry about. Just let him go and have a good time. Senor Begal has it all worked out."

He was wrong. They were wrong. And Senor Begal was wrong to send his son. Miguel knew too well the dangers.

Sure, if he was successful, he would be back and all would be well. But what about those boys that did not make it back home? What if he got caught?

He wanted his son to go to the great

United States of America, to school maybe, to work perhaps. But not like this. Not as a mule carrying freight. Yes, he knew what The Factory did. He knew that truckloads full of Marijuana left there each week. He knew that when he got his son a job there.

But packing the chuppa in cotton bales and running tow motors to load trucks was quite different from being a mule.

His boy would be crossing American soil with enough product in just one of those thirteen bales of cotton to put him in an American prison for life.

What if he gets caught? What will I tell his mother, Miguel thought, as he hugged Marco goodbye.

"Quit worrying, Papa. I know what I am doing."

With the confidence of youth and inexperience brimming from his face, a smiling Marco climbed into the large moving truck and drove through the opened gates, as a worried father watched his oldest son head north toward the border.

~~~~~

In spite of the uneventful-trip projections by Senor Begal, Marco felt uneasy, as he neared Nuevo Laredo. But he decided it was just his Papa's words bouncing in his head.

He had been working on the docks of the

3

factory since he was sixteen--almost three years. But this was the first time the boss had asked (told) him to make a delivery.

He handed the uniformed American his papers. Except for the California driver's license and social security card, he didn't know what was in them, but Senor Begal had told him what to say.

The guard at the border began his litany of questions: "Where are you from? What is your cargo? Anything to declare?"

Marco watched, nervously as dogs circled the truck, their armed masters watching them for any reaction, as the canines were directed toward particular parts of the truck, holding them sometimes, forcing them to sniff longer.

Now comes the real test, Marco thought, as he was made to get out of the truck, as the dogs climbed into the cab, sniffing at the seats. Then he watched as the trailer door was hoisted and they climbed on top of the cotton bales.

Nothing.

"O.K.," the guard said as he handed Marco his papers. Have a good trip."

So far so good.

Not many cars, Marco thought, as he pulled into Cowboy's Used Car Lot just off the southern bypass. *I am tired*. The three hour drive to San Antonio from the border seemed much longer.

Climbing out of the truck, he walked toward the glass-walled office at the back of the lot, past the dozen or so cars. There was water on the asphalt. *Oh, they just washed them*, Marco thought. *I wish I could drive that one back.* He stopped beside a red freshly washed Ford Mustang, its windshield lettering of 'nothing down' and the overhead flapping in the breeze of yellow and red flags strung across the lot helping to act as catalysts of desire for a boy who had never driven anything but his papa's thirty year old truck, a tow motor, and of course the monster he had just parked.

Marco knocked on the glass door. Through the glare of the afternoon sun, he could make out a man sitting behind a desk motioning for him to come in. The room was filled with smoke. Marco's cough caused the young girl bent down behind the desk to look up. She was young with reddish-blonde hair and peered from behind the desk, her eyelevel just above the desk top. Quickly she stood, a mild look of surprise on her face, as she straightened her disheveled sleeveless blouse over her short shorts, then climbed onto the man's lap. Her right hand slipping over his shoulder, as Marco walked in. Both she and the seated man stared at Marco as though he were an intruder who had no business being there.

The man abruptly stood, pushing the girl from his lap while placing his black Stetson hat over his black curly hair. Walking

5

past the girl to the side of the desk, he loudly said, "Howdy pard, Whazup?"

He had a disapproving, intimidating scowl on his face as he waited on an answer. He looked Marco up and down, as though sizing him up for a reaction.

Donnie Ray Tarpley was not a towering figure who could inspire immediate fear. He was short with legs that bowed out like the sides of a barrel full of apples. He had a ruddy, tanned complexion with an indented and very deep scar across his left cheek, which looked as though a cut had not been properly sutured.

With his brash loud tone and his black hat pulled down low next to his brow, Tarpley seemed to be attempting to inspire fear.

Marco appeared unfazed. Perhaps, because the fearsome look was tempered by this comic, cartoonish presentation of a cowboy outfit surrounding a prominently large nose, much larger than was needed for his face, which contrasted greatly with his small, beady, constantly blinking eyes that seemed to blink faster when he talked.

Before there was time enough to fully appreciate the miscellany visual, Tarpley spoke again, "Well, what do you want?"

Marco still did not answer. He was uncertain of what he should say, particularly since the man's costume looked so comical. *Should I laugh?*

The last thing he wanted to do on his first trip to America was insult an American.

But if I am supposed to laugh, it would be rude not to. At the carnivals at St. Sebastian Church, sometimes the priests would bring in someone dressed as a clown.

I always laughed, then. Of course that was expected.

There was more than just the black hat. He was dressed in a multi-colored, sequined cowboy shirt and blue jeans with a gold, shiny, thick bracelet on his right arm, with a heavy looking gold-ringed necklace-to match. The left hand wrist was wrapped in a turquoise stone bracelet, surrounded with engraved silver--fashioned as a coiled snake, with a matching snake motif on his belt buckle.

For Marco, this eclectic collection of gold, silver and turquoise jewelry mixed with the cowboy costume and the enhanced facial features, created a cartoon character presentation which was difficult to take seriously. Ray Tarpley looked as an actor without a stage. The gruff Texas drawl, the incessant blinking, the wide brimmed, black Stetson and his alligator-skin boots--the bookends for this costume, all made him appear more thespian than threat.

He was a pretend-cowboy, Marco was sure, and an answer to this character's questions did not come immediately, for it was more than a kid on his first trip from Mexico could take in and be expected to answer without some thought. Besides the costume, the blinks he made with those beady eyes were enough to keep any boy of mild curiosity occupied counting: three words--six blinks; and the blinking intensified as he spoke again.

"You da man Ken sent up here?"

During the entire presentation, the girl stood in modeling form, her head cocked to the side, her long slender legs predominant, as though waiting for a nonexistent photographer's instructions. Her look of allurement, however, came off as confused.

Looking back at the cowboy, Marco began to assimilate all that had been said about this stranger on leaving this morning from Mexico: *Blinky,* his friends called him; known for repossessing cars, selling cars, carousing with wild women, and--drug running. $10,000 to $20,000......that's how much he was going to be paid, *they said*, to take the load from Mexico deeper into the states--Atlanta, maybe the Carolinas.

The girl walked past Marco. The jingling sound of the door closing, as she left the office, jarred Marco's senses past the visual.

"I am sorry, what did you say?" Marco asked, finally responding.

"You da man Ken sent up here?"

"Who?"

"Ken Begal, at da Factory."

"Yes," Marco said, remembering that Senor Begal wanted only English spoken across the border. In fact Begal had told Marco that his command of the English language, as well as his youthful appearance, was the reason he was chosen for this trip.

"What's yore name, kid?"

"Marco Antonio Esgivas, sir."

"Sir?" Tarpley looked somewhat disbelieving at the show of respect.

"You a polite little motha ain't cha. Speak English good too."

Looking past Marco, he continued talking after the girl who was already out the door, "They sent me a kid dat just got off his mama's tit."

Moving to the front of the desk, he crossed his hands and propped against it. Pushing his hat back, he said, "How old are you, Marco Antonio Esgivas?"

"Nineteen, sir."

"I bet you ain't ever been laid yet, huh? Grinning, reaching back across the desk, he picked up an unfinished cigarette, exhaling the smoke slowly, then laughing to himself. It was a dirty laugh.

Motioning in the direction of the now exited lady, "I get attention all the time. What about you?"

Marco didn't answer--again, and Tarpley seemed to enjoy the prospect that his brash demeanor and off-color questions might be a little disturbing to the baby-face in front of him.

Indeed, Marco was feeling uncomfortable. There had been some sense of security in having another person in the room, even if it was a flighty looking, possibly drug

9

induced, skimpily dressed girl. He turned to see if she was anywhere in sight. She was gone.

Tarpley stepped closer, his salesman's smile revealing the lone gold front tooth glistening in the remaining light of the setting sun.

"Well, Mr. Marco Antonio Esgivas, I'll do my best to help develop yore education while I gotcha. Me an' you gonna be buds by da time we get back. Gimme a second to lock up and we'll get goin'," he said, as he moved behind the desk, fumbling in the drawer.

"Sir, I need to be heading back. Here are the keys," Marco said, anxiously taking a step forward and laying them on the desk, as though delivery of the keys would stop this nonsense. "My instructions were to drive one of your vehicles back."

"Been a change in plans, Marco," Tarpley said, as he picked up the keys. "You goin' with me."

"What do you mean?"

"I mean, you and me goin' to Hilton Head to make da drop."

"Sir, I cannot . . . "

"Look, we ain't got time for dis discussion. Jus' understand I been doin' dis for a long time and I need you taggin' along, ridin' shotgun so to speak."

"*It's a simple trip.* Senor Begal had said to his father, as the truck was being loaded this morning. *He'll have money for fast food and be back by tomorrow morning.*"

10

Tarpley, still searching in his desk drawer, looked at Marco and smiled as he pulled out a handgun--a revolver, gave the cylinder two quick spins, half checking the amount of bullets in the gun, then shoving it into his jeans, he motioned for Marco to step outside.

Marco thought briefly of running. *But where*?

Locking the door, Tarpley turned, looking for the first time at the truck parked in the middle of the used car lot.

"Dat's a big truck for a kid like you. I'll drive. Get in," he said, putting his office keys in his pocket and then tapping the handle of the gun shoved in the front of his blue jeans.

Marco crawled into the passenger side.

This morning when he arrived at work, he knew nothing of this truck, nothing of this trip, and nothing of this Ray Tarpley. His father and mother knew nothing of it, and his father stood on the loading dock of The Factory begging Senor Begal to let the father go instead of the son.

No, we need Marco, Begal said.

His father did not understand, but knew enough to be afraid; and, as this gold-toothed, drug-running, pretend-cowboy drove the factory truck out onto the streets of San Antonio, Marco's excitement on getting to go on this adventure was over, and he was ready to admit that like his father, he too was afraid.

TWO

Heflin, Alabama is a quiet, sleepy, southern town; a one street, rural conglomeration of shopkeepers whose southern beginnings date to just before the turn of the twentieth century. A place where time is marked more by who was sheriff or probate judge than by other measures.

Located halfway between Birmingham and Atlanta and only ten miles from the Georgia line, this last city in Alabama on Interstate 20 before entering Georgia is one of the top fifty places to live, according to a recent Sports Illustrated article.

Atop the rise overlooking Ross Street, in the middle of town sits the Cleburne County courthouse: dull, white-washed brick, climbing two stories into the air and topped with a shining silver dome; a smaller poor man's version of the Capitol Building in Montgomery, some had said.

"All rise," the bailiff said, as 59-year old Judge Samuel A. Munroe, the presiding Circuit Judge for the Seventh Judicial Circuit entered the main courtroom.

He had an impressive appearance and his neatly trimmed gray hair blended well with the flowing black robe. Criminal defense lawyers viewed him as dictatorial, domineering and harsh; prosecutors generally viewed him as amenable, authoritative and just. Regardless of the perspective, neither could deny that he seemed to relish in inflicting ceremonial pain from the bench with denials for defense motions or stiff sentences for the guilty.

The trial of Thomas Henton was about to resume. A local boy, Henton was a notorious chop-shop operator who had made the mistake of allegedly stealing the sheriff's truck, then bragging about it. Not able to get him for that crime, the sheriff had found a boat in his possession with an altered identification number, and if convicted (because of previous convictions), Henton could be sentenced to life.

Believing with certitude that a trial was a nuisance that delayed justice, Judge Munroe threatened William Davis, the defense attorney, that if the case had to be tried and the defendant lost he would be inclined to give his client at least twenty-five years.

"Let the record reflect that all the members of the jury are present and accounted for," Judge Munroe said, as he sat down in his black judge's chair.

"Ladies and gentlemen, just before we broke for lunch, you heard closing arguments from the prosecution. Now we will hear closing arguments from the defense. Mr. Davis."

All eyes were fixed on him as he approached the jury of his 37 year old client's peers: two elderly farmers, two middle-aged

13

housewives, five males, aged 30 to 40, employed in various businesses in neighboring Anniston, one 35-year old male school teacher, and two unemployed females in their twenties. The seated jurors resembled rows of multicolored Easter eggs, with their plaids, solids, and stripes, the color varieties of shirts worn by the gentlemen, some with overalls and some with work pants. All of it somehow blended eclectically with the ladies best print flannel or cotton dresses and nylon pantsuits.

"May it please the court, Madame Prosecutor, Ladies and gentlemen: If what we have seen and heard in this courtroom is enough to put Tommy in that jail at the bottom of the hill, then we are all in trouble. For I will never again buy a used car, a used lawnmower; and I certainly will never buy a used boat. What has the state proven? Well, they've proven that Tommy bought a boat. They have proven that he bought a tag for the boat, and they have proven that he borrowed money using the boat's VIN number. And, he used the same number that was given to him when he bought the boat. The banker had no problem loaning him money on that boat. Why should he? Tommy had a bill of sale showing it was his, and he had a valid tag, purchased right here in this court house. All of that is something you or I would have done if we bought a used boat or a used car or any used contraption that you have to buy a tag for."

He looked the part of a southern lawyer,

Davis did: long gray hair bouncing as he walked back and forth, a graying mustache-- darker than the hair, a three-piece Hart-Schafner & Marx charcoal colored suit, with a 21 carat gold pocket watch and chain hanging from the vest. The suit, along with the stiff windsor-collared, white shirt and cuff links from New Orleans, gave him a provincial, staid, almost conservative look. The hair, however, and the way he spoke gave him the persona of a southern rebel.

He had lost only one case in his career and it was in front of this judge some twenty years ago. The courthouse checker players predicted he would lose. He had proven them wrong before.

"What have they not shown you? The State has not produced one witness to prove that the boat was even stolen. Why haven't they? Well, maybe because it wasn't stolen, and if it wasn't stolen, why would anybody change the Vehicle Identification Number? And why would Tommy change the number? He wasn't trying to sell it. He wasn't trying to do anything with the boat except maybe do a little fishing. Besides all of that, they haven't even proven that Tommy changed the VIN number. Remember, the bill of sale he showed to the probate office had the same exact number on it. The Cleburne County Probate Office issued the tag for it. They didn't have a problem with it. Tommy paid for it and Tommy used the boat and now he sits before you to see if all of you are going to put him in jail for that."

One hour and ten minutes later, the jury announced their verdict: 'Not Guilty.'

"Ladies and Gentlemen, I want to thank you for your service," Judge Munroe announced to the jury with a stunned look on his face. Please follow the clerk and he will give you your pay of $10.00 a day. Thank you and you may be excused."

Both Tommy and his lawyer politely stood as these benefactors of justice and freedom left the jury box.

Judge Munroe watched in disbelief, as did Davis, as the foreman of the jury, a young, male agriculture schoolteacher from Ranburne High School, walked across the courtroom and shook hands with the newly proclaimed innocent defendant.

"You make sure you stay straight, you hear," the teacher/juror said, the matter-of-fact comment an obvious reference to Tommy's known reputation of running a chop shop.

Sheriff Sykes, the man whose Chevrolet Silverado truck had disappeared over a year ago and was never found was seething in anger as he walked over to congratulate Davis.

"Well Mr. Henton, your lawyer kept your ass out of the crack and out of my jail for the moment, but you'll be back. I'm sure of that." Congratulations counselor," he said, somberly offering his hand.

16

Sheriff Sykes had been the sheriff of Cleburne County for one and a half terms--six years in a county that had only once in recent memory elected anyone sheriff more than two terms.

A stocky-built man with salt and pepper hair, he was not the most intelligent of men; but, since intelligence had never been a prerequisite for election to anything in Cleburne County; and, since Sykes was a good talker and had experience (in his younger years) with the DEA in Texas; and, since he was the most Worshipful Master of the local Masonic Lodge, his election to arguably the most powerful office in the county had been easy, the last one without a runoff.

Looking at Henton, while still shaking Davis' hand, "Somebody like you won't be ready to retire yet. We'll get you next time," he said with a sardonic laugh, as he turned and left the courtroom.

"Good argument, Mr. Davis," Judge Munroe said, as he stood from his chair, behind the bench, an astonished expression of disbelief still on his face.

"Thank you," Davis said, as he packed files and notes into his bags, making ready to exit behind the deputies and his client.

Walking down the courthouse steps, Davis laughed to himself as he thought about the look on Judge Munroe's face as the jury foreman walked across the court room to shake the newly freed defendant's hand. *That's not something you see every day.* And from the look on the Judge's face, he hadn't seen it either.

Reaching the bottom of the steps leading from the courtroom, Gloria Jenny, Tommy's girlfriend stood alone, waiting on the man responsible for her boyfriend's freedom. She was not unattractive, in a country song, tight blue jeans sort of way: dirty blonde hair, an hourglass figure that was wrapped reasonably tight in those blue jeans and a white, skin-tight blouse. Her eyes were green, mesmerizing; if you were fortunate enough or unfortunate, depending on the situation, to stare into them.

She was without a doubt the best looking thing in the courthouse today, and as she came closer and closer, Davis was sure he probably had the same Judge-Munroe-type-stupefied-look on his face, as she wrapped her arms around him, kissing him squarely on the lips.

"Thank you, you got me my man back," she said, turning, walking away, the trailing of her cheap, sweet smelling perfume lingering for a moment on Davis' face, even after she disappeared around the corner.

The newly victorious lawyer, temporarily and delightfully dumbfounded, collected his thoughts and resumed walking in the direction of the courthouse exit.

Darryl Joe Whitman, the Circuit Clerk and long time friend of Davis, stood across the hall, a broad smile on his face, having just witnessed the unusual thank you.

"Congratulations, William, great job. Don't worry, I'm not going to kiss you."

"Thank you, Darryl Joe--on both counts."

"No wonder they call you Matlock. I can't believe you got him off."

"All in picking the right jury," Davis said, smiling.

"Whatever it was, congratulations. Hey, since you've been in court all day, I bet you didn't hear about the state trooper gettin' killed on I-20?"

"Somebody from around here?"

"He's from Mobile. Found him before sunrise this morning."

"Did he have any family?"

"Don't know. They got a Mexican boy charged with the murder."

"Who's his lawyer?"

"Don't know. You interested?"

"Probably not. I stay in the courtroom too much as it is. You know a lawyer can't make any money in the courthouse."

THREE

8:00 a.m. on Monday morning, found Davis attempting to return a week's worth of calls. By 10:00a.m. he was ready to see his first appointment of the day.

"Mr. Davis, Demarcus Greenwood," his secretary, Jenny, said, as she ushered in a young, over-weight man in a brightly colored t-shirt and blue jeans. Davis had represented Greenwood some months earlier on a drug charge in Calhoun County.

"Hey man, good to see ya," Greenwood said, as he reached across the desk to shake Davis' hand. "I never did thank you for gettin' me off. I knew you was gonna do it though, man."

"You're welcome. I'm glad to see you are doing well. What can I do for you?"

"See here, what exactly do you do? I mean do you do lawsuits and shit like dat? I mean, I know you got dat little drug case of mine throwed out, but I mean, check dis out man. My buddy, Icehouse got me dis job at the Golden Dragon Tattoo parlor in Jacksonville, and instead a payin' me--"

Davis hated to interrupt the flow of such an interesting story, but felt compelled to ask. "Icehouse?"

"Yeah, Icehouse. His mama named him after a beer."

"Oh." Davis said, feigning complete understanding.

"Anyway, dis chick name of Doris owns dat place and she started my tattoo and now she won't finish it."

Without invitation, Greenwood stood and began the arduous task of pulling his shirt up to create a visual exhibition to add to his story.

"I mean look at dis shit!"

Davis had never seen anything quite as unique as what was now before him: An artist's rendering of a dragon, located on a great deal of white, untanned fat, beginning in the middle of Greenwood's chest between two hair-covered breasts. The dragon's tongue extended in an obvious but unsuccessful attempt to breathe fire and proceeded down Greenwood's orbicular stomach, disappearing at the halfway point.

Time stood still as Davis tried to absorb all that was being placed before him; one of those moments where the gouging of eyes having to view such a piece of art seemed appropriate, while trying to recall whether this man had truly been this fat six months earlier when he had represented him.

"Just look at dis shit, man," Greenwood said, again, as he attempted to raise his t-shirt even higher.

"I mean, she owes me a bunch a money, and she's supposed to finish dis and she says she won't till I pay her back for some shit she claims I stole." Defiantly Greenwood's lips puffed as any wrongfully accused patron of the arts would as he stated his innocence.

"I didn't steal any of her shit, man."

Davis, having seen more than enough, had already slid his hand under his desk pressing a button which would bring his secretary to the rescue.

"Come in," Davis said, responding to his secretary's knock.

"Mr. Davis, you have a phone call-- Judge Munroe."

Standing, Davis held out his hand to the visitor.

"I'm sorry to disappoint you Demarcus, but I'm afraid that suing the Golden Dragon Tattoo parlor would not be something I would be interested in."

"Ah, man, what am I gonna do?"

"Tell you what, I'll write her a letter. See if I can convince her that it would be in her best interests to settle with you. Give Jenny the information."

"Go ahead, I'll be out in a minute," Jenny said to Greenwood, as she closed the door behind him.

"He wants his tattoo fixed," Davis said, in answer to the questioning look from his secretary. "Take his information. I'll dictate a letter to Doris at the Golden Dragon Tattoo Parlor. And bring the next one in."

"Your call," she said, pointing to the phone.

"Oh, I thought you were just getting rid of him."

Laughing, Jenny said, "Judge Munroe is really on line two."

Davis picked up the phone.

"I'm sorry to keep you waiting Judge; I had to get someone out of my office. Yes, sir. Ah hah. What's his name?" Davis wrote the name on a yellow legal pad, as Jenny leaned over to see the name.

"O.K. I'll go down to see him tomorrow. Thanks judge," Davis said, as he hung the phone up and stared blankly at his secretary.

"The one that killed the trooper?" Jenny asked, blandly, with some hint of trepidation in her voice.

"Allegedly, Jenny. I've been appointed to represent Marco Antonio Esgivas.

FOUR

The Cleburne County jail was a three story brick structure. Built in 1904, it sat just down the hill on the northern side of the courthouse.

Looking very much like a pile of red bricks with a tall wired fence and razor-barbed wire at the top, the only side of the Cleburne County Jail with windows, except for the office, was the courthouse side, where the fortunate prisoners are placed. Fortunate, because on mild Alabama nights, in an attempt to catch the semblance of a breeze they could hang their arms through the bars, their noses pressed in between. Plastic had covered the barred windows, but it had been torn for years, the result of inmates trying to escape the putrid smell of leaking sewage, century-old mustiness, sweating men, and burned unchanged cooking grease.

Those courthouse-side fortunate's could not see William Davis and Malcolm Caide as they pulled into the jail parking lot at sunset. But they could hear them getting out of Davis' Jaguar, talking about the age of the jail and why the Feds hadn't made the county tear it down.

On hearing two new visitors in the parking lot, the sounds of locked up men always increased to a full crescendo: '*Hey you!*

Who is that! Come talk to me! I've got money! I know your mama! Senseless, meaningless chants for the most part, vulgarities of ignorant and angry men who have nothing but time on their hands.

"Just men?" I don't hear any females," Caide said.

Davis grinned. "That's because there aren't any. This jail's too nasty for females. They send them to Anniston," he said, as he climbed the one step into the office, holding the door open for Caide. "Hello Jerry. This is Malcolm Caide, my interpreter. Got some new buckets I see," Davis said, as he and Caide walked into the front office.

Hanging over the jailer's head were several small, white five gallon buckets tied with a wire to the ceiling. There were no less than six other buckets in the downstairs area of the jail. Their job was to catch the steady drip that appeared about every half second; the smell, from years of leaking sewage had already permeated the walls, floors, mattresses and pillows, leaving even the visitors battling to regain their sense of smell hours after leaving.

A Federal Court Order in response to an inmate's lawsuit had been in place for some time. It mandated the tearing down and replacement of the jail, but the County Commission seemed to always be without the necessary funds. Another lawsuit by another inmate might force the issue, but since none

25

had been filed, the lack of money was seemingly forgiven until the next fiscal year and the old jail and the buckets and the smells remained.

"Yea. Sheriff got some that don't have cracks. We just have to empty 'em twice a day."

"Do they get full twice a day?" Caide asked.

"Well, some of 'em get pretty full. We have to empty 'em twice a day anyway! Who you need to see Mr. Davis?"

"The boy y'all arrested last Friday, Marco Antonio Esgivas."

"The one that killed the trooper? You got him? Huh."

"Allegedly, allegedly, Jerry, and yes I am his attorney," Davis said.

With that short exchange, the jailer reached for a ring of very large, dark, iron looking skeleton keys.

"I guess I can miss the beginning of *I Love Lucy*. It'll take me a little bit to get the tonk. I'm the only one here and I gotta climb to the top."

"The tonk?"

"Yea," That's what the sheriff said them boys that work the border patrol call em: Tonk! Says that's the sound it makes when you hittum in the head with a flashlight. Ain't that funny?" The jailer said, grinning, as though he had said something profound.

The stairs leading to the jail cells were

like climbing into a lighthouse or the guard tower of a castle. Concrete steps that circled around a conical form making their way to each floor, looking and sounding like something from a B-grade horror movie from the fifties.

The inmates that were shouting as Davis and Caide got out of their cars had obviously found other pursuits. The night was quiet, and every step by the jailer on the concrete steps could be heard as his shuffling, dragging feet went round and round, making their way to the top floor of the jail. With each step the huge skeleton keys clanged, as the reverberating sounds of opening and closing of cell doors bounced and echoed on the hard surface, louder still as jailer and inmate descended.

"Here he is," the jailer said.

Before Davis and his interpreter stood a young man with loosely hanging, jet-black hair, sporting the usual orange suit, but unlike most of Davis' clients, Marco's orange suit and disheveled appearance was overshadowed by his very bruised face and almost swollen shut eyes.

"Is the jewelry necessary?" Davis asked, pointing at the shackles on the prisoner.

"Yep, sheriff's orders. Good thing you brought your man. Don't think he speaks English. They couldn't get a word out of him. Might think he's a deaf mute, except I did hear him holler a little, that one time he got rough."

"What do you mean, got rough?" Davis asked.

"Well, the sheriff said he was tryin' to make a move so they had to get rough with him."

Davis got up from the couch and walked to where Marco was standing near the stairs, examining his hands and swollen face.

"Did you see any of this?" Davis asked, as he went back to his bag on the couch, taking the warrant on Marco from the bag, and reading as the deputy talked.

"Naw. I heard it. Got pretty loud. Didn't last too long. Don't think he gave em any more trouble after that."

"He's five feet five inches and weighs a whopping one hundred fifteen pounds," Davis said, reading particulars from the warrant without looking at the deputy.

Marco still stood near the stairs, without emotion, looking at the two new people in the room.

"As big as he is, he would certainly be hard to control. How many people did it take to subdue this . . . dangerous man?" Davis asked facetiously, his insincere tone completely lost on the jailer.

"Ah, I'm not sure. Probably two or three. Y'all can sit in here," he said, motioning to the small space in between the front office and the kitchen, that housed the drink and candy machines where lawyer/client visits usually took place.

28

Closing the glass-paned door that separates the break room from the front office, the deputy left the three alone and went back to watching television.

Two old metal chairs and a small couch whose springs were attempting to gain freedom from their cracked, open cushions made up the available seating.

Davis sat down on the couch, his Hartman bag already there, placed strategically between protruding springs, while Caide and Marco took a chair around the adjacent table.

Looking beyond the bruises for the first time, Davis was amazed at how young and how American his Hispanic client looked.

"Well, Mr. Caide, if you would, please begin by explaining who I am and who you are. Tell him that I have been appointed to represent him as his attorney; that, I am here to fight for him and let him know that anything he tells me is confidential. Explain what confidential means."

"Sir, I speak English. I know what confidential means." Marco said.

Both men were stunned.

"Well, good. My name is William Davis. I am a criminal defense lawyer here in Cleburne County. I have been appointed by Judge Munroe to represent you. This is Malcolm Caide. He came to be my interpreter, but it appears that we don't need him. Do we, Mr. Esgivas?"

"No, sir," said Marco.

"Mr. Caide if you will please step outside. I hope you brought something to read. Looks like I won't need you."

"That's O.K., you can pay me by the hour to watch *I Love Lucy* with Jerry," Caide said, as he left the room.

Davis took out his client information sheet and began asking questions, background information, mostly, letting Marco ask as many questions as he wanted, spending about an hour with him before finally packing his bag to head home.

"Goodnight, Marco. Maybe you'll sleep tonight." Davis said, as he tapped on the window for the jailer.

"The gate's open Mr. Davis. I'll take him on up and get him tucked into bed."

Nothing the lawyer said necessarily gave Marco hope; and maybe his perception of the lawyer was not entirely correct, but it was comforting—to Marco, believing there was someone who at least *thought* he was not a killer.

It was late. Marco laid down, ready for sleep. The three others in his cell, and most of the other inmates, were already sound asleep, the usual useless talk replaced by loud snoring reverberating on the concrete-block walls from every level of the jail.

First, he slept. Then he settled into a wonderful dream of home: Work with Papa in the fields was always long, for there were many rows of corn to hoe and water and many times there was still work to do as the sun was disappearing. But today the work was finished early and Marco was walking the half mile or so past his home to a cluster of trees--ebony, mahogany, rosewood, some walnut. There, a small stream fed by a bubbling spring falls over rocks, smoothed by time. The stream, with its clear cool water gives life to those trees, along with flowers and birds and animals that choose to call this spot in the desert, home.

Under a very tall, very wide mahogany tree, Marco sat; the tree's roots spreading on the ground on each side, resembling an octopus spreading endless thick tentacles. With the stream nearby, the ground cover of roots was perfect for nap-taking. Wildlife of every imaginable type staked their claim to life here in this oasis, this Garden of Eden refuge in the desert.

In the distance, beyond this haven of shade and greenery was a totally different view: cactus, scrub bushes and tumble weeds abound; rattlesnakes control the walk and the hot sun bakes its claim on the weary.

But, here, the magnificent trees create a canopy of cool shade filtering the sun. Here, a breeze is always blowing. Here, the azaleas, geraniums and orchids wave as they sway with the gentle breeze.

That smell! Lilac? Honeysuckle? Their

aroma filled the air, as though someone had just crushed different leaves in the air and threw them just ahead of the breeze.

Birds, the kind he wasn't sure, cluster overhead, staking their claims to a perching spot on the limbs of their desired trees, resting, enjoying their reflection in the water below, flapping their wings in ritualistic show, singing songs of freedom, launching, soaring into the air—free, then re-landing on the branches again.

An osprey? White with a gray breast, lands, shaking twigs and leaves to the ground. So pretty are these birds, not exotically pretty like the quetzals further south, but amidst this oasis, they are exceptionally beautiful. To watch them play and sing and be free with the backdrop of that bubbling stream is joy itself.

This small secluded spot was not far from Marco's home. Even when Marco and his family lived in a hut near Padres Nagres, he would come here to play, to think and plan—at least in his dreams. King of the world he was, at the base of this mahogany tree—in his dreams.

Startled, Marco looked behind him. "Papa, I didn't know you were here."

"Son," Miguel said, stepping from behind the mahogany tree where Marco was sitting. "Stay true to your roots, to your family, to God. This will sustain you."

"I know, Papa. I know," Marco said, as another osprey flew over their heads.

Time means nothing here; minutes seem like hours, and hours like minutes.

Turning back to his father, "Papa, I. . ." Oh Mama, how long have you been there? I must have dozed." Tears begin to swell. "I miss you Mama."

"Let me rub your back," his mother says. "I know you are hurting."

"Mama, I need you." Marco turns over on his stomach as his mother's soft hands gently caress his shoulders. He doesn't want her to see him cry.

"I know, son. Remember how I used to do this for you when you were little?"

"Si, Mama. Don't stop," Marco says, as tears roll down his face and he basks in the joy of his mother's touch. "I don't want you to stop."

The wonderful sounds are alive: water flows over the rocks, louder it seems, gushing forcefully from the ground. Singing birds compete, their songs intermingling with crashing water on the rocks, as the faint beginnings of whippoorwills create a backdrop signaling the end of another day.

A twig cracks. Startled, Marco turns and sits up. His mother is gone.

"Adidra," he says, as he wipes the tears away. "How beautiful you are. I had forgotten how beautiful you are."

The young new plantings of the girl that Marco had grown up with, had fallen in love with, had ripened and matured. Resplendent

33

with both the innocence of youth and the provocative stimulation of sexuality, she walks closer, bending down to Marco, kissing him with a long, lingering wet kiss, leaving his lips warm and moist as she pulls away.

Stepping back she loosens the sash from behind which holds her bodice-work white blouse together. Just as quickly as she appeared, her top falls to the ground revealing two soft supple breasts, the nipples appearing as though they had been pinched and made pert, ready for Marco to observe.

"Don't stop," Marco said.

She continues loosening and untying, allowing the long flowing skirt to drop to the ground alongside the blouse.

"I've never seen you like this," Marco said, as she steps forward, bends down, kisses him again, her clean natural scent competing with the flower's fragrance. Stepping back, again, Marco can see all that she has to offer.

Breathing is hard, intense; restraint becomes impossible; both of Marco's hands slowly reach for the heaven in front of him.

"Let me have you."

"I'll let you have me," she said, smiling. "I'll let you have all of me," she said again, but this time her voice much deeper, coarser; so deep, it startled Marco, and he began to wake.

"I'll let you have the back of my hand you stupid tonk," the voice said.

Marco sat up. Now fully awake, his eyes wide open, he looked at the sheriff standing over him, a half smile, half scowl creeping over his face, the jailer's ring of black metal keys in his left hand tauntingly held close to Marco's head, his right hand resting on his gun.

"You want these, don't you?" the sheriff said, referring of course to the keys. His deep voice, his uniform, his derisive look and ridiculing tone all combined to create the unpleasant return to the pain of his harsh world that was now Marco's, again.

Papa, Mama, Adidra; all were gone; Marco's beautiful sanctuary of trees and water and birds and family--all just a dream.

"I know you can understand me. My deputy told me you speak English."

Bending down closer to him he said, "Don't think just because they appointed you the high-dollar lawyer around here that you're going get to go back home. No, sir," the sheriff said, as he stepped back outside the cell, re-locking the cell door and shaking it for good measure.

"I plan to personally see to it that they put a needle in your arm. We don't like people that kill law enforcement."

The jingling keys made their way down the concrete steps, becoming more distant, finally quiet.

For the first time since Marco had found himself here, he began to cry. The warm tears were almost comforting; a relief that made him feel normal. The moldy smelling pillow was soon soaked and his face completely wet.

I saw Papa, Mama and Adidra. I got to go home, and I can close my eyes and go again.

The sheriff can't stop that.

The moon that night was full, larger than Marco ever remembered, shining bright as day on a clear winter night. His face and pillow, soaked, glistening like a wet puddle on the street in that tender bright light.

That same moon would just about now be rising over the Sierra Madre Oriental Mountains east of home, and that same light would soon be shining on Marco's family as they prepared for bed.

Down below a car door slams as the jailer for the next shift arrives. *Reality trying to steal my joy*, Marco thought. *Talking in the night, I can't make it out. I don't want to make it out, I want to go home.*

Tighter, he squeezes his arms, wrapping them around. He can almost see his mother standing in the doorway. He can almost hear her calling: *Where are you, baby?*

Marco closed his eyes and with a warm smile mixed with warm tears, he went back home and stayed for the rest of the night.

FIVE

"You remember, I told you I was applying for Youthful Offender Status," Davis said to his client, as he took a file from his bag, while looking over at the prosecution's table where Joseph Hudgins, the District Attorney for Calhoun and Cleburne Counties was seated with one of his assistant D.A.'s.

"Yes, I remember." Marco said.

"If the judge were to grant it, you would be treated as a kid instead of an adult and would face no more than three years in prison; the trial would be in front of the judge instead of a jury. Anyway, we are here for the judge to rule on that."

While Davis was talking to Marco, Judge Munroe entered the courtroom without ceremony taking his place behind the bench.

"Mr. Davis," the judge began without pounding the gavel or giving notice that he was ready to begin.

"I have examined your motion, and your attached application, as well as the report prepared by the state probation office. After considering this report along with the fact that your client is in this country illegally, I am denying your application for Youthful Offender Status."

"Your Honor, Defense would request that a bond be set for my client. I can make arrangements for him to stay here in this county until trial. My understanding is that he has no criminal history. He is only nineteen years old, speaks English and certainly would not have the funds or the ability in any other way to be a flight risk."

The expression on Judge Munroe's face did not change and the district attorney did not wait for the judge to respond.

"Your Honor, first of all I have no idea about his criminal history. We're not getting a lot of cooperation out of Mexican authorities. I frankly am not sure that they have a system in place to know whether he is a criminal or not."

"Is there anything on him in the NCIC?"

"No, your honor nothing here in the states."

"Alright, continue." The Judge said.

"Secondly, I don't care if he used to be a Mexican boy scout. Here, he is charged with killing an Alabama State Trooper who was in the course of his sworn duty as an officer of the law and the murder weapon was found in the defendant's hand. Even if Mr. Davis personally tucks him in at night and feeds him pancakes every morning, I don't think allowing a killer on the street after he calculatingly shot and killed an officer in cold blood is something the state needs to do."

"Your Honor, I know Mr. Hudgins had to take Constitutional Law to get out of law school, and--"

"Mr. Davis, I would love to hear more

argument, but I am going to deny your motion for a bond. This is a capital murder case and I believe the sheriff will make your client quite comfortable in the Cleburne County jail."

"Your Honor, I would ask that a preliminary hearing be set as quickly as possible."

"Very well, I'll look at my calendar and set it by separate order. Anything else?"

"No Sir, not at this time."

"Alright, Sheriff you can take the defendant away."

Sykes' deputies walked toward the defense table and stood in front of Marco motioning for him to get up. Marco stood but made no moves toward the deputies.

Maybe they were the ones that beat him, Davis thought, as he watched Marco's reaction.

"Your Honor, I need to talk privately with my client before he's carried back to the jail."

Motioning to the jury room, Judge Munroe said, "Alright, deputy, please escort the defendant to that room and let Mr. Davis talk to his client."

"Thank you, Judge. I'll be right in Marco," Davis said, as he walked to the left of the defense table where the sheriff was standing.

"Sheriff, I need to speak with you."

"Talk away." The sheriff said, blandly.

"In private," Davis said, as he turned

and walked toward the storage room on the other side of the courtroom, adjacent to the room where the deputy had carried Marco.

Sykes followed Davis and closed the old wooden door to what was an early twentieth century law library.

"This place sure needs cleaning," said Sheriff Sykes, a small attempt at a smile, as he propped his left hand up against dusty, old law books, his right hand on his gun.

"Well, it's your nickel, Counselor. What do you want?"

"I've got one question sheriff that I hope you'll be man enough to answer." A pause, slight, but effective, preceded the question. "Why did you beat the shit out of my client?"

The abruptness of Davis' tone seemed to startle the sheriff, who stopped patting the top of his gun and made a step toward Davis, as though ready to launch into the accuser.

"What in the hell are you talking about?"

"You know damn well what I'm talking about. You and I have known each other a long time, so cut out the bullshit."

The sheriff stared at Davis, the attempted smile now overcome by a face of consternation, and after just a moment spit out the answer.

"He fell down and my deputies had to help him up."

"That's one helluva fall. With all those bruises on his face, he must have fallen several times."

"You son-of-a-bitch," Sykes said, angrily, as he moved still closer, pointing his finger in Davis' face.

"You shysters are all alike. You dress up in your suits and ties and think you can control the world with your words. Well, let me tell you something. You don't control mine! I have a jail and a county to run and if I need to beat the shit out of a Mexican, I will."

"Why did you beat Marco?" Davis tone was loud, demanding and unrelenting.

"I beat him because I felt like it," Sykes said, his speech faster than before, more determined, matching his progressively angrier demeanor. "And, since you're aggravating me about it, I think I'll carry him back and beat the shit out of him again, just for good measure. What do you think of that, counselor?" he said, now stepping even closer, less than a foot of difference between his face and the face of an unflinching, determined defense attorney. "Is that plain enough for you?"

Davis pulled a tape recorder out of his coat pocket, rewound it and pressed play:

"*I beat him because I felt like it and since you're aggravating me about it, I think I'll carry him back and beat the shit out of him again, just for good measure.*"

The astounded look on the sheriff's face was evidence enough that he had underestimated this lawyer from the southern end of the county. His recorded words hitting him in the face, harder than the slaps he often received from women in the strip clubs in Birmingham and Atlanta.

"Alright." The sheriff's controlled words now slowly emerging, as he took a step back from the antagonist.

"You win. . .for now. I'll leave the little tonk alone."

Turning to leave, Sykes said, "You're a mighty ambitious lawyer for somebody that's appointed to represent this wetback. Better watch yourself counselor, too much ambition can get you into trouble. Lawyers have accidents all the time and you can record that if you want to."

Davis stepped in front of the sheriff, opened the door and turned to go into the jury room where Marco was waiting. The deputy that was guarding Marco stepped outside and Davis closed the door behind him.

Marco was sitting in a straight chair, staring out the north window toward the jail.

"That's a strange sight," Davis said aloud, as he watched with Marco: Courthouse-side inmates were hanging their arms through the barred windows exercising the very limited freedom of loosely hanging their arms, waiving, like dozens of broken clock pendulums, with no particular beat of time. Stranger still, the arms in a particular window did not necessarily belong to the same body; the lengths, the movements, all different, but moving. The unnaturalness of those hanging limbs and the animal-look created was something you didn't expect and didn't relish the thought of seeing again; ridiculous, amusing, even entertaining, as long as you're not the one sleeping there.

"Listen Marco, I know they have hurt you, but they won't bother you anymore."

"These walls are pretty thin," Marco said, unmoving, continuing to look out the window, as Davis stood behind him next to the long jury-room table.

"I heard what you just did. You are very brave, but not very smart," Marco said, now turning from the jail, looking up and down at Davis, as though expecting some damage from what he had heard.

"Well, I don't know about either of those things. But . . .you're welcome."

"You do not know me but you risk your life to save me. You make an enemy out of a powerful man. In my country that means you will soon die.

"I think you'll find he's full of hot air," Davis said, as he switched his briefcase to his left hand and stretched his right to shake Marco's hand.

"Thank you," Marco said, as both shackled hands lifted for the handshake.

"I'll see you soon," said Davis, who walked out into the courtroom, nodded toward the judge, as he made his way past the sheriff toward the double doors.

~~~~~

On his return to the jail, Marco was placed in a different cell on the top floor, with a view of the courthouse; a 10 x 12 foot cell with one double bunk at the back and two double bunks on each side.

Usually, six inmates would be in a cell this size, but three had been transferred that morning to the Alabama Department of Corrections and the sheriff hadn't brought anybody else in. So, for the moment, there were just three: Joe Frank Erwin, Dale Carter, and Marco.

Joe Frank Erwin was a big black man; blacker than most of the coloreds anywhere around Heflin; so much so that the contrast of his wide smile with his pearly white teeth against the extremely black backdrop would seem to light up a room. He was so big the jail didn't have a uniform to fit him, not properly, anyway; the front buttons appeared ready to pop, as they attempted to hold the stretched orange material, allowing more of the white t-shirt underneath to be seen. His broad chest, huge arms and a neck that was fairly wide, made him appear to have once been physically fit. Still, in spite of some rolls of fat, pushing against the suit, he looked like a man that could still give a good account of himself in a fight. And although you would not know it by his appearance: the shaved head, orange suit and physique, Joe Frank was an ordained

Baptist preacher. His caring heart (rescue of a young girl being molested) had gotten him charged with assault. But his overly indulged libido was the cause of his recent problems with local law enforcement, for he was being held for contempt by Judge Simmons for not paying child support.

As Marco appeared with the deputy ready to enter the cell, the preacher and Dale Carter were talking.

"Aw, you know how it is round here," Joe Frank said, "A black man beatin' up on a no account white-trash man, even if he had no business with the girl is always gwoin to gitcha arrested."

"And not paying child support will sure get you in here, too," Dale Carter, the other cellmate said with a grin, as he puffed his cigarette, and both men watched the jailer as he took the shackles off their new roommate.

The jail door slammed loudly behind Marco, as he walked in without ceremony or introduction, and the jingling keys re-locked the cell door. Marco looked first at the two men, then to his new surroundings, not exactly sure which of the two empty bunks he was to take.

The preacher smiled his seemingly irrepressible smile. "I'm Joe Frank. Dis here's Dale." Dale, unresponsive, sat in the corner, watching, quietly shuffling a deck of cards.

"Marco Esgivas." Marco said.

As though feeling a need to welcome the

new man, Joe Frank got down from his bunk.

"Dis place ain't dat bad," he said, laughing, and then lowering his voice, as he stepped over next to Marco so that only he could hear.

"If I was to want out, all I'd have to do is get my brother to make me a skeleton key."

Marco did not understand and did not respond.

Continuing to whisper, Joe Frank said, "Dis jail jus' like da ole west, jus' old locks dat use skeleton keys. Ain't nothing for a bona-fide blacksmith like my brothah."

Joe Frank turned and jumped on to the upper bunk across from Marco, as he continued to talk, this time so that Dale could hear. "Your lawyer from down toward da southern end of da county ain't he?"

"I do not know," Marco said, climbing into the upper bunk across from Joe Frank.

"Dat where he's from. My grand pappy used to tell me some stories 'bout Abel."

"Abel?"

"Dat what day calls da southern end of da county."

Sitting up in his bunk, a smiling Joe Frank began to tell a story: "Dis heres bout when my pappy was a little boy in Clay County, just below here."

"Aw, come on preacher, nobody wants to hear one of your stories," Dale said, still shuffling a deck of cards. "Let's play some cards."

Undeterred, Joe Frank continued: "They would ride in a wagon all day long on ole, dirt farm-to-market road, and snake up beside Cheaha Mountain till they reached Abel Gap-- jus' over da line in Cleburne. Good spring water at Abel Gap. They could make it in about a day and rest da team, build a cook fire, camp out at Abel for da night; at dawn, get up and go into town bout ten miles into Oxford to trade, den drive back to Abel Gap fo nightfall, spends da night, den up at dawn again to head back home. Took ole Sal and Mauch, accordin' to pappy, da two best mules God evah made, all day to get back home to Millerville."

Joe Frank paused in obvious reflection, viewing in his mind all that he was describing, smiling that illuminating smile that Marco would soon become accustomed to, his teeth gathering the reflections of the only source of light--a power pole light at the edge of the fence surrounding the jail, just outside Marco's window.

Until now, Marco had never been around a black man before. He liked him. His storied face and his smile seemed genuine, free from hypocrisy and evil. Besides the lawyer, this was the first man of any color who had given him cause to believe that there were good people in this country.

In school he had studied the American Civil War. Sister Tiana had said that slavery of the black man was the reason for that war and Marco had developed a negative opinion of the

47

black race--believing that the Negro was inferior, a race incapable of existing on par with the rest of the world. Listening to Joe Frank, he realized how wrong that was, and how artificially elevated his view of his own mestizo (those mixed with Spanish and Indian blood) race had been.

No, this man was not educated, not even to the extent that poor Mexicans were. But in spite of his backward-slang, country way of talking, he was intelligent, knowledgeable and caring. And there was this light. Not a reflection, but a deep, inward glow, subtle yet powerful, that seemed to give him strength of mind and body .

In the short time that he had met Joe Frank, he already knew that there was more to him. For even in this wretched place where all that Marco had seen was evil with its accompanying darkness, there was a light that shined in this man, subtle yet powerful; an inner glow that caused his countenance to shine.

Some of the priests back home were just like him, the inward strength, that glow. And he remembered meeting an old Indian woman during a trip to market that had this light, her face shining like a beacon in the night as she told her tales of the Apache and Comanche of long ago.

As Joe Frank sat on his bunk in this God forsaken jail basking in that same light, Marco felt compelled to tell his story: "We would leave home with a two-wheeled wagon, Friday afternoon after school, packed with things to sell at the market in Piedras Negras. Since we just had one donkey to pull it, my brothers, sisters, all of us would have to walk."

"We always got to town right after sunset and set up for camp near the livery stable at the edge of town. Cook, clean up, go to bed, and sleep on the ground, sometimes on hay at the livery if they weren't too busy."

As Marco began talking, his story was carrying him back, just as Joe Frank's had done for him, and soon Marco lay back on his bunk, his hands under his head, looking up at the cracked ceiling as though pictures of what he was describing were being painted overhead, visualizing every detail, as though he were there, again.

"That was so much fun lying up in that loft, the smell of clean, fresh hay that would stick to your neck when you turned over, looking through the cracks of the barn roof, trying to find the Big Dipper. Sometimes we would take turns telling stories, first Papa, then Mama, and on down. This gave the little ones time to come up with their stories. On the ground, on blankets around a campfire was fun too, and sometimes that's where we ended up because there was no room in the barn. Outside was always colder, harder. Mama would wrap us up in her quilts, and we would watch for falling stars. One night we saw two within minutes of each other. Papa said that

49

was a good omen--two in the same sky. Mama would tell all the children that we were under God's special night blanket, and she reminded us what a privilege it was for God to allow us to be together as a family under that same blanket of stars. In the morning we would get out our goods and set them up on tables in the square: goat's cheese, milk and knitting Mama had done; Papa would repair farm tools, sell corn and cotton seed along with the other members of the ejidra."

"What's dat?" asked Joe Frank.

"Ejidra is a group of people who join their lands together to raise their crops and carry their goods to market, pooling their goods together to get a better price," Marco said. "If, while we were there at the market we could not get enough pesos to buy what we needed, Papa would work a trade. We never went hungry. Papa always got what we needed. We would stay into the night, then pack up early the next morning and get back in time for Sunday Morning Mass."

Marco stopped. Silence, it hardly ever happens in a jail. In Marco's short time at this place, he had learned that clanging tin pans, constantly ringing phones in the downstairs office, and fights—all of that was the norm. But right now at this moment, in a break from storytelling there was absolute silence; something you long for if you are in a jail; something you would pay for if you could.

Two men--strangers, one old, one

young, both from different worlds that only yesterday did not know each other; and, except for life's strange fates would never have met, and never would have exchanged pieces of their lives.

Neither of them wanted to say anything else; not now, not at this moment, not until this wonderful silence was concluded and had allowed them to absorb and experience afresh and anew every detailed picture that had been so masterfully painted by two stranger's words.

"We entire worlds apart," Joe Frank said, still looking at the imagined pictures on the ceiling. "We still jus' people and families, jus' tryin' to live, love, work and be happy; jus' some ah God's little chil'rens under dat one big blanket of stars yore Mama talk about."

Turning to look at Marco with that wonderful smile, he said, "I like yore family already, Marco; reminds me of families I used to minister to when I was pastorin."

"You are a padre?"

"A preacher? Well, I used to be," Joe Frank said, looking back up at the ceiling, no longer smiling. "Did a little sinnin' and don't nobody want to hear me preach no more, I reckon. Preached a long time though. Done more baptisms in da Tallapoosa river dan any preach-brethren 'round here, black or white."

"You ever seen a good Holy Ghos' preacher?"

Marco shook his head.

51

"Watch dis," Joe Frank said with a deep resonant laugh, as he jumped down to the floor from his top bunk and began dancing a two-step, back and forth jig.

"He, He, He, yessah, me and da Holy Ghos' made a good team; a good team, if I sez so myself."

His smile lighting the room, he held up two fingers side by side.

"I mean we was jus' like dis, me an' da Holy Ghos'. I would begin my little walk back and fo'th in da pulpit, thowin' in a few *'shouts'* and *'well glorys'*, an purty soon da whole chu'ch was a shoutin' an' a praisin' an' a liftin' their hands in da air, and you ain't nevah seen such."

"Scuse me, Dale," he said, almost stepping on the third member of the cell, who quickly pulled his feet from the floor back into his bunk, and seemed to watch Joe Frank with as much jarred enthusiasm as did Marco. Dancing faster and faster in the dimly lit room, left to right, right to left, both Dale and Marco watched with amazement from their bunks as the preacher took over the floor.

"Yea, you go, preacher," Dale said, as he smoked his cigarette and pushed his loosely hanging hair back behind his ears, bobbing his head up and down, and clapping his hands to the preacher's rhythm.

Dale had a shades-of-Elvis kind of look, with his dyed jet black hair combed straight

52

back inside his ears and curling on the ends. Up until now, he had been shuffling his deck of cards, staying quiet, filling the room with smoke from his Marlboro cigarette.

He had patiently waited on these two story tellers to get tired of talking so they could play cards with him. He had memories he could share, but he'd rather play cards.

Besides, his memories would have been drastically different. They wouldn't like them: an abusive stepfather, whose primary contribution to Dale's education was teaching him how to raise marijuana at the age of fifteen. Or his sixteenth birthday party at Junior's Bar, across the Georgia line in Tallapoosa, the night his step-dad tried to show him how to be a real man by getting them both stone-cold drunk. Too inebriated to walk home and unable to perform with one of daddy's prostitute friends, they both slept it off in between the garbage cans in behind the bar. The next day their truck was gone, so they both walked the eighteen mile trek home from Tallapoosa, Georgia to Heflin, Alabama.

As a grown man, the Carter legacy of dysfunction had been continued by Dale, passed on to his son, Dale Junior. At the time of Dale's most recent arrest, he was caught demonstrating the scientific and very dangerous art of cooking crystal-meth in front of *his* sixteen year old boy.

Watching Joe Frank demonstrate his preaching did not bring back any pleasant memories for him. Church-going was not something he was accustomed to, and Dale had only seen a 'holy ghost' preacher one other time in his life: He was a teenager; dating was a new thing then; and, in spite of his father's attempt to expose him to carnal knowledge on his sixteenth birthday, girls were still a new thing, and he really wanted to date one particular girl--Sarah Allen, who lived up the road in Oxford.

"The boy's got to go to church with you first, before you go out with him," Sarah's mother had said.

Mrs. Allen's preacher was similar to Joe Frank: one of those loud, Holy Ghost, bench-jumping, speaking-in-tongues type of preacher, but the one at Sarah's church seemed to be more comfortable preaching about Hell than Heaven. At seventeen, Dale's one-time experience with going to church, and more particularly with seeing a Holy Ghost preacher, had left him with so much anxiety that he decided no girl was worth having to endure that kind of ordeal. It was Daviston Church of God, Hell and Heaven had been preached, mostly Hell, and the invitation was being given. Dale ran out the door. He was out of the church so quickly; Sarah Allen didn't know he was gone until she reached over to hold his hand as everyone stood to sing *'Just As I Am.'*

Now, as fate would have it, here he was

in what ought to be the safest place on earth from a fire and brimstone preacher, and a colored one had just jumped down out of a cell bunk, practically on his feet--preaching to him and a Mexican murderer!

Dale stopped clapping and curled up tighter toward the wall.

"Lot a times after I do dis shuffle, if I feels dat da Holy ghos' is in da room, den here I go like dis: *Weeeee*, here we go a preachin' tonightah. Me a preachin and a preachin, harder and harder, and movin' up and down da aisle and tellin' folks, Whooo, da Lawd said, if *I* be lifted upah den I gonna draw you unto meah. *Well glory!! If any man hear my words and believe nottah, den I gonna judge him nottah thus saith the Lawdah. . .for I came not to judge yo world, but to save yo worldah. My sheep, day hear my voice and I know dem an day follow me—Whooo, Glory.*"

The preacher stopped dead in his tracks, panting as though just finishing a hard run, the sweat from his forehead shining as it rolled from his rounded cheeks and dripped to the concrete floor; his hands resting on his knees as he looked at the two members of his audience.

"If I jus' had my Bible," he said, between the panting of breath-catching, "I believe I could still do it," he said. "What chu think 'bout dat boy? I betchu ain't neva heard nothin' like dat down in Mexico."

"No," Marco said, smiling, his eyes as

large as shells from the Gulf. "I have never seen anything like it."

The sermons Marco was used to as a boy were always sanguine, always meaningful, never lively and never more than twenty minutes long. The priest might tell a joke from time to time; he might even turn to the left or to the right, but he never came down from behind the sacrament banisters--at least while preaching.

As the preacher rested, Marco asked. "Why is it you add *ah* at the end of words?"

"Emphasis," Joe Frank said, still panting. "You sees how I has to put da emphasis at da ends of someah dem words." Dats da way us ole-time preachers preach in da south. Black and white ones preach dat way. My pappy preached dat way and his pappy did."

Having caught his breath again, Joe Frank began to prance around the room, again, like a rooster that controlled the barnyard. "I tell you me and da holy ghos' had it a goin' on. I brings em in with my preachin' and da holy ghos' grabsem an' shakesem, an' day would spout out in tongues you ain't nevah heard afore. And den dem women would always start ta fallin' out in da spirit, and as they fell, 'Well Glory's' and 'Hallelujah's' rang from God's people."

Dale, who had been resigned to shuffling cards, listening and re-living his own life story for the last few minutes, got up from his bunk, clapping, ready it would seem to participate.

"Yeah, and kid," he said, grinning a large grin, his cigarette hanging from his mouth as he clapped, "I bet every time those girls fell out, the reverend's big black ass was right there to catchem." He laughed insultingly as he continued to clap, and Joe Frank continued to dance.

"In fact, kid, I heard those black girls liked him so well he got half his female congregation knocked up; spends most of his time in one jail or another cause of child support. Ain't that about the way of it preacher?"

Joe Frank stopped, frozen, looking as though he had been slapped, a stunned, back-to-reality-look on his face, his arms still outstretched in his preaching posture.

Marco was just as stunned, insulted that this other stranger would talk this way to his new friend.

"Please," Marco said, "you should not talk to him that way. He is a man of God."

Dale was laughing, uncontrollably. "Man ah God my ass, a man for every black woman, as long as he can get his hands up their skirt, that is. Hey, preacher," Dale said, louder, more determined, acting as though he had just remembered something important. "I remember now. What was her name? She worked at Sewell's as a seamstress, back around ten years ago. Let's see, what was her name?"

Maybe it was Marco's naiveté, or Joe Frank's kindness, but for the first time since being placed in this Alabama hellhole, Marco found himself caring very deeply about another human being. Thirty minutes ago he had never laid eyes on either of these people, and now he watched as this card-shuffling, retro-looking man with his unwanted tales was trying to destroy another human being with words. Marco had no idea if Dale's accusations were true. It didn't matter.

Dale snapped his fingers as though the rhythmic sound would jar his memory of more sordid details. Moving closer to the now stationary and subdued messenger, who stood breathless, a testament of dejection, still appearing shocked at the recounting, Dale's look of destruction was becoming more anticipatory, as though expecting that the preacher might give up the name.

The effect this preacher must have had on others at one time, Marco thought. *How mesmerizing.* For indeed, watching him for a few minutes, Marco had forgotten he was in a jail; this preacher with his stories and wild antics, his shuffling feet and hallelujahs, had taken Marco to a different, happier place. It was obvious that his new friend wanted nothing more tonight than to climb back up to that level of achievement in his past, a time when what he said and did mattered, a time for him that was happy, where everyone around him felt as Marco did a few minutes ago.

Now, with Dale's foul mouth and lurid tale, the dark reality that is a jail cell once more filled the room. Joe Frank stood subdued and exposed, having been reminded by a sinner that *he* was a sinner-- unworthy to preach to anybody, even if the congregation *was* made up of inmates in a county jail.

"Donita or Akisha or Aleatha or some name like that, and the last name was Baxter. Yeah, that's it," Dale said, amazed and pleased with himself at his ability to recall the name.

"Yeah, kid, I guess she just got too big a dose ah that Holy Ghost, got on her so much she got pregnant."

Dale lay back down on his bunk, shaking with laughter, holding his stomach with his empty hand, the lit cigarette still occupying the other.

The preacher still did not move. Like a New Orlean's mime on Jackson square, he stood frozen in his tracks, his arms still outstretched, looking as though any moment he might take up where he had left off. But he couldn't. Like a Biblical Satan, Dale's fiery darts had hit the target, immobilizing the would-be messenger of God.

Still laughing, Dale got up from the bunk and walked around the preacher like a wolf circling his prey before finally closing in for the kill. Used to a world of cerebral depravity, Dale had figured this preacher out, and intended to put a stop to this preaching madness. And he was proud of it; and, as any good predator would, he was ready for the kill.

"Yeah, I worked for a while at Moore Business Forms, on the hill," Dale said, "loadin' trucks one summer, and I heard them talkin' about this black preacher."

Dale moved his head side to side, in front of the preacher's face, trying to get a response. Nothing. The preacher didn't move. He didn't look at Dale. He didn't look at anyone, just a stupefied, straight-ahead stare.

"The girl was just seventeen or eighteen, and the preacher here was pastorin' a black church in Anniston, and she goes over there to his meetins', joins the church, and he does such a good job pastorin' that bout nine months later, they gottem' a new piccaninny."

The kill should have been complete, but Dale wasn't satisfied.

Marco's Papa always said a wolf kills to survive. Hunger is the motivation. Not Dale, he was a different kind of predator. Destroying this preacher was not for survival, just destruction for the sake of destruction. A coyote may kill to survive, his Papa had said, but he also kills for the sake of killing. Dale could have stayed quiet and shuffled his cards, but he was destroying--like the coyote, because he wanted to.

"Yea, I heard she would wait till the church was a rockin' with music, everybody clappin' and singin' and shoutin', and here she would walk in right in the middle of church;

down the aisle bigger than life with that new baby in her arms."

Marco could not stand anymore. Taught from childhood to defend anything that was helpless when attacked, he especially did not like someone who would kill for the sake of killing. Jumping from his bunk, he said, "I am not listening to this."

"Yes sir," Dale continued, not paying attention to the kid from Mexico. "She'd come walkin' down that aisle with that baby, a new bonnet on the kid's head--*his* baby," Dale said, pointing at Joe Frank. "And she walked all the way to the front of the church and she'd sit on the goddamn front row, next to his goddamn wife," pointing the finger at Joe Frank.

Overtaken, clutching his knees, Dale was bent over with laughter; an incessant, annoying and evil laugh that befitted the predator's moment.

"Can't you see him?" Dale said, in between the spitting laughter. "Dressed in his Sunday best, a new tie and shined shoes; the band at full crescendo in a cut-time beat in front of a packed house. The bass player looks toward the back door of the church; the piano player turns, then the drummer; the choir stops singin'. Then the music dies, and the congregation turns, row after row, to see the late arrival. They already knew her. They had already heard and they knew why she came. Hell, the deacons had already been to her house asking how they could help, and she

61

made it clear that she wanted the pastor to acknowledge *his* baby. And, of course, she wanted money and they gave her some money. But today the money wasn't enough. She wanted more, maybe some hide, some retribution heaped on the heads of the powers in the community--starting with the preacher. The preacher, the deacons, and the congregation watched as she walked that aisle, came right up to the front, getting her pound of flesh. Can't you just see the good reverend up there trying to get it going, trying to do his thing dressed in his starched shirt and fancy store-pressed suit, ready to lead everybody to that Sunday morning promised land, and in she walks with that baby. How'd it feel preacher to watch her come in the door at the back with that baby? I bet you saw her first. I bet that starched collar got to chokin'. I bet you ruined that suit, shit in your pants and I bet she walked *slow* up that aisle--"

Before he could finish, Marco's left hand was around Dale's throat, squeezing just enough to prevent effective breathing and swallowing.

Dale tried to bury his lit cigarette in Marco's arm, but the surprise pressure had bent it into between his useless fingers. He took both of his hands, while still holding on to the cigarette, and attempted to push against Marco's lone arm maintaining the stranglehold.

Somehow, Marco stood straight and

solid, an untapped reservoir of pent up anger and hurt boiled to the top, as his hold on the predator-turned-prey grew tighter by the second. The strength he seemed to possess, the will to use it, and the temper to fashion it, surprised even Marco.

He had never done this before. It didn't matter. The room became a blur. The bunks, the cell bars, the smelly concrete; none of that mattered, and all of it gave way to the determination of the moment. All Marco could sense was the terrible wrong this man was doing. He had to be silenced, and all he could see was the horrific reality of his gripping left hand wrapped around the throat of a man he had just met; squeezing tighter, his bruised and beaten face within inches of Dale's, leveraging Dale's head against his bunk, refusing to let go until there was complete capitulation.

Dale quickly relented, collapsing, and Marco lessened his grip.

"You are a vile man, and you will stop," Marco said, in a soft, determined manner, as he loosened further, then released what was a death grip.

Marco picked up and shoved a completely subdued Dale Carter into his lower bunk, much like you would throw a sack of picked cotton on the back of a wagon.

Dale began to gasp for air, laboring to swallow while gently clutching his red, hand-imprinted throat.

"You're just a killer," Dale said, coughing, trying to breathe deeply. "Don't matter whether you got a gun or not."

Amazingly, Dale was still holding on to the burning cigarette that miraculously had survived the fracas. Mashed between middle and forefinger, and with a trembling hand, he brought its remnants up and took another draw. "Ah, you and this bag of air ain't worth getting scratched over," he said, rolling over in his bunk, seemingly content to try and finish the almost broken cigarette.

As though he were unaware of what Marco was doing, Joe Frank had not moved or said anything during the affray.

"Go on, my friend," Please, I will listen. He will be quiet," Marco said, turning to look at the defeated predator rubbing his throat,

Joe Frank turned and walked the one step to his bunk, silently climbing in, laying down with his back toward the outside, curling in a fetal position, his right hand like a pillow under his head.

Dale Carter and his story had done the job. The life, the light and the preaching had been sucked right out of Joe Frank. The positive energy that had so inundated the room only a few moments ago was gone, an aura of emptiness all that was left.

Like a wounded animal withdrawing to die, the preacher lay quiet, motionless.

Not knowing what else to do, Marco rubbed and patted him on the back like his mama used to do for him.

Under his breath, almost inaudibly, Joe Frank, his back still turned to Marco began to explain: "I messed up; I did, and good Christian folks, well most, don't have a problem forgivin', 'ventually, its jus' dat forgitten comes purty hard."

"Ah come on guys. I's just funnin'," Dale said, shuffling his cards again, and looking back over his shoulder toward his cell companions, as a man would look with the realization that he had messed up the chance for having a card game tonight. "Hell, preacher, I don't blame you for knocking up that girl. I've had a few, myself," he said, laughing again; the level of gusto replaced by a conciliatory whine. "Shit, I don't understand you goody two shoes kind of people. I's just funnin' a little," Dale said, as he threw the cards at the foot of his bunk, and turned again toward his own wall, silent.

"My friend," Marco said to the preacher, continuing to pat his back and ignore Dale.

"Father John, the headmaster of my Catholic school, had a sermon called '*The Evil Wind.*' God allowed the Devil, he would say, to use destructive force all around Job, destroying all he had worked for, but God would not allow him to touch Job, and he soon regained sevenfold everything he had lost."

Marco could not see the preacher's face, and tried to look over Joe Frank's huge frame to see if he was listening.

"Any man that causes harm to another, Father John would say, or tries to destroy another--even with words, even if some of those words are true, is evil. These people, he would say, do not have the salt to stand for anything. They become controlled by this evil wind. Like tumbleweeds on fire in the desert-- destructive and powerful with no control over their own path, not even for the length of time they will burn."

"Hell," Dale said, "is everybody in this Goddamn jail gonna preach tonight?"

"I assure you I am not, but if you say another word, I will finish putting the wind out of you," Marco said.

This is rich. Here I am charged with capital murder, strangling a no-good and instructing a preacher!

"I do not remember a lot of verses," Marco continued, "but there is one from the book of Psalms: '*Fret not thyself because of evildoers. For they shall soon be cut down like the grass and wither as the green herb.*'"

"Dat's da thirty sempth Psalm," Joe Frank said, breaking his silence, his back still turned to Marco. "Somewhere in dare he talks about when a good man fall he ain't gonna be utterly cast down, for da Lawd uphold him with his hand."

Marco breathed a sigh of relief.

"I believe dat," Joe Frank said, his back still to Marco. "And I believes what you done said bout dat wind. Yore padre sound like he a purty good preacher."

Marco smiled, thinking of the comparison between Father John and Joe Frank.

"Nothing like you, my friend," Marco said softly, smiling, his hand still on Joe Frank's back.

The evening's events had left everyone in the jail cell drained of all energy. Both the predator and the prey and Marco were emotionally spent, leaving sleep as their only escape.

But Marco couldn't sleep, yet. He had never felt such rage before.

Was it really Dale and his castigating words? Or is it just my frustration at being here? In one of his classes, Father John had said, "you really don't know what you are capable of till you are put to the test."

Was this the test? Being here? Sharing a smelly cell with a loud-mouthed, Elvis-reject? Or was that just a test within a test; a small window view of a picture within the bigger picture, struggles and encounters while foreigners in this strange land wait for trumped up charges to conclude so they can kill?

I wish this were a bad dream. Then I could wake up at some point and say I had passed the test—in my dream.

His thoughts were again of home, but this time not so much of longing, but of thankfulness for roots, for teachings and lessons learned.

Everybody needs a friend, Marco thought. And for whatever reason he was here, if he had to be here, he was proud to have met this black preacher.

He stayed by Joe Frank for probably half the night, patting him on the back, just letting him know that he believed in him and that he was his friend.

SIX

From his bedroom window, looking past his courtyard beyond the entrance gate to his 10,000 square foot palatial home, Antonio DeMarcos could see the SUV making its way up the graveled road, in the hills below. Juan Fernandez and Roberto Ochoa, both second generation businessmen from Columbia, South America were arriving for a pre-arranged visit.

Their business was illegal narcotics, particularly cocaine, heroin and meth. Both of their fathers had been instrumental in the production and export of illegal drugs from Columbia, particularly to the United States since the late seventies.

"Why are you meeting with these people if you are not interested?" said Elizabeth, as she helped her husband with his jacket, brushing the lint from his shoulders.

"Respect. They asked for the meeting. They are very powerful people. That demands respect. Besides, it never hurts to listen as long as you do not say too much."

Pulling his wife close to him, he kissed her soundly on the lips.

"How long will this take?" she asked.

"A couple of hours. We can't talk business until a respectable time has passed for socialization. They'll eat lunch, have some drinks, talk business and drive back to their plane. I'll see you at dinner," he said, as he made last minute adjustments to his tie.

"Tony, please be careful. These people are ruthless."

Saying nothing, he nodded, knowing that what she said was true and involvement with these people was indeed dangerous.

She was a smart woman; if the truth be told, she probably was much smarter than he was.

She and Antonio had met at Yale at a soiree. She found him charming, handsome enough and rich. He found her attractive, intelligent and American, and in spite of Antonio's attitude toward America and its historical colonialism, he was attracted to her.

Tall, slightly taller than he was, her long blond hair was a stark contrast to his. She was everything he needed and wanted in a wife. The fact that she did not come from money also seemed to be attractive to him.

International business was her major. She always intended to work for a major conglomerate; negotiating deals, traveling to the outermost parts of the world, or possibly working and negotiating on behalf of some government.

Instead, just after her graduation from Yale and the summer before he was to graduate, a simple, yet dignified ceremony was held on the DeMarcos property in Mexico, and Elizabeth Renée Bryant and Antonio Alfonso

DeMarcos IV were married.

Their two children, Luis and Sara, came in successive order, one and a half years apart. Like their mother, after her marriage, they also wanted for nothing. Private tutors, swimming and tennis lessons; all were included, together with English, World History and Economics as part of their education.

"Hey, how about some dessert tonight after dinner?" The gleam in Tony's eyes and the smile on his face making it clear to her that he was not talking about food.

"Well, Mr. DeMarcos, I'll see what I can do," she said, as she began loosening the silk robe. "Right now I have to take a shower." The robe dropped to the floor and she stood facing him with nothing on, her right knee tilted, like a modern version of Venus De Milo.

"Too bad that you don't have the time. We could have dessert before lunch," She said.

Tony sighed, his eyes gazing up and down and across her body, admiring the beauty that stood before him.

He turned and walked out of the bedroom and down the stairs.

My wife still looks good, even after two children.

Tony loved art and history and his house was full of both. Reaching the bottom of the stairs, he paused in front of the mural depicting the revolution of 1910. He remembered his grandfather and the stories he would tell about that time. As a young boy, he would climb into his lap and revel in those stories his grandfather would tell as he smoked that dark brown pipe with a long stem. As though it were yesterday, he could still smell it: a strong commanding tobacco that would inundate the room and linger on your clothes long after the visit and the stories were finished.

He remembered the whimsical look on his grandfather's face as he puffed and enjoyed; a look of intelligence, kindness and sternness all wrapped together, a face with the markings of a man who had weathered many storms, fought many battles, and was here ready to share his triumphs and failures with an eager listener.

Between puffs on his pipe, he would speak almost in riddles, reminding his young grandson of lessons learned:

"Don't ever let the other side know what you are thinking. If your enemies know what is inside you, there is no need for a battle, for they have already won. If you are engaged in business with associates, don't let the left hand know what the right hand is about, for if they know, there is no need to be in business with them, for they will eventually take advantage of you and destroy you in the night when you least expect it."

A philosophical man, he was always ready with a story of struggles and battles, those that had helped the family to improve its standing in the country, as well as those that held them back.

His grandfather's favorite book was by General Sun Tzu, *The Art of War*, an ancient Chinese text written over 2,000 years ago. Many of his grandfather's conversations reflected Sun Tzu's words: "*If you know the enemy,*" quoting Sun Tzu, "*and know yourself, you need not fear the result of a hundred battles.*"

I remember talking to him just before he died, Antonio thought. *I was twelve or thirteen. We were in his home about ten miles from here and I had managed to catch him by himself. He walked over to his desk and picked up 'The Art of War.'*

"*Do you read much? Show me what you read and I'll show you what you are. You become what you think about.*"

I wonder what grandfather would think about these people today?

"*Anyone who is not your friend has to be viewed as an enemy or a potential enemy, and a friend is only a friend after he proves himself over and over,*" Antonio remembered him saying.

Sitting on his lap you wanted him to talk, to teach, to tell his stories, to share his wisdom. The words, slow and deliberate at first in deep contemplative tones would soon evolve into a soothing continual cadence of memories, recollections and anecdotes.

"Tell me about your father," Antonio would often say, and he was always ready to tell of the founder of the DeMarcos fortune, Alfonso Antonio Luis DeMarcos (Great Grandfather): a General in the Mexican Army under Porfirio Diaz, who helped Diaz to seize power in 1876. With his prominent role in Diaz' new government and with DeMarcos' new position of authority, he managed to lay claim to some ten thousand acres of the most fertile land in Mexico along the Plateau.

The rest of the family history, Antonio knew about first hand: Alfonso's son, DeMarcos II (Antonio's grandfather) did little more than hang on to the land; however DeMarcos III (Antonio's father) did very well as a steward of the DeMarcos wealth: educated in Mexico, at the National Autonomous University of Mexico, in Mexico City, he started the factory in 1957, primarily producing cotton and corn for export. His genius lay in his ability to negotiate deals with tenant farmers who produced goods on his land, as well as their own for shipment to the rest of the world.

For the first eight years his business was completely legitimate. Then in 1965 it was brought to his attention that the same ground that grew corn and cotton could also grow marijuana with a much greater return per acre. And Americans loved it, and were willing to pay a lot of money for it.

Upon taking over the factory at DeMarcos III's death, the present Antonio DeMarcos (IV) or Tony, as he liked to be called, began to expand the business, negotiating deals allowing him to control most of the old haciendas and the majority of the ejidos in the area, including the one that a young Miguel Esgivas had worked on since he was a boy.

In exchange for the control of these areas, he provided the workers with modern machinery and advice on rotation of crops, replacing the hand tools and ancient farming practices which resulted in an increased production in cotton, corn and marijuana.

The increased production of marijuana combined with Antonio's control of a powerful gatekeeper in Nuevo Laredo and Mazatlan, propelled him in the mid-1990's to the position of a cartel head.

As leader of one of the five major drug cartels in Mexico, Tony became a voting member in what was loosely known as the Federation, the organization that attempted to peacefully control drug trafficking in Mexico.

The Federation was headed by Osiel Cardenas, head of the Gulf Cartel, arguably the most powerful of the cartels because of their enforcers known as Los Zetas: trained by the United States Army at Fort Benning, Georgia, having been sent to Mexico to help fight the cartels, Los Zetas ended up joining them. Feared even by the Mexican military, their name had become synonymous with killing, and anytime there was killing near the border, Los Zetas was usually blamed--most of the time rightfully so.

Each cartel had their own division leader who was responsible for all stages of smuggling into the U.S., and each cartel had at least one division leader who was loyal to a particular cartel head, with gatekeepers working under them, controlling all major ports of entry, and facilitating trafficking across the border.

So far, Tony had no trouble from the Gulf cartel. Osiel Cardenas with his enforcers (Los Zetas) primarily supplied the west with a variety of drugs, including marijuana, crystal meth, and cocaine. His territory, the Pacific side of Mexico, with its inroads into California and Arizona, seemed to keep Cardenas occupied supplying to that lucrative area; and, at the moment, he seemed satisfied with the fees paid by the other cartels for the use of Los Zetas.

Tony had managed to remain outside the infighting that occurred quite often between three of the most aggressive cartels: Gulf, Juarez, and Tijuana. Attempting to avoid trouble, he had even allowed some encroachment into his Federation-authorized territory and had kept his production at its current levels for the last three years. But in spite of his efforts to avoid confrontation, trouble was now at Antonio DeMarcos' door: the Columbians.

Ken Begal and Phillip DeMarcos, Tony's brother, were standing on the veranda waiting for the arrival of their guests. Phillip's presence wasn't necessary for a meeting like this, but Antonio thought it a good idea to show foreigners the strength of his family. Begal was directly under Tony and was in charge of day to day operations at The DeMarcos plant, which they commonly called The Factory.

Phillip, twelve years younger than his brother, had been unsuccessful at a one year stint in college and had not shown a great aptitude for business. At twenty two years of age, he was in charge of security over The Factory and his brother's home.

"Both of you understand that you are to be seen and not heard," Tony said, as he continued to watch the progress of the SUV which was now entering the estate.

The security for the day had been increased, and the passengers in the white Cadillac Escalade watched with interest, as they passed a dozen or so guards armed with semiautomatic handguns, or Israeli uzi's hanging to their sides from shoulder slings; and some sporting scoped semiautomatic Ak-47's, with most of the men posted on the second story walkways above the courtyard parking area at the front, all entrances, including the gate with two prominent guards.

Stopping in front of the veranda, the suited, front seat driver and front seat passenger both exited quickly opening the door for the two backseat passengers.

"Welcome to Mexico. I am Antonio DeMarcos, but please, call me Tony," the head of the DeMarcos Cartel said, as he greeted the first visitor.

"Senor DeMarcos, Tony, I am so pleased to finally meet you. I am Roberto Ochoa, my associate, Juan Fernandez."

Tony shook hands and smiled at both his guests. Roberto Ochoa was close to fifty years of age and in good shape. Tony knew that this man's father had started the Medellin cartel and that both he and his father had worked closely with the late Pablo Escobar.

Juan Fernandez was younger, even though his receding hair line gave the opposite appearance. His father had started the Cali Cartel, Medellin's competitor in the seventies, eighties and early nineties. The awkward smile on his face made him appear insincere and his wayward eyes that refused to meet Tony's added to that perception.

"Gentlemen, let me introduce you to my brother Phillip DeMarcos. I think you have already talked with Ken. This is Ken Begal."

As everyone shook hands, Tony turned toward the house and began climbing the stairs to the veranda.

"Gentlemen, please follow me. I will show you where to freshen up before lunch."

(Tony wanted no down time for investigatory chatter from these Columbians; he wanted to eat, talk, and get them back to their plane.)

The dining table was appropriately decorated with freshly cut flowers, with settings of silver that had been in his family for at least 100 years. Everything, except the main course had been prepared in advance, and Tony had anticipated the timing of his guests' arrival, instructing his staff to be prepared to serve lunch as soon as they arrived: mesquite grilled chicken with wild rice, salad and flan for desert with red wine.

Fernandez was the talker.

"Last year we went to Israel and every time you turned around, there was a goddamn Jew with his hand stretched out wanting some money. It is a carnival. 'Get your tickets here! See where Christ and Mary stood! See where they prayed!' They have turned Christ into a moneymaking show. I didn't really like the place, but you know how wives are--Spend! Spend! Spend! You work hard to make it, and they work twice as hard to spend it."

Everyone at the table gave complimentary laughter or at least the complimentary smile.

As the dinner-table talk was winding down, Tony thought again of his grandfather: "*All warfare,* quoting Sun Tzu, *is based on deception. Hence, when able to attack, we must seem unable; when using our forces, we must seem inactive; when we are near, we must make the enemy believe we are far away; when far away, we must make him believe we are near.*"

Tony stood at the head of the table with his glass raised. "Gentlemen, I wish to propose a toast: to friendship and our mutual success in business; may the two find a place with us, together."

With that, he reached to his right and to his left, touching glasses with his seated guests, and drank down the last of his wine, smiling as though he meant every word.

"Gentlemen, if you will please join me in the library. I have some fine cigars and some very good French cognac."

"Senor, let me compliment you for the fine meal, I must get your cook's recipe for the chicken. Your home is lovely," said Ochoa, as everyone made their way through the hall, with its historic murals, through the double doors and into Tony's study.

"I understand you also have a beautiful wife and two children. We were hoping to get to meet them," said Ochoa.

"Yes, perhaps next time," Tony said, curtly, then quickly changing the subject. "Are you married Roberto?"

"Oh, si."

"Any children?"

"Si, two also."

"How about you Juan, I know you are married. Any children?"

I will be damned if either of these killers gets to see my wife and children.

"Si, I have three children, one ex-wife and two girlfriends," Fernandez answered, with an exuberant and hearty laugh, as though he had said something extremely funny.

Again, the complimentary laughter, as Tony picked up an engraved mahogany box from his desk and opened it to his guests, then to Phillip and Begal.

"Please. Try one of my cigars."

"Cubans?" asked Ochoa as he picked up a cigar and smelled it.

"No, the maduros are from Nicaragua, the habanas from Mexico. The Nicaraguans are made in Estelí. The man's family that makes these fled Cuba when Castro took over," Tony said, as he watched Fernandez take two, placing one in his pocket and lighting the other. "If you like a cigar with a little more spice, the Mexican habanas are excellent."

"I usually like the darker ones," Ochoa said, referring to the maduros. "Thank you."

"Now, gentlemen before we get down to business, I want to thank you in advance for honoring me with your presence," Tony said, as he motioned for everyone to be seated.

Ochoa and Fernandez sat down on the blue Italian leather sofa, while Tony and the others occupied chairs in the seating area of the room, all of the seating centered around a huge oak coffee table.

Tony observed that Ochoa was the stronger of the two, not quite as boisterous, yet he had more of an air of calm assurance and intelligence to that of his companion. Indeed, when it came time to conduct business, instead of bragging about girlfriends, wives, and relating minutiae of the same, Ochoa was business-like, always a serious tone.

"Pablo Escobar was a friend, a close friend of mine and my late father," Ochoa began.

"My father, Jorge Ochoa, started the Medellin Cartel in the late 1970's. Pablo was just a young punk, a street kid, who started out giving protection to the local businesses in Ehvigado."

"Later he went into business with my father in Medellin. Pablo's strength grew to the point that my father, while still involved in the day to day operations of the business, allowed him to take charge. Together they did great things, things that were never dreamed of before and have not been duplicated since. They had an airstrip in the Bahamas. The planes flew in from Columbia, completely loaded and would fly out to routes across the United States and Europe. At one time, we were moving as much as fifty metric tons per month, heroin and cocaine; all that we could produce, over one billion dollars a year; hundreds of millions in profits. The Medellin Cartel and the Cali Cartel, run by Juan's father had control over the entire market."

"Anything moving out of Columbia, we had our hand in," Fernandez said.

As Ochoa paused to finish the last of his cognac, Tony stood up and reached for the decanter to offer a refill.

"No, I am fine," said Ochoa.

"Sure, I will take some more," said Fernandez.

Ochoa waited for Tony to be seated, and then continued.

"Pablo was a good man. He built over 3,000 homes for the homeless in Medellin."

"His brother has written a book about Pablo," said Fernandez, who, except for the one previous interruption had seemed satisfied to smoke Tony's cigars and drink his cognac.

"It is called *Mi Hermano Pablo*," Fernandez said, laughing in an almost disrespectful tone. "In the book he talks about Pablo being a modern day Robin Hood," he added, his tone bordering on disrespect to the deceased Escobar.

Tony could tell that Ochoa was annoyed at being interrupted by his companion, and even more annoyed at the derogatory tone used toward the revered Escobar.

"The killing," Ochoa continued, "that Pablo had to do was just business for him, but he let it get out of hand. He let some things become a personal contest. The press devoted so much attention to it that every headline cost us millions. Soon it destroyed everything, at least as we knew it. Today the business is nothing compared to what it was."

When Ochoa paused again, Tony decided to help his guests get to the point of their visit.

"I certainly appreciate all that you have

said, and I know the greatness . . . the history of your organization is unparalleled."

Pausing, to take a puff from his cigar, Tony looked upward at the cigar smoke floating in the room. *An appropriate physical metaphor for the storm clouds these Columbians brought with them*, he thought. For part of the history lesson that Ochoa was failing to mention was that Columbians had a history of getting their way and did not mind killing to achieve their goals.

Certainly Mexican cartels had shown an aptitude for getting their own way in business. And while their reputation for killing was well known, Columbians seemed to have a far greater aptitude and an accompanying zeal for it, as well as a much longer history of killing, particularly when the records of the Medellin and Cali Cartels were considered.

Not wanting his next question to sound too insensitive in regard to the regal story of the glory days of Columbia, he stood, poured himself some more cognac, and then slowly began.

"But . . . what does any of this have to do with me?"

Roberto Ochoa set down his almost empty glass and placed his unfinished maduro on the ash tray on the table beside him.

"I am reorganizing the Medellin Cartel," Ochoa said, his slowed speech making it obvious that he had now gotten to the point of the visit.

84

"Senor Fernandez is reorganizing the Cali Cartel. Together, we intend to make more money than anyone in the drug business has ever done, join together and pool our efforts. But to accomplish what we want to do we need a partner in Mexico," Ochoa said.

"We need a partner in Mexico who is reliable. Your reputation is clean, cleaner than any of the other cartel heads in Mexico," Fernandez said.

"I already make more money than I can spend. Why would I want to try and make more?" Tony asked.

"Usted no quiero hacer mas dinero? You don't want to make more money?" Fernandez said in a slow, mocking tone, his head tilted downward, his eyebrows arched; the incredulous look enhancing the insolent stare and intensifying the sarcastic question as he laughed in disbelief.

"It is not just the money," Fernandez said, continuing with his disbelieving, insulting manner, "It--"

Ochoa looked toward Fernandez with an expression that a father would give a young child when he wants the child to be quiet.

"Opportunities," Ochoa interjected. "We all have opportunities in our lives. We either take advantage of them or we leave them for someone else."

Not responding, Tony smoked his cigar. Phillip and Begal remained silent with their cigars and cognac.

"Senor DeMarcos . . . Tony," Ochoa continued. "Since the fall of Pablo Escobar, it has become more and more expensive for us to get our product into the United States. The air strip in the Bahamas has long since closed down. With a few exceptions, the United States Drug Enforcement Agency and the present administration in Washington are content to basically ignore Mexico, but they want continual arrests coming out of Columbia."

"Mexico, unlike Columbia, has potential voters, Hispanic voters, relatives of Hispanic voters that make it politically incorrect to come down too hard on the Mexican border problem. You saw that in the last American presidential election."

"Neither Republicans nor Democrats," Fernandez inserted, "want to address the border problem with Mexico.

"Columbia, however, is another matter," said Ochoa. "We are expendable. We can't bribe enough people to get our product out anymore, at least in the quantities we want to ship. We have become the whipping-boy poster for every politician in America."

"Every time a politician talks about getting tough on drugs, all they see is Pablo Escobar and Columbia."

"With all due respect, Senor Ochoa, I still don't see how any of this involves my family. Just like you, we are subject to what the world offers," said Tony.

"Yes," said Ochoa, "and what the world

offers today is an opportunity for all of us to make money, the likes of which your family has never seen using the Mexican border."

"You have been carrying elephants across the border to make millions. What I offer is a way to carry mice across the border and make more."

"You want me to carry your cocaine and heroin across the border instead of my marijuana."

"No, no. Expand. Still carry the elephants. It is your bread and butter, but carry the mice too. With all due respect, you have achieved great things, but neither you nor I have achieved our potential."

"We can produce the highest quality product, and we have the fields and the production capabilities. We need a partner in Mexico who is ready to share billions."

"Why me? Why not the Gulf Cartel or Amezcua-Contreras or the Juarez or Tijuana?"

"You are the perfect fit," said Ochoa. "Right now, we are not competitors. Our business is cocaine and heroin. Yours is marijuana. Our businesses complement each other. Together we increase one hundred, two hundred-fold on what we make now."

"The people that run Amezcua-Contreras Cartel for instance, Luis and Jesus are too volatile, too violent, the same with the Gulf Cartel and Cardenas. We also do not like what we see from The Juarez Cartel either—hot heads, all of them."

Fernandez reached for the decanter--more cognac.

"And Los Zetas is a little frightening to us. I understand they get the job done, but it looks like Pablo Escobar killings all over again, and as businessmen we know from experience that we cannot afford that. If the Gulf Cartel and Los Zetas do not change their ways, these violent killings close to the border could cause the United States to come down on you, killing your business like the Americans have in Columbia."

"Hell," Fernandez said, "Los Zetas is already crossing over into New Mexico and Arizona to do their killing."

"Someone who looks Hispanic is not safe in Arizona without his papers, all of that because of Los Zetas," Ochoa said.

"But, why now? For all these years the Caribbean and Aruba has been your route. Why change now?" Tony said.

Ochoa, still business-like, realized more convincing was necessary. "Tony, we have great success going to Aruba, to the Caribbean. From there we can land shipments wherever we want in Europe. But, as I have said, with the U.S., it is getting harder and harder and here you sit just to the north of us, our neighbor, Mexico, with eighteen hundred miles of virtually unprotected border; and on the other side is the richest market in the world."

"I am afraid the border is not as

unprotected as you think. It is struggle every week to get our product across," Tony said.

"But you are still successful, and you have the supply routes to get product across. Understand, we don't want to interfere with what you have going. We simply want to tap into what you have developed, and allow you to tap into what we have developed."

"It is a marriage made in financial heaven," said Fernandez, staring into his almost empty glass, as though looking for something lost at the bottom of his cognac.

"What would be my cut?" said Tony.

"Your share would be at least twenty to thirty million a month for starters, and that would grow. We would need to use some of your gatekeepers to get the product up to The Factory, and part of it would come in through another way that we have arranged."

"What way is that?"

"Well, Tony we can't share all the secrets until we are truly married, you know," said Ochoa, laughing now for the first time while looking over at Fernandez, who still seemed consumed with his glass; the cognac having obviously taken effect, he appeared disengaged from the conversation.

Tony smiled. The people in the room could have thought he was pleased at what he was hearing. But, his thoughts were lined with cynicism at the thought of a meaningful relationship with these killers. They dressed well. They acted reasonably well; but no matter their front, they were killers, and he did not trust anything about them.

His grandfather certainly would not have trusted them. *But, would his grandfather have done business with them, anyway?*

"So," Tony said, "once your product gets to The Factory, I use my supply routes to get it across the border to your buyers."

"With this, you and I and Fernandez can make history together," Ochoa said.

"Would you not agree that for history to be made, for this wonderful financial marriage to work, more sharing of the costs would have to be done?" said Tony.

"What do you mean?" Ochoa asked.

"I mean out of that twenty or thirty million a month you talk about, a third or more will be paid out to division heads, gatekeepers, federal and state authorities--and to Los Zetas."

"Those figures are just a good starting point. We have the same type payoffs to get the product out of Columbia. We'll all sit down and come up with numbers to your liking," Ochoa said.

Tony finished his cigar. It was an awkward moment. If he said no, these potential enemies would become enemies, immediately.

"Gentlemen, I am sure that with an offer of such magnitude you did not expect an immediate answer."

"No, no, of course not," said Ochoa.

"We want you to come to Columbia. Take a look at our operation, and of course we would like to look at yours at some point," said a smiling Fernandez, now appearing not nearly as inebriated or distracted as a moment ago.

"Yes," said Ochoa, who along with Fernandez now stood up to leave. "We would like to meet again, say in a couple of weeks, schedules permitting. You come to Medellin or Cali. Let us return your gracious hospitality."

Stepping back into the hallway where the murals of famous moments in Mexican history were on display, Ochoa stopped in front of the painting depicting the Alamo.

"By the way, your artwork is truly amazing. Mexico has certainly had its share of fighting."

A slight nod came from Tony as they continued walking outside.

"We will talk again soon," Tony said, as the men made their way down the steps to their vehicle.

As the Escalade pulled out of the driveway, Tony stood next to Ken Begal and Phillip looking from the veranda at the courtyard of his home, waving goodbye to his guests.

His thoughts were deeply troubled. He had tried to be so careful in his alliance building, so careful not to make enemies. All of the deal-making had been contained in his country, and now these foreigners were at his doorstep, and the options he was left with were not good.

Columbians did not like to be told no, and he knew if he said no to their proposition, they would move to eliminate him, something they were very good at doing.

If he said yes to their proposition, once the Columbians were entrenched and using his supply routes, his gatekeepers and division leaders, they would still very likely move to eliminate him.

"Well, Tony, what are you going to do?" Begal's expectations of being answered immediately did not have an effect on Tony. His reflective pause was extremely long before answering.

"I am going in to see my wife and enjoy the evening."

"But what about the Columbians?"

Tony walked in, closed and locked the front door behind him without acknowledging Begal's insistent questioning.

Tony looked at the same mural complimented by Ochoa on his way out: the triumphant scene from The Alamo, as the Mexican army is hoisting the country's flag above the shattered wall. *Why are we always having to fight to keep what is ours?*

Sitting down in the hallway outside his bedroom, he wanted to think before confronting Elizabeth. His concerns would be nothing compared to hers.

I have better security than any of the other cartels, he thought, as he pictured the buildings, the grounds that made up his factory; all 150,000 square feet inside a 110 volt electrified barbed wire fence. Both types of businesses operated in the stone, brick and concrete space in the middle of barren land, less than one hundred miles from the border, halfway between Piedras Negras and Nueva Rosita: The first involved the shipping, processing and packaging of corn and cotton. The products arrived by truck, railcar and sometimes wagons. After packaging, finished products were sent to wholesale distribution to a subsidiary in San Antonio, Texas. The wholesale commodity business, while certainly profitable, also provided a needed air of respectability for the entire operation.

The second and most profitable business was dedicated to one 5,000 square foot building, partially underground, in the middle of the compound. This building had its own fence, gate and armed guards at the main entrance, with a password activated elevator operated by still another guard that ran to the underground portion. It was a world-class facility, capable of turning out 20,000 pounds of cured, processed, double shrink-wrapped marijuana per week.

What bothered Tony was that up until now he had grown and still managed to remain off of the world's radar screen, operating virtually enemy-free.

But now the Columbians were at his door, trying under the pretense of partnership to take over his business. Notwithstanding their attempt to convince him of their desire to remain nonviolent, Tony realized that these men had been involved--firsthand, with more extreme levels of continued violence than he had ever used, and this violence had resulted in gaining power.

They could talk money and profits all day long, but what motivated these men was power.

They feel their grasp on the world slipping, or they would not want to involve a Mexican. Nothing about this is good. I will have to tell Elizabeth.

SEVEN

The knock at the door interrupted William Davis' dictation. He had a law office to run, and while he enjoyed doing capital murder cases such as that of Marco Esgivas, the tyranny of the urgent was keeping the bills paid--a constant drain on his time. There was a Will to do for an elderly client, a letter to a judge concerning a bond reduction, and at least 30 phone calls to answer, some of which could be potential employment, and of course, there was the planning of the fast-paced trial of Marco Esgivas.

Davis' secretary appeared at the door.

"Mr. Davis, Dennis is here."

"Good, send him in. Oh, and call Shelly Harmon's office and get her secretary to give you some times when we can meet. Judge Munroe is appointing her as my second chair."

"Who is she?"

"She's new, and probably more trouble than help."

Dennis Allenger was Davis' investigator. A college drop out after one year, he went to work for the Anniston police Department, and after ten years of being underpaid, decided to become a private investigator.

Tall, slender, and youthful, his good looks were not in any way lessened by his slightly receding hairline, the rest of the hair shoulder length; and, he had the attributes that made him very much in demand: honest, tenacious, resourceful, and he made a great witness in front of a jury. Equally important to Davis, he was willing to wait about getting paid until the conclusion of a case.

"Hello, counselor."

"Dennis, I'm going to get the judge to authorize you to be my investigator on this new case."

"What kind of case?"

"Murder of a state trooper on I-20."

"Oh, the Mexican kid."

"Here's the information I have so far concerning the stop," Davis said, as he picked up a piece of paper from his desk and handed it to Dennis.

"According to this report, the officer stopped the driver for following too closely. Then the officer never reported anything back. He was found dead and our client had the murder weapon in his hand."

"They arrested him with the weapon?"

"He was unconscious, lying on the interstate."

"What kind of vehicle?" Dennis asked, as he sat down in one of Davis' office chairs. Pulling out a cigarette, he was preparing to light it, but because of Davis' stare thought the better of it. "I thought you smoked in here?"

"Not cigarettes," Davis said. "A moving type van with Texas tags. The officer was on the drug interdiction team.

"What was in the truck?"

"I don't have an inventory yet. But according to one of the deputies, nothing was in the truck. There is a guy in Texas I need you to check out, his name is Donnie Ray Tarpley."

"How is he connected?"

"He forced Marco to make this drug run with him. That's how Marco ended up in Alabama and on the interstate. Tarpley has a car lot in San Antonio, Texas, called *Cowboy's*. According to Marco, they made several stops at strip bars; one in Mississippi and one of them in Birmingham."

Dennis looked at the incident report, as he talked. "So it was a drug run—but nothing was in the truck?"

"Yep, go figure."

"According to this, your client was the only one there, lying next to the dead officer on the interstate."

"Yep."

"So Mr. Tarpley is our main suspect. Does the sheriff's office know about him?"

"I don't know. I also need you to find out as much as you can about Marco's parents."

"O.K. How much do you want me to spend?"

"The state will pay eventually and I'll front some expense money, if I have to," said Davis, in a sardonic tone.

"Alright, that means Day's Inn instead of the Hyatt."

Davis continued, seeming to not pay

attention to Dennis' response. "You and I will possibly be going to Texas, maybe Mexico to talk with his family."

"I hope you got a rabbit to pull out of a hat, cause this sure doesn't look like a winner," Dennis said, as he glanced at the incident report.

"Oh, you know me," Davis said with a grin, "I always have that hat ready, provided my brilliant investigator supplies the rabbits."

"Hm," Dennis grunted. "Anything else?"

"I suggest you be very careful. This very possibly is one of the Mexican cartels we are dealing with, and they may not appreciate the questions a nosy investigator from Alabama will ask. I need you to get going on this ASAP."

Davis, finished with the meeting, went back to dictating a letter. His mind was on Marco.

Particularly disturbing to him was how this kid from Mexico, with no reason to be in Alabama, and no apparent motive to kill an Alabama State Trooper, ends up unconscious on the side of the interstate with a dead state trooper by his side and a Smith and Wesson snub-nosed 0.38 revolver in his hand. He hadn't asked his client for an explanation—yet. There was plenty of time for that. *Besides, the jail has ears.* He planned to pick a time when they were at the courthouse to ask that pointed question.

Davis got up from his chair and looked outside through the shutters as Dennis' car was pulling out of the parking lot.

A rabbit indeed. I hope you can find one!

EIGHT

Every day was busy at The Factory. Shipments, arrival times of raw materials, and the maintaining of equipment to process the cotton or the corn, and of course the marijuana, was just part of the demands of this multi-million dollar facility, along with keeping enough workers to operate the plant-- ones that could be trusted to work and also keep their mouths shut.

Quality control issues were always springing up. Even the crops in the field had to be monitored. Sprinkler systems sometimes needed repair, and coordination between crops in the field, picking times, processing as well as the ultimate shipping of the final product for wholesale distribution, whether legal or illegal, were constant concerns.

Kenneth Begal was the man in charge of making sure all these problems were short-lived, and Tony had no qualms calling him early or very late on a given day to solve the latest problem that had presented itself.

It was Monday morning, 6:00 a.m., ten days since Marco was arrested, when the call came from Tony: "Meet me at The Factory, immediately."

"Come in, Ken," came the almost unrecognizable, gruff response to the knock on Tony's office door.

"Ken, you know Miguel from shipping."

Ken stood in the door, surveying the scene: Miguel Esgivas stood in front of Tony's desk, hat in one hand, his back to Ken, seemingly immovable, holding an envelope in the other hand. Phillip sat in the corner sipping orange juice, and Tony, looking very displeased stood behind his desk.

"Sit down Ken," Tony said. I have been talking to Miguel about his son, Marco. He did not come back last week from the delivery you sent him on. I know you did not know about it, or you would have told me," he said, as he looked at his nonresponsive employee and long time friend.

Tony did not give time to respond.

"Miguel, I am going to need to discuss this with these men. I assure you I will do everything in my power to bring your son back home."

Miguel got up and slowly headed toward the door as Tony followed. Just as he reached the door, Miguel turned to DeMarcos.

"Senor, I trusted your father. I trust you. But . . ."

"Thank you, Miguel. Let me work on this."

Tony opened the door and looked down the hall, then closed it, waiting to allow Miguel time to get down the hall before speaking.

"What the hell happened here? This man shows up at my home standing at the gate at 5:00 a.m. this morning, waiting to see me

101

about his son. This kid was supposed to deliver the truck to our man in San Antonio and head back home."

"I don't know, Tony. I. . ."

"Why did you not tell me that this had happened; and, if you tell me you really did not know, then explain to me *why* you did not know." Whether for dramatic pause or to give Begal time to answer the question, Tony waited a moment before continuing. "Do you realize what this development could do to this entire operation?" Tony said.

"It's just one kid," Begal said, with far too much flippancy to suit his boss.

Tony slammed his hand on his desk.

"It is not just one kid. It is one kid whose father runs our shipping department; whose father designed our current methods of shipping; and, who knows too much about our business for his son to be at the disposal of the Americans."

"Look Tony, I knew the kid had not come back, but sometimes the drivers stay over in San Antonio a few extra days after a run. I have no idea how this kid ended up in Alabama."

Seated in his chair, an exasperated Tony looked at Ken and said, "How did you know he was in Alabama? You knew. So not only did you not tell me that he had not come back, you also kept from me the fact that our shipment was lost, and the fact that he was arrested--in Alabama."

He did not answer.

"Ken, you and I have been friends since college, the best man at my wedding. But, I tell you this. I don't care about your reasons. You keep something like this from me again and I will deal with you like I would any other disloyal employee."

Begal still did not answer.

"When I see you again," Tony said, "I expect some answers," he said, accentuating his disgust by sitting down and turning his chair and his back on everyone in the room.

"Gentlemen, close the door on your way out."

NINE

Every large town has a sleazy side, a place where strip clubs, adult video stores, pimps and prostitutes monopolize an area, ply their trades, sell their goods, and call it their own. In Birmingham, Alabama, First Avenue North, just off Oporto Road is such a place.

Most city's managers will usually turn one blind eye to the sin on the seedy side of town, while the other eye remains steadfastly focused on the tax money generated; and, from time to time, when necessary, strong words of consternation are offered up by the politicos, placating the right-wing, churchgoing voters, assuring them that their fair city is not turning into Sodom and Gomorrah.

We have it contained in a particular area, would always be the politician's answer to any worrisome questions from those opposing factions.

Here, neon signs of red, white, pink, and blue molded plastic, advertise their wares: *Completely nude girls. Adult novelties. Must be 21 to enter. XXX rated*! Here, the signs line the avenue, beckoning those who would partake of a different side of life, an *adult's only* amusement park behind closed doors with no windows, ready to take you for an adult ride with your adult money. Here it could all be bought, sold or rented: toys, adult games, videos, video sex games, marital aids and of course, women or men.

As an investigator for the Anniston Police Department, Dennis had made several trips to this part of town with local law enforcement looking for suspects or witnesses. It had changed since then, flashier, more like a Las Vegas-style strip.

It was a Friday afternoon, 5:10 p.m. The traffic was intense as he exited I-20 west onto Oporto Road and headed north, toward the Adult strip and *The Show and Tail Club*.

He decided to forego the parking behind the club and parked his Toyota Tundra in the metered parking spaces down the street in front of an Adult Video and Toy store.

Dennis had his hair pulled back in a short pony tail and was wearing faded blue jeans, boots, a fake earring in his left ear, and a t-shirt with a message that would be appreciated by the people he expected to encounter.

The sign on the Video Store door said 'MUST BE AT LEAST 21 YEARS OF AGE TO ENTER.' No windows, just the door.

On entering, Dennis saw what he would believe to be every type of adult sex-toy ever created by mankind: vibrators of every shape and size, artificial penises, artificial vaginas, and of course it looked like at least a thousand pornographic movies, both disc and VHS, for sale or rent.

"Hi, can I help you?" said the slender, tall, not-too-young lady with mousy blond hair standing behind the counter.

"Just looking around," Dennis said, pretending to be interested in an assortment of lubricants in the case below the counter.

"I like your shirt," she said.

"Thank you."

"Let me see," she said, "turn around." Dennis turned and she began to read his shirt: *'STICKS AND STONES MAY BREAK MY BONES BUT WHIPS AND CHAINS EXCITE ME!'*

Laughing out loud, she said, "Ooh, I like that."

"Might let you wear it sometime," Dennis said, feeling extremely silly as he said it.

"But if I did that, I'd have to take mine off," she said, turning around so he could read the back of hers. *'SAVE A HORSE RIDE A COWBOY,'* "And I like mine better."

"Tell you what," Dennis said, "We'll swap right now if you want to."

"I ain't that easy. Sides, you ain't a cowboy," she said, giggling like a school girl.

"Well I'm as close as you're going get around here."

"Anyway you want somethin' took off, you need to go next door or wait till I get off and see if you get lucky," she said with a sultry grin, as she chewed her gum.

"Well, what time do you get off?"

"7:00"

Looking down at his watch to check the time, Dennis continued the repartee.

"Tell you what, if I'm still here, I'll come over."

Motioning with her right hand, she said, "Well, you want a movie to warm up with."

Still grinning, holding his hands up, he said, "Got no way to look at it in my truck. Maybe I just need to warm up next door."

"They got three or four girls right now. Don't really get any action goin' till nine or ten."

"What kind of action?"

"What kind you want?"

Dennis grinned and shrugged his shoulders.

"I can tell by that grin, you want what every other man wants."

Dennis leaned closer, not wanting any customers to hear.

"Well, what happens when a girl won't give ya what you want unless she gets a joint first?"

"Oh, you can get that over there, anything you want. Just ask for Speck. He's the owner's brother." Lowering her voice, she leaned across the counter and said. "He can supply you with weed, meth, cocaine, crack, ice, you name it."

"I'm real particular," Dennis said, whispering. "The best stuff comes from Mexico."

"Oh yea, Speck's got it. He gets a delivery bout every month or so. Hey you're not a cop are you? You got to tell me if you are. You know it's the law," she said, becoming extremely serious, her smile disappearing.

"Please, do I look like a cop?" Dennis held out his arms and smiled.

"I guess not," she said, smiling again.

"Well darling," Dennis said. "What's your name?"

"Linda. What's yours?"

"Just call me Cowboy. I tell you what, come on over there when you get off, and if I'm still there I'll buy you a drink."

"Maybe, we'll see."

"Alright. See you around," Dennis said, as he began to head toward the door, stepping aside, as a customer walked in.

She motioned up to the clock.

"I'll be here till seven."

Dennis smiled and tipped his hat to his new acquaintance and walked out of the windowless store turning left toward the 'Show and Tail' next door.

"Come on in. That'll be five dollars," said a bushy-browed, Neanderthal-looking man, wearing a tuxedo, sitting on a stool outside the door.

A cave-man in a tuxedo, Dennis thought. *Now, that's funny. They must be shooting an insurance commercial!*

"Five dollars? What for?"

"Parking."

"I didn't park in the back. I parked on the street."

"I don't care. Anybody gets in has to pay for parking."

"Is Speck in yet?"

"Yea, he's here. You a friend of his?"

"No, I was just told to ask for him. Here you go," Dennis said, as he handed over the five.

Dennis was greeted by the loud music as he stepped inside a corridor filled with pornographic advertisements: Coming attractions: current and former Playmates of the month for the top selling magazines. *You saw her in Penthouse, Swank, Gallery, Velvet and more; 34D-24-25, seen in High Society, Easy Rider, Club and Hustler. Amateur Contest–$500 Prize; All Female Wrestling Show-- starts @ 9PM; Babes Battling Babes!*

The autographed, less professional looking pictures has to be the local talent, their attempt at a seductive picture hampered by the lack of professional lighting, all with a plentiful display of cellulite.

Just ahead was a glass, double-door, which allowed you to see just enough flesh through the cigarette smoke to whet your appetite. The room vibrated with the bassy sound of music within.

Behind a poorly constructed counter, made with cheap paneling and counter top material stood a scantily clad, big breasted blonde, possibly in her late twenties who bore a strong resemblance to one of the women he had just seen on a poster in the lobby.

"Hi, that'll be five dollars," she said with a smile that would make refusal difficult.

Maybe it was her big blue eyes with the long fake eyelashes or her smile, remarkable primarily because of the obvious lack of dental work. Or maybe it was the bleach-blonde hair combined with the see through mesh shirt, cropped off just above her navel ring. Whatever the reason, Dennis didn't argue.

Has to be for a good cause, he thought, as he handed the second five dollars in less than two minutes. *Whhh.*

"Devon working tonight?"

"You a friend of hers?"

"Sort of."

"Well, here," she said handing him back his money. "You don't have to pay. Go on in."

"Thank you, sweetheart," Dennis said.

Tonight's the night, gonna be alright. . .

The music of Rod Stewart, while loud to the point of annoyance in the corridor, was deafening inside, as Dennis walked in.

The room was filled with tables and chairs surrounding the three light-lined stages filled with female figurants of varying degrees of dress; on the floor below the stages at small round tables sat the patrons who could not find a seat closer to one of the stages, served by at-break performers, all scantily clad—of course, mostly just topless, some with trays of drinks and empty glasses held high, as though posing for an artist's rendering, as they maneuvered their way between the tables, others taking orders or wiping the tables making it presentable for a newcomer.

The stage in the middle had been built wider than the others, to allow the four almost nude girls a place to stand, as they danced for eager customers, flashing dollar bills for a close-up look.

At the end of the bar, Dennis watched as a guy with an Atlanta Braves baseball hat carefully set his drink down and picked up one of the dollar bills that were lying in a stack in front of him. Holding the money with his right hand and using his forefinger and thumb of the left, he creased the dollar bill down the center, then waved it in the smoke filled air toward the tall girl dancing on the bar.

Showing great skill and balance, she maintained eye contact with the gentleman, as she shifted her long black hair back and forth, creating a sensuous border for her rather sexy face. Slowly, she began to slide the only remaining piece of clothing she had left down her thighs until it dropped to her ankles, resting on top of her black platform high-heeled shoes.

Gracefully, she stepped out of her black laced panties with her right foot. Then, with the toe of her left foot she gave them a sling upward and caught them effortlessly with her left hand. Still holding them, she stepped in front of him and squatted down, opening both legs, allowing the stranger with the cap, a full, unobscured, eight-inches-away view.

The viewer with the Braves cap had no eyelashes batting, no change in expression, and no inference that there was brain activity. He stared at her private area, like a man that had just found everything in life that he had been searching for and intended to commit every aspect of the visual treat to permanent memory. His stupefied, hypnotized look unchanging until she took the stiff dollar bill and placed it in the black garter on her left leg along with the six or seven others she had collected during her strip-tease performance. Like a catcher for a baseball team, she slowly and gracefully stood up, and then repeated the exposure to three or four other gentlemen along the bar's edge.

With equal suspension of all brain function, they were treated to the same viewing while *their* extremely stiff and creased dollar bills were tucked into her garter.

"Hi, my name is Candy," said a topless, red-haired lady, who had appeared next to Dennis, holding a tray of empty glasses. "Let me know if there is anything I can get you." She said, shouting above the music.

"I'll have a Margarita," Dennis shouted back, sitting down at a nearby table.

"You want salt on the rim?" The young lady asked.

"Yes ma'am, please. Say, can you tell me if Devon is here yet?" Dennis said, still having to almost shout in her face due to the music.

"No, not yet," she shouted back. "She doesn't get here till a little later. Do you know her?"

"The girl out front said she was here."

"Well, she is, but her shift doesn't start for a few minutes."

"How much does she get for a private lap dance in one of those rooms?"

Grinning, the girl said, "You'll have to talk with her about that. How about me while you're waiting?"

Dennis smiled, looking the topless beauty up and down, as though considering her offer.

"How much do you get?"

"For you, if we can go on now, maybe two hundred."

"Well, I need a drink first, don't you think?"

"Sure, honey. I'll be right back."

This place is so loud! If I have to come back, I'm putting some cotton in my ears, Dennis thought.

His table was between the center stage and the main stage to the right, which looked like a smaller version of a Miss America stage, complete with a well lighted runway. The silver pole at the back centered the widened area of the stage and allowed the girls a prop to augment their performances as they stepped out from the curtain.

"Let's give her a hand folks, Miss Zoe

Lynn," the announcer said, as the music stopped just for a moment at the conclusion of the act. A smattering of applause erupted for the plus sized dancer, as Dennis watched Ms. Lynn bend down to pick up her discarded clothing and some scattered money that had been thrown on the stage before scurrying off and disappearing behind the curtain.

Dennis was glad that the music had stopped. "Here you go sugar. That'll be $6.50," Candy said, handing him his drink.

"Keep the change," Dennis said, handing her a ten dollar bill.

"Thanks honey. Oh that's her about to come out on stage."

"Who?"

"Devon," Candy said. "But I'm still the one you ought to get in the VIP room with," she said, looking back, as she walked away.

A strong cut time drum beat began that got progressively louder--again.

"All right, it's time for a little Devon in the afternoon. Here she is folks, last year's Miss Nude Birmingham, and former winner of Zombie magazine's country centerfold contest, Miss Devon Wolf."

The curtain moved slightly, almost like a tease, then swung back, as a short, nicely built brunette came out from behind. She was clad as most every other girl was—not very much, along with black platform shoes.

Her dance was a real dance, choreography accented by the blaring music and flashing lights. On-cue, collective 'Ahs' came from the audience as she swung round and round the silver pole.

She was totally in rhythm with the music, dismounting, landing with her legs split, in rhythm, rolling until one leg extended past the edge of the stage over the bulbs, propped on to the shoulders of a very excited oriental man, his glasses fogging up very quickly, in close proximity to the leg.

Except for the opportunity to lose your hearing, this has to be the greatest job in the world (mine not hers), Dennis thought, as he lit a cigarette and watched the first and second article of clothing leave Devon's body and sling through the air like a new bride giving away her garter.

"Let's hear it for Birmingham's own, Devon Wolf," the announcer said, as Devon left the stage.

"Don't forget the VIP rooms are ready for you when you're ready for private entertainment. Just talk to the lady of your choice and she'll make all the arrangements."

"Can I get you another drink or anything, honey?" This one was a red-head he hadn't seen before.

"Could you tell Devon to come over, please?" Dennis said, as he sipped on the drink.

"Sure," she said with a dejected look similar to Candy's earlier look.

The entire bar was now a maze of open

sexuality. The main stage was going strong, with somebody named Gina, a very tall, athletic girl performing extortion techniques as she waved her blonde hair in a circular motion; the middle, smaller stage was filled with three different women attempting to stay out of the each other's way as they danced. Out on the floor around the tables were five other girls who were now doing individual dances for patrons at their tables.

"Hi there, my name is Devon. What's yours?" As she said this, Devon climbed into Dennis' lap, and with her arms around him did not wait to hear his name.

"I heard you wanted to see me. What can I do for you? Ooh," she said with a high shrill voice. "Your belt buckle is cold!"

Dennis always felt he was quick on his feet and could exchange one-liners with the best of them, but he realized that his tongue and brain moved much slower when a pretty half-naked brunette was in his lap.

"How much for the VIP room?" He said, finally managing to get the words out.

"Well it depends on what you want done."

"Just the usual."

"How about five hundred?"

"Well, I was hoping to get you for a hundred."

"I'm worth five."

"Can't argue with that, but if I spend five hundred, I won't be able to come back tomorrow night. How about two hundred?"

"O.K. you're on."

Getting out of his lap, Devon reached for his hand and led him to the back area of the club, past the bar, up a short stairway, and into a large hallway with three doors.

The yellow neon sign with the red lettering, 'VIP PRIVATE LOUNGE' was above the doors, reflecting off the bright red carpet. Black plastic letters on each door completed the information: 'NO ONE UNDER 21 ADMITTED.'

Devon, holding Dennis' hand, led him into the first room: not very big, possibly ten feet wide and just a little longer, with one surveillance camera in the right hand corner.

The red carpet continued on the floor with a rounded black leather seating area, in the shape of a semi-circle, with a small, lighted, round table, centered and fastened to the floor in front of the seat. The mirrored walls made the room appear larger.

"I haven't seen you in here before. How did you know about me?" Her tone, inquisitive, suspicious.

"The Texas guy," Dennis said.

"Texas guy? Oh, you mean Ray. Yea, he comes in here all the time, about every month or so.

"Yea, he supplies some really good stuff," Dennis said.

"Oh, you do know about him." She seemed relieved. "That's funny, you don't look

117

like y'all would get along."

"Really, why do you say that?"

"Well, I don't know. You sorta watch people. Oh, here, I'm sorry, I'm just talking away. Go on and sit down, honey. Well, I have to go ahead and collect the money," she said, holding out her hand, and pointing to the camera on the wall with the other. "I trust you, but it's the rules."

Reaching over to an intercom system mounted on the top of the leather seats, she pressed a button, and immediately music began piping into the room from inside the club.

"Is that loud enough?" she said.

"Too loud," Dennis said.

"Yea, I work three nights and my ears get pretty tired," she said as she reached over to turn the volume down, then mounted the table and began her exotic moves.

"I really don't know him that well," Dennis said, keeping to the conversation about Tarpley. "I just met him a few times."

"Well, you're so nice," she said, as she began taking off her high-heels, "and, he's--"

"An asshole?"

Laughing out loud, she almost lost her balance. "Yea, I didn't want to just come out and say it. Now he's a great tipper, and a lot of fun, but . . ."

"But, you just don't like him."

Grinning from ear to ear she said, "Now ain't that awful of me?"

118

"Why don't you like him?"

"Oh, I don't know, just a feeling you get. I like you though," she said, sweetly, walking closer and placing her hands on his shoulders.

Dennis decided to take his chance.

"I'm a private investigator hired by one of his wives."

"One of his wives?" Devon said, as she climbed down from the table and sat down next to him, her top still lying on the table, very interested in what Dennis had to say.

"What if I were to tell you that Tarpley has three different wives in three different states, along with seven children?

"Seven children?"

"How does he support them?"

"Well, that's the thing. He doesn't. Poor kids are starving to death, and their mothers are . . . well, one of them has to wait tables during the day and strip at night to keep food on the table. I'm just trying to help out. I need to find the guy and let these poor ladies start divorce proceedings, one at a time I guess, and see if they can get child support."

Dennis' head dropped in sad fashion.

"Oh, that sorry piece of shit!" Leaning closer, her tight lipped words were barely able to come out.

"I knew he was no good. You can just tell. I see a lot of men and I can tell. You know the last time he was in here he brought a real young guy in, a boy, really," she said. "He kept laughing at the little guy because he was

119

uncomfortable. Ray got mad at me, because I refused to strip till he let the kid go outside. Wow. That sorry piece of shit! Seven kids, and him spending his money like it was water over here and them babies hungry. I wish I could help you. I'd like to fry his ass."

"Well, you could help me by telling me what you know about him."

"Sure, honey. O.K. He comes in about once a month. Stays maybe one night or two, a big tipper, like I said."

She stopped talking, obvious that she was trying to think of more to tell Allenger.

"Oh, "He usually meets some guys here."

"From here in Birmingham?"

"No, uh, uh, out of town. One guy comes all the time up here from over towards Georgia."

"From Georgia?"

"No, next to it." Snapping the fingers of her left hand to help her memory, she said, "Sheriff! Yea he's a sheriff, kept telling me if I ever was going to Atlanta and needed help over that way to give him a call."

"Do you remember his name?"

"No, I don't remember."

"Was the sheriff from Cleburne County?"

"Cleburne County. I'm not sure."

"A town called Heflin?"

"Yep. I think that's it. Heflin. Yea, because they kept making a dumb joke, calling it Hell-fell-in."

"What did they talk about?"

"They were always talking business of some kind, you know, money being mentioned."

"You said another guy came."

"Yea," Devon said, as she snapped her fingers again to help her memory. "And he was a state trooper. I told both of them the last time they were here that they ought to wear their uniforms and scare the shit outtah Speck."

"Devon!" A deep voice from the intercom startled both of them. "Is everything all right?"

Devon looked up at the surveillance camera and motioned that everything was O.K.

"They get antsy if I'm not dancin'," she said, starting to climb back up on the table.

"Look, I'm going to run on," Dennis said, having gotten the information he wanted, and feeling a little unsettled at being watched.

"Don't you want me to finish?"

"I would love to stay, but I need to get cracking on this. If anybody wonders why I left, just tell them I got sick."

"O.K. honey; I hope you catch him and make that worthless piece of shit pay. I'm so proud of you," she said, her hand around his waist. "If it wasn't against the rules, I'd kiss ya," Devon said, as she began fastening her top back on.

"Well, next time I come, we might need to just break the rules."

121

"Wait, you better let me walk out with you. If they don't see me they might stop you--think something's wrong."

Dennis opened the door. The loud music rushed in.

"Thank you again, Devon," he said, as he headed out the door, with her beside him.

Dennis noticed two men, rough looking with ill-fitting cheap suits, talking and watching him, just to his left, near the back of the large stage. They continued watching him as he made his way across the room, past the bar to his right through the maze of tables and dancers. In a matter of seconds, he made his way back through the glass double doors, past the entrance foyer of advertising to the outside walking swiftly past the tuxedo-wearing Neanderthal.

It was beginning to rain. Dennis was very excited about the information he had just gotten and the connection of Ray Tarpley to the Cleburne County Sheriff and to a state trooper--very possibly the dead one.

The rain was coming down harder.

Wow, they got out quick, Dennis thought, as he looked up ahead at the end of the street, seeing the same two men that had eyed him from the club, now standing on the sidewalk between his truck and the video store.

With keys in hand, Dennis stepped from the sidewalk into the street heading toward the driver's side of his truck, as the two men left the sidewalk and stepped in between.

"Speck wants to see you," one of the men said, his hand inside his jacket pocket intimating that he had a gun.

"I'm sorry. I don't know a Speck."

One of the men, the more clean-shaven of the two, smiled, and as he chewed his gum said, "He don't know you either, but he wants to see you. Says he never seen a man come into a strip club to talk--especially about his friends."

The door to the video store opened and the light from the store flooded into the rainy darkness, shining on all three men and the truck. Linda, the girl behind the video store counter that Dennis had met earlier, walked out and provided the diversion that he needed.

"Hey, there you are," she called out to Dennis, from the edge of the sidewalk. "I got off early. I'm ready for that drink."

Both men had turned to look at Linda, but immediately turned back around on hearing screeching tires and horns blowing. Dennis was running across the street.

A changing light and the onslaught of increased traffic delayed their pursuit, as Dennis disappeared around a corner and up the street.

Out of view, and taking full advantage of the chance to build a lead, Dennis ran outright for three blocks then hid in an alley behind a Church's Fried Chicken, watching from behind a dumpster as the rain continued to fall. He stayed there for at least fifteen minutes before finally getting the courage to walk to the street and wave for a taxi.

After three passes in front of and behind the club, Dennis had the taxi driver drop him off at his truck, and as quietly and quickly as possible he slipped into the driver's side, turned the ignition, pulled into the street, and headed south on Oporto road. Five minutes later he was on I-20 east heading home.

Too dangerous to use the cell, he thought. *It would have to wait. Davis would be pleased with wh*at he had to tell him in the morning.

TEN

He had never been north of the border. But *they* had his son. He was not even sure that *they* would let him see his son when he arrived in this place called Heflin, Alabama. But he had to try.

Senor DeMarcos understood. He was a father. He bought the bus ticket. He even gave me five hundred American dollars for traveling money, Miguel thought, as he felt again of his wallet in his back blue jean pocket, as the bus headed north on Interstate 35 out of Laredo, Texas.

Even kindness had its limits, particularly in business, and more particularly in the business that Senor DeMarcos' family was in.

"I want to remind you," Senor DeMarcos said. "You are going into a foreign land, foreign to everything you and I hold sacred. It is a place where they put food on their tables by lying and stealing from the bounty of others. Watch what you say and remind Marco that both our family's survival is depending on him."

While not used to hearing veiled threats, Miguel could certainly recognize one, and the true meaning of Senor DeMarcos' words was clear.

Except for the fact that the signs were in English, the land that was being passed looked like the northern part of Mexico that he called home. Flat, with more clouds than mountains on any horizon, and a worker's sun in the sky that seemed to always be hotter than any other part of the world, and always seemed to take too long to set.

Miguel had a window seat, but its greater purpose seemed to be as a prop to rest his head against. His eyes barely open, only occasionally did he see the coyote or prairie chicken or road signs referring to small towns like Encinal, Artesia Wells or Cotulla.

His mind was on home, and he passed the time thinking of home, his family, and particularly of Maria:

~~~~~

His wife of 20 years had been extremely quiet for the past month. But in spite of Marco's captivity, it seemed she had not allowed it to dampen her spirits. At least that was her facade.

She celebrated the *Posadas* at St. Sebastian's, where for nine nights before Christmas, the members of the church met there with family, friends and neighbors to act out the journey of Mary and Joseph to Bethlehem, and to watch the children play the *piñata* game.

Miguel did not enjoy the festivities. Watching children play was difficult. To Miguel, every little blindfolded boy who

126

attempted to break the piñata with a stick was his boy--a little Marco. Bursts of laughter that would come as the candy and fruit and toys spilled to the ground were not made by other children. To a grieving Miguel, they all sounded like his son.

He would watch and listen to their squeals of joy, then turn to look at Maria. She smiled, but would not look at Miguel.

He knew that she dared not, for indeed, the usually sought after expressions of glee and laughter from children at Christmas time served now to deepen her pain—their pain. At least that was how Miguel felt and he was certain she felt the same, her façade just a show of strength.

There were no tears when Maria had first learned of Marco's arrest. He did not question it, for he knew she cried them alone; he knew, because he had heard the sobbing late at night when she thought everyone was asleep.

She knew this was coming, she told Miguel. God had given her a dream: a little boy, lost in a faraway place. Miguel knew she prayed and cried many times in the course of a day, for all her family, but particularly for Marco.

"Miguel you must stop blaming yourself," she said, "you think you have killed him just because you chose work at DeMarcos' Factory instead of the fields, but you were just trying to be a good father, supporting your

127

family. And as she kissed Miguel goodbye Maria said, "Tell him I love him and I know he will be coming home. Tell him that."

As Miguel and his youngest son, Carlos Diego prepared to leave for the bus terminal; Maria appeared clutching a beige, shawl-type, knitted blanket that was lined with fringe. Strangely she looked happy, joy on his wife's face that he had not seen in months.

"I wrapped this *rebozo* around Marco when he was a baby," she said, weeping for the first time in front of him. "I have kept it neatly folded in my dowry chest to use with Marco's children. Just as I dreamed of my boy being held in a foreign land, not being allowed to come home, God has also given me a dream about this *rebozo*."

She held it up, and with a huge smile said, "It will be wrapped around a new baby--Marco's baby."

She waited for a response. There was none.

"No, I am not crazy," Maria said. "I have seen this, Miguel. He will come home."

Her expression changed, more thoughtful, stern.

"He must come home," she repeated in a deliberate fashion, as though saying it aloud and seriously would make it so.

~~~~~

"Papa, do you think Mama is alright? I mean, does she seem alright to you?" Carlos Diego said during the drive to the bus terminal in Nuevo Laredo.

"No. None of us will be alright till Marco comes home," Miguel said.

~~~~~

After a brief stop in San Antonio, the bus continued in a northeastwardly direction to Austin, through Waco and finally to Dallas.

More people, strip malls, Wal-Marts and skyscrapers began to appear. Miguel had seen big cities. He had been to Monterrey, even to Mexico City. Those places, even with their tall buildings had a feel of home, but *these were places where a man could lose everything*, he thought, as he again felt his back pocket.

In Dallas, a mandatory bus change took place for all those heading east to Birmingham, Alabama. An old man boarded the bus and sat down next to Miguel.

I was only doing my best to support my family, Miguel thought. *I wanted my boys to go to college, to make something of themselves besides a poor, dirt farmer.* "Is that so bad?"

"What did you say?" said the old man. He had begun reading a newspaper, but looked up, stirred from his reading by Miguel's sudden outburst.

"Oh, I am sorry, Miguel said, realizing that he had spoken aloud. "I was thinking about something else."

Miguel wanted to ask the old man where

he was going and where he was from, some polite conversation between two travelers. Since the business with Marco, there had been no one for Miguel to talk to, and he had so much inside him that needed to be said--to somebody. But he could not talk to this man. He could not talk to anyone.

How do you tell someone that you are on your way to visit your son in an American jail in some place called Heflin, Alabama? How do you tell them that your son is accused of murdering a law enforcement officer? No. The guilt is mine. The problem is mine and I will have to bear it alone--solve it alone, Miguel thought, as the bus left the terminal in Dallas, Texas, and proceeded from downtown Dallas on Interstate 20 heading east.

There wasn't a bus terminal in Heflin. As a courtesy to those few passengers who wanted to go here, Greyhound Bus line would accommodate them by getting off the interstate and making the one and a quarter mile trip to a stop in the middle of Ross Street, the main thoroughfare in town. Except for the obvious signs of modernity such as concrete and two traffic-lights, Ross Street and Heflin, Alabama still looked much as it did in 1906: a one dimensional town with one main street and stores lined from east to west.

The trip from Nuevo Laredo, with all its stops, had taken almost twenty hours, but the next day's sun was still high in the sky as

Miguel, the lone passenger getting off at this stop stepped down off the bus.

His plaid shirt, naturally washed out blue jeans, wide Texas-looking belt buckle and straw cowboy hat certainly did not look out of place, although there were few people that walked the street that early afternoon to compare with.

The driver opened the compartment underneath the bus to retrieve Miguel's canvas duffle bag and a tired Miguel began to look over this Alabama town that held his son. He was surprised at how small Heflin was; surprised that a town with one four lane street through its middle would have so few businesses, all of them in a row on either side, broken only by an old train station on one end and a Methodist Church and a Chevrolet dealership on the other.

Plain-dressed people with overalls and jeans. Nothing that bespeaks of wealth, he thought, as he viewed the entire town from the sidewalk in front of The Cleburne News office.

Must be a lot of sick people to be this small and have two drug stores.

Sitting on a slight hill to the north was the courthouse: a massive two story, silver-domed building; its importance, obvious by its elevated, central location and its ornate architectural design. Monstrously larger than the other buildings, it stood in stark contrast to the plainer less elaborate shops of the rest of the town. The dome's grayish silver color and trim work glistened in the afternoon sun, looking to Miguel like a giant piece of historical jewelry reaching to the sky.

No different from home, Miguel thought, *the courthouses and banks have all the money.*

"Excuse me. A place to eat?" He asked a man in overalls, who pointed to an old block building with a dilapidated, plank-front façade and cook smoke coming from the back, with the smells of bar-b-que permeating the air on both sides of the street.

It was 3:00 in the afternoon. Miguel was hungry, and except for a bag of chips, sunflower seeds and several bottles of water gotten at the bus station in Dallas he had not eaten since leaving home the day before.

Arguably, *The Pool Room Cafe* was the most unpretentious building in a town that seemed to pride itself on plainness. He stood in front of the restaurant, with its scratched, flecked and dented, badly-in need-of-new-paint wooden doors, not knowing whether to go on in. Miguel knocked. He heard some response, but not understanding exactly what was said, decided to knock again.

The door opened.

"Come on in, honey," a lady said, as she opened the door. "You don't have to knock."

Miguel took off his cowboy hat, holding it in the same hand as his duffle bag.

The inside was just as unpretentious as the exterior, except that the cinder block walls

132

were newly painted and the gray concrete floor appeared shiny clean.

There were no windows and only two small tables in the front part of the restaurant. Larger wooden picnic tables were in the back. There, adjacent to the tables was a large, smoke-filled, well lighted room, filled with four commercial, eight-foot pool tables. An opened pack of Camel cigarettes was on one of the tables, with cigarettes spilling onto the table and floor. Two young boys, both looking as though they should be in school were shooting pool, loudly experimenting with curse words, smoking the Camel cigarettes, and drinking Dr. Peppers.

The hard surface interior provided an acoustical bouncing of sound where every strike of pool stick and ball combined with talking and laughter and shuffling feet were loudly pronounced, all of it reverberating as though inside a metal drum.

From the right, behind an unstained, plywood counter, more sounds escaped through short, saloon-type, swinging doors: kitchen noises of clanging pots and pans, and the sizzling sounds of cold meat and cold potatoes meeting with hot grease.

"Order up", someone called out. Chatter erupts from the waitress taking a customer's money and jingling from the cash register add to the compendium; all of it combining in the hard-surface room, creating an overwhelming audio-sensory awakening, where individual

133

sounds become meshed.

Miguel's eyes darting from side to side, tried to reconcile the visual with all he was hearing.

After a moment of hesitation, he sat down in a wooden straight chair at a small wooden table near the front door and picked up a menu. Even though he *could* speak English--enough to get by, he could not read a word of it. But that didn't stop him from trying to appear that he could.

"What can I gitcha?" The waitress who had opened the door for him said. Her pad and pencil outstretched, ready to take Miguel's order, vigorously chewing gum as she spoke.

Well beyond her prime, she dressed as though she were not: tight blue jeans, tennis shoes and beige turtleneck sweater that left nothing to the imagination.

"Cheeseburger, fries and water please," Miguel said, trying not to look at her, as he put the menu back in its place between the salt and pepper.

"Be right out," she said, scurrying to the kitchen.

He turned and watched the young boys with their pool game. They were oblivious of him, chattering about a girl, laughing, talking smack about the next shot, both sucking on cigarettes as though it were a straw, then attempting to blow the smoke to the ceiling.

"Here you go," the waitress said, several minutes later, setting his food on a plastic plate in front of him.

"You want some ketchup?"

"Si, yes." Miguel said, quickly remembering he needed to speak English.

"That'll be $3.84," the waitress said, as she tore the ticket from her pad and laid it on the table.

Miguel handed her a five and immediately began eating.

"Could you please tell me where the jail is, and lawyer William Davis?" Miguel asked, as the waitress walked back over to the table to give him his change.

"Sure. The jail's across the street, behind the courthouse." Pointing in a direction, she said. "Just walk up here to the red light next to the old bank building and turn left. You can't miss it. Now, Davis, that's a little harder. He ain't in town. He's about fifteen miles from here out in the country past Hollis Cross Roads."

She laid his change and an extra napkin on the table then walked back toward the counter. Miguel continued to eat. The waitress was now staring at him. Her right hand on the counter, her head turned over her right shoulder toward Miguel. Her feet were planted in the opposite direction and she looked back at Miguel in that fashion for quite a long time before laying her pad on the counter and quickly walking through the small swinging doors into the kitchen.

In a moment she reappeared, followed

by what appeared to be the owner: a short, stocky man, in his late fifties, sporting a full length, white apron on top of the blue jeans and white t-shirt. The anchor tattoo on his forearm and the crew-cut made him look very much to be a former Navy man.

The cracking sound of the balls at the break of a new game startled both the owner and the waitress. They both jumped, as though a gun had been fired. Holding her chest from the fright, and looking back and forth between her aproned employer and Miguel, the waitress carefully approached Miguel's table, as though she expected some injury to result from the movement in his direction.

Miguel realized that he was the center of attention, but continued to appear disinterested in anything but his food.

"I didn't know you *was* Mexican," the waitress said, now standing next to his table, her statement made without the benefit of the chewing gum. *Swallowed it during the fright*, Miguel thought, as he dipped his french-fry in ketchup, calmly chewing, staring straight ahead at the door.

In an almost scolding manner at not being forewarned of his nationality, she said. "Everyone ofem that works at Tyson's looks Mexican. But you don't. They sound Mexican, and you don't."

Finishing the last of his meal, Miguel finally looked up at the now seemingly disturbed waitress.

136

"Could I have some more water, please?" he said.

The waitress looked around at her boss, as though she needed approval for the request.

He nodded, and as she filled his glass she said, "You kin to that Mexican they got in the jail? The one that kilt that trooper?"

Miguel drank the water, emptying the glass, and as he picked up his canvas bag and stood, the waitress backed up toward the counter next to her boss and watched as Miguel headed to the door without answering or looking at either of them.

He debated whether to talk to them, whether to tell them who Marco really was. He would love to explain how his boy was raised; how it would be impossible for him to commit such a crime, any crime.

No. They would not listen and they certainly would not believe.

Miguel walked through the door. In a moment, he was in front of a three story brick building surrounded by fencing and barbed wire—the jail.

Sprinkles of light rain were beginning to fall as the electronic gate opened, allowing Miguel to enter the jail yard.

Nothing was as he expected. This jail looked no better than a cheap, three-story motel with a fence around it. No guards. No cameras. He had expected more from the great United States of America.

~~~~~

The case of The State of Alabama v. Marco Antonio Esgivas was moving faster than any murder case William Davis had ever tried.

The autopsy report, which could take as much as six months to one year, had already been delivered to Davis. A special grand jury had been convened by the court for the express purpose of indicting the young man from Mexico and a special arraignment had been set for the following Monday morning: a non-event where a plea of not guilty would be entered and a date set for trial, a date which Davis had already been told would be in one month with no continuances.

"Good, I'm glad you got on over here," said the jailer, Sam Watkins, as Davis walked in.

"I think the boy's father did pretty good to get this far, but I don't know if he could find your place," he said.

"Family visitation ain't till Sunday, but I figured if you came down, I could get by with lettin' him and you visit, at least as long as the sheriff don't show up"

"Where is he?" Davis said, referring to Marco's dad. I'd like to meet him first."

"He's in here," the deputy said, leading the way to the middle room, adjacent to the front station, the same room where Davis had first met Marco.

"Mr. Esgivas, this is your son's lawyer, Mr. William Davis."

"Senor, it is a pleasure to meet you."

"Well, I'll go up and get him," the deputy said, as he headed up the stairs.

"Please sit down, Mr. Esgivas. I appreciate your coming. You must be very tired. How did you get here?"

"The bus--Nuevo Laredo."

"Do you have a place to stay?"

"No."

"Well, there's a Howard Johnson out by the interstate. When we get through, I'll carry you there. I have a lot of questions I want to ask you, but not in here. After you visit with Marco, we'll go somewhere and talk.

"Si. That will be good," Miguel said.

"Papa? Hello Papa," Marco said, as he and the jailer entered the room.

Miguel had traveled over one thousand miles to see his son, and now that he was standing in front of him, he could not speak and for just a moment Miguel went back in time when Marco at nine years of age had begun helping him in the cornfields:

"Papa I can work just as hard as you can. You will see," Marco said as the two began to hoe the corn that day.

"Careful, you will hurt the small leaves. Bring your hoe out this way and chop the weeds like this. Good. That's right."

Miguel was shocked at his son's

appearance. Perhaps it was the weight that Marco had lost or maybe the bruises that could still be seen on his face; or, maybe it was the shock of seeing his son in an orange jail uniform with the dull silver ankle and wrist shackles and red swollen wrists. *This was America? The place everybody wants to come to because they have all these rights and protections?*

"Mr. Esgivas, I am going to let you visit your son, but I've got to search you. Please turn around and put your hands against the wall and spread your legs," the jailer said.

Looking anxiously toward Davis, Miguel did as he was told. Sam Watkins started the pat-down process at the bottom of Miguel's pants legs. Reaching in each back pocket, he came across Miguel's wallet and as he pulled it out, Miguel's hand immediately came down and stopped just short of grabbing the jailer's hand.

"Hey, I'm going have to search it. You need to simmer down," the jailer said, as he looked inside. "This Mexican's like the rest. They always got cash money. I ain't never seen one yet with less than five hundred." he said, as he handed the wallet back.

"O.K. you can turn around now. Let me know if you need anything, Mr. Davis."

"Sam, do you mind if I step outside with you and let them visit for a few minutes?"

The jailer looked apprehensive.

"You've already searched him. They

haven't seen each other in months."

After a moment's hesitation, he said, "I guess it's alright, long as I can see through the glass. But keep in mind," the jailer said, more loudly, sternly. "Ain't anybody going to question nothin' if I have to shoot one of you."

With that, Davis followed the jailer into the front office leaving Marco and his father alone.

Miguel wrapped his arms around his son.

"You still want to take me to the United States to get a steak?" Marco asked.

"You remember that, hah? Our fishing trip on the Salado River, about ten years ago, I think."

Stepping back to look at Marco at arms length, he began speaking in Spanish. "Are you alright? Did they hurt you bad?"

"Not bad. They got rough one time," Marco said, continuing in their native tongue.

"Why--"

Before he could finish his question, Marco began answering.

"The cowboy, Ray Tarpley made me go with him."

"How did the man end up dead?"

"It was night time, very late. The law man pulled us over. Tarpley got out. They talked. I stayed in the truck. With the traffic, I could not hear everything that was said. After a few minutes, Tarpley came back and told me the trooper wanted to talk with me. I got out and went to the back of the truck. He told me to spread my legs and feet and he began to search me. Then--"

"Fellows," the jailer said, standing in the doorway between the room and the front office. "I'm afraid we'll have to cut this short. Come on, Mr. Esgivas."

Still standing in the doorway, the jailer turned back to Davis. The sheriff's car could be seen just pulling in front of the jail.

"You'll need to get him on out, Mr. Davis. The sheriff'll be in here any second."

Davis stepped into the room. "Mr. Esgivas, if you would, please come in here. The visit is over."

"Do not worry," Miguel said to Marco as he was walking out the door. "Your Mama, she dreams her dreams. She said to tell you everything will be O.K. You will be coming home."

"Come on Mr. Esgivas," Davis said.

"Tell Mama I love her. I think about home every night."

"Come on, now," Davis said to Miguel, pulling him through the door, and breathing a sigh of relief. "Stay in here. I need to see Marco for a moment and then I'll be out."

Miguel stood in the small office in front of the counter for a moment watching Davis talking to his son.

"If you would, have a seat Mr. Esgivas," the jailer said, pointing to one of the straight chairs lined up against the wall. Miguel picked

142

his bag up next to the counter and set it beside the chair as he sat down.

For the first time, Miguel noticed the white, five gallon plastic buckets hanging from the celetex ceiling just over his head and above the counter.

"Alabama ingenuity at its finest," said the jailer. "I'm sure y'all have these problems down your way."

"Water?" Miguel asked, as he continued looking upward.

"A little of everything. Don't think you'd want to drink it."

Aviator sunglasses and a cowboy-styled felt hat, similar to his own, was the first thing Miguel saw as the door opened and Sheriff Sykes walked in. His khaki uniform looked almost military: crisp with a large black belt adorned with the requisite flash light, ammunition packet and Glock 45 caliber pistol; finished at the bottom with black military boots.

"Sheriff, this is Miguel Esgivas, Marco's father."

Looking at Miguel without emotion the sheriff said, "Did you search him?"

"Yes sir."

"Well, you came a long way didn't you?" Sykes said, as he looked through the glass door at Davis and Marco. Walking past the counter toward his back-room office, Sykes turned back to the jailer and said. "Family visitation isn't till Sunday. I guess you can tell him that."

143

The jailer busied himself with the shuffling of some papers. "Yes sir," he said, as the sheriff walked into his office and closed the door.

~~~~~

It was dark, and the rain was coming down extremely hard as William Davis' black Jaguar splashed its way into the parking lot of the Howard Johnson near the interstate.

Davis and Miguel had left the jail some time earlier and had sat talking at the Huddle House just across the road. Information on Marco's family was gathered by Davis, as he watched a perfectly good ham and cheese omelet with hash browns being smothered with an entire bottle of hot sauce.

"You're not going to put any on the grits?" Davis asked, grinning.

"No. I do not like grits," Miguel said, as he continued eating with obvious enjoyment. For the better part of two hours and with great pride, Miguel eagerly talked about his family, their values, their convictions, as though he felt it necessary to convince Davis of Marco's innocence.

Finished, they drove in the still pouring rain across the highway to the motel.

"Do you need me to help you check in?" Davis asked as he parked the car.

"No. Gracias."

"I want you to know it was a pleasure

meeting you. I wish I could meet your entire family--"

"Can you save my boy?" Miguel interrupted Davis in mid-sentence.

"Mr. Esgivas, what your son is facing is the worst possible thing a man or woman can be charged with. If he is convicted --"

Again, without giving Davis a chance to finish, Miguel interrupted, finishing the sentence for him.

"He will be sentenced to life in prison without the possibility of parole, or killed."

"Yes," Davis said.

"Can you save him?"

"I have a great deal of experience, Mr. Esgivas, and I will do everything I can under the law to help him, but--"

"I know. The deputy, he say you are best," Miguel said, obviously unsatisfied with Davis' perfunctory answers. "But, can you save him?"

Davis knew that Miguel was desperate for words that would give him hope, and Davis wanted so much to be able to say what this desperate father wanted to hear: 'that everything would be alright; that he would win the case.'

He wanted to say that. He wanted to say anything that would change that hopeless look in Miguel's eyes and allow this man to go back to Mexico with the longed for relief he had traveled so far to attain. But he could not.

There was too much against Marco: the

murder weapon; a dead law enforcement officer, and the fact that the accused was a foreign citizen, with no legal right to be here certainly did not help. None of that would give any reasonable person, much less a trained criminal defense attorney reason for optimism.

"I don't know. Frankly, in most cases such as these, if a lawyer is successful in avoiding the death penalty it is considered a win," Davis said,

Miguel sat in contemplative silence, and Davis waited a moment for more questions.

"Are you going to wait here till Sunday to see Marco?" Davis asked.

"No. I am going back to Mexico, tomorrow--if the bus comes tomorrow. I can do nothing for my son, here, by myself."

"I don't understand," Davis said.

"Goodbye," was Miguel's answer, as he shook hands with Davis and quickly climbed out of the car into the rain.

Davis watched Miguel as he went into the motel. *I'd better wait and make sure he doesn't need any help*, Davis thought. When he saw a room key handed to Miguel, he backed his Jaguar up and headed toward the highway.

What did he mean by 'nothing for my son by myself, here'? Certainly, there was nothing he could do here. It was the way he said it. Oh well, it's Monday. He's just a father that doesn't want to wait almost an entire week to visit his son for an hour. Probably needs to get back to work.

Davis leaned his head back on the headrest, turned his wipers to the highest speed, and headed toward home.

~~~~~

Dawn was breaking as a cloud-hampered sun was trying to show itself just beyond J.A. Owens's old lumberyard, across the street from the jail.

The rain of the night before having long since moved on to the east was now replaced by colder temperatures that served as a stark reminder that it was still wintertime in northeast Alabama.

The red-brick, three story jail outlined in the darkness by a power pole street lamp near the entrance was now giving way to silhouette outlines of brick, concrete and wire fencing and barred windows. As these shapes took on form with the natural light, Miguel could be seen near the back of the courthouse crouched near the ground, next to the steep angled, concrete steps that made their way from the parking lot through a steep grassy embankment down to the jail. It was used by the deputies to escort shackled prisoners to and from their judicial appointments.

He had been there since 2:30 a.m., squatting, sometimes in the rain, his cowboy hat and light jacket the only protection from the elements. From his vantage point, he could see two sides of the jail, including all traffic in and out of the jail parking lot.

He hadn't stayed in his motel room very long. He couldn't sleep. Finally after hours of staring at the ceiling, he got up, left his key on the table, picked up coffee and biscuits from the same Huddle House where he and Davis had eaten the night before and walked the one and a quarter miles in the darkness. The last three hours had been spent eating his ham and biscuits, mentally measuring distances, and recording times and facts concerning the comings and goings of the jail.

His bus would not arrive until 2 p.m. Until then, he intended to finish his biscuits, drink his coffee and water and think.

He came for answers. They were as expected. He knew he could not rely on the American justice system to save his boy. The bruises on Marco's face and the lack of confidence by his lawyer, as well as the sense of distrust of him by the people in this town had convinced him that he had to do something or he would never see Marco in Mexico again.

He had nothing to write on or to write with, but he kept the notes he was making, and had made when he was inside the jail clearly in his head: *one relatively untrained guard; 19th century, old west styled keys to the cells hanging on a hook within arm's reach--as you walked in; gates easily opened, no cameras, and, according to the motel manager, the most traveled road in the United States (I-20) less than two miles away. And it would take you all the way to Texas on a tank of gas! 5:00 p.m. to 7:00 a.m. appeared to be the slack times.*

Miguel was tired and cold, but gratified that he now had the information he needed to help his son. He would stay there most of the day, until his bus arrived. By the time he got back to The Factory, he intended to have a plan to present to Senor DeMarcos to bring his son home.

ELEVEN

"The Columbians are behind this," Ken Begal said.

"Why would the Columbians feel a need to disrupt our shipments?" said Phillip.

"They want us to have problems so we'll bring them in," Begal said. "The timing of their visit, their urgency to meet and do business, the arrest of one of our own; all of it points to them."

"That doesn't make any sense," Tony said. "How would the Columbians know enough to be able to get one of our own arrested, without the cowboy getting arrested, too?"

"How should I know. For all we know the cowboy just happened to get away."

"Have you asked him—how he got away?

"No, Tony, I have been a little busy to talk to one of our mules."

"Maybe you should ask him," Tony said in a detached manner.

Since the meeting started, all of Tony's questions or comments had been without emotion, as a man would contemplate a detached philosophical preponderance, only wishing to calmly propose a debatable issue. Begal and Phillip had been in Tony's office for the last hour, discussing a smorgasbord of Factory issues that seemed a waste of time: the potential fallout of the Marco situation. Were the trucks properly registered in American names? Had the driver's been properly prepped?

It was early, and in Tony DeMarcos fashion, he had called both of them at 6:00 a.m., telling them to be at the factory for a meeting, 7:30 a.m., sharp. It was as though Tony had brought them in to talk so that he could watch them.

"For the Columbians to be behind this, they would have to have inside information," Phillip said.

"Well, maybe they have bugged the place, or . . ." Begal said.

"You know I sweep for listening devices every other day . . . "

"Or, they got to somebody on the inside," Tony said, still without emotion, finishing Begal's statement.

The phone rang, rescuing everyone from the seemingly endless round song of a debate.

"I do not have time. Did he tell you what he wants? Alright, send him back. Tell him to wait outside with the guards and I will be right with him."

Tony hung the phone up, continuing to stare at it, as though he were expecting another call. He was pre-occupied in an extreme way; both Phillip and Begal still had not been told why they had been summoned so early. His questions and comments had a ring of distrust or lack of confidence, yet, there were no accusations. To both men, Tony certainly would have looked like the proverbial poker player, his cards close to his vest, his face devoid of expression, his mind intently contemplating how much to bet--or maybe which employee to bet against.

For Tony, thoughts of his grandfather, his words, his wisdom, milled through his mind. How he would love to talk to him now, to get his approval on what he was about to do.

Do not let the right hand know what the left is about, he would say. Tony was sure of that. Indeed, not even his own brother knew of his plans: tomorrow, he and his family would do what no other DeMarcos had ever done--he would leave Mexico--for good, and leave the fate of the DeMarcos Empire to someone else.

He and Elizabeth had decided to leave the night Ochoa and Fernandez had come to the estate. The situation in Mexico, at least for Tony, had become unwinnable. There always had been interference from the Americans; always the other cartels that tried to take part of your business, and these problems had been and were acceptable parts of doing business. But now he had the Columbians to deal with. And they would take what they wanted--from him or whoever was in charge of the DeMarcos Cartel, and he was certain that whoever was in charge would die, relatively soon.

He intended to grow old with his wife and family. He wanted grandchildren on his knee, giving them the benefit of his wisdom, just as his grandfather had done for him.

He so wanted to tell his brother of his plans, but he dared not.

Today, business as usual.

In the morning he would finish transferring the rest of his bank accounts to Bank of America in Miami Beach, and by noon tomorrow, his children, his wife, and he would be gone. Florida would be their home. If saying the *Pledge of Allegiance* and singing '*My Country Tis of Thee*' was necessary to live without concomitant fear of dying, then so be it.

He did not have time for this unscheduled meeting, but he certainly could not meet with this man tomorrow. Tomorrow he would be gone.

Tony refocused his thoughts on the two men in the room. He would give orders as though this place held something for him tomorrow. Useless orders, for certainly, whoever took charge after he left could change them. He no longer cared.

"Phillip, Ken," Tony said, as he refocused his thoughts on the meeting he had called. "Phillip I want some increased security, particularly until we sort out this Columbian thing."

Phillip looked puzzled, for the guards at both Tony's residence and the factory had been doubled since the Columbians' visit.

"Do you want more guards?" Phillip

said, tentatively.

"I'll leave the details up to you."

"What do you want me to do?" Begal asked.

"Double check all the trucks, the registrations. And don't lose any more shipments."

"But," Begal said, "it is a given in our business that probably 50% of the shipments will be taken."

"Yes, and I'm tired of that. I want a report from you in the morning on how you plan to keep that from happening," Tony said, as he stood. "I will expect reports from both of you . . . in the morning. Please excuse me, I have to see someone."

Begal got up and headed out the door. It was apparent that Phillip, who was hesitant to leave, was not satisfied with the instructions; he wanted more explanation before leaving.

Tony smiled at his younger brother. "Tomorrow, my brother. Please, excuse me, I have to attend to this," he said, as he ushered Phillip out and closed the door.

Outside Tony's office door, Ken Begal waited, talking with one of the guards, looking down the hallway watching Phillip leave and curiously waiting on Tony's urgent visitor.

Miguel Esgivas hurriedly rounded the corner, wearing the same clothes he had on when he left three days ago. He was weariness itself, tired, unshaven and dirty; a haggard representation of a powerless father whose innocent son was facing death in a foreign country, a nonstop traveler who had been without sleep and little food in a quest for information, and as he rounded the hallway corner, his brusque demeanor, determined gait and insistence on seeing DeMarcos, made it apparent that he was on a mission. The fact that he did not smell as good or look as presentable as Ken Begal did not concern him.

"Miguel, it is good to see you," Ken said in the most caring tone he could muster.

"How is Marco?"

Miguel did not want to talk to anyone but Antonio DeMarcos, and he certainly did not want to talk to the one he blamed, almost exclusively, for his son's desperate plight. For it was Begal that had insisted Marco make the run to San Antonio, and Begal who had pointedly told Miguel that he could not go in Marco's place. Thousands of miles of Greyhound bus travel had severely heightened his already sharpened disposition, and his unsociable tone matched the cold look of disdain on his face, as he curtly answered Begal's question.

"He is in jail."

"Ponga sus manos en alto," said the guard, motioning with his Krinkov rifle that hung from his shoulder in a two point sling, for Miguel to lift his hands and turn around so that he could use a metal detecting wand to check for weapons.

For the second time in as many days,

Miguel was searched. He understood those Gringos doing this to him in Alabama--but not here. *Not my own people.*

He was tired, but the anger, frustration and guilt had combined with his exhaustion to create a sustaining energy. *I will explain to Senor DeMarcos that I have to go back and get my son. He has to help me with my plan,* Miguel thought, as Tony DeMarcos opened the door.

"Come in, Miguel," DeMarcos said, holding the door open. As Miguel went into the office, Ken Begal, still in the hallway, looked on as the door closed.

~~~~~

Visitors to the Miguel Esgivas home were infrequent at best; usually consisting of friends and family, particularly friends of the children, and usually on the weekend. But, visitors during weekdays and even more especially at night were unexpected. So, a knock on the door at 9:20 p.m. at the Esgivas home was all the more surprising, especially considering Miguel had just gotten home.

After a supper of gazpacho andaluz, a cold soup made from tomatoes, onions, garlic and peppers, Miguel had long ago fallen asleep amidst the telling of tales of his non-stop three day trip.

For the sake of his wife and children, his descriptions of Marco and his trip to Alabama were embellished: *How wonderful Marco looked,* Miguel had said. *His lawyer is the best and expects to set him free.* Nothing was said about shackles and bruises and the candid evaluations given by Davis.

Miguel knew that to tell Maria of what he saw would break her heart, and fortunately for him the questioning had soon ended. He was tired and needed rest.

Maria was greatly relieved to know that Marco was alive, but knew that her husband of almost 20 years was not being forthright. As he headed to bed, she wondered of the truth, but did not want to press the issue until he had rested.

Even though she knew in her heart that Marco would be coming home, *tomorrow I will insist he tell me the truth,* she thought. For tonight she would accept his story and have faith in her dream.

Maria was sitting with Carlos Diego in the main room of the house when the late night visitor knocked on the door.

"Who is it," Carlos Diego said, getting up to go to the door. Maria motioned for him to wait.

"Senor DeMarcos sent me," he called from outside. "He must see Senor Esgivas now, tonight, at The Factory.

Maria walked over and stood by the door, not convinced that she should open it.

"It is about your son, Marco," the stranger said.

On hearing Marco's name, Maria opened the door just enough to see who she was talking to: a young man, possibly American, dressed in a suit, his hands opened in front of him, as though making a point to show that he did not have a weapon.

"What is so urgent that could not wait until tomorrow? My husband is exhausted," Maria said, as she looked past him to see that he had arrived in a pickup truck, and that he was alone.

"What about Marco?" Carlos Diego asked, as he joined his mother, looking over her shoulder, peering at the visitor through the small opening Maria had created by continuing to hold the door open only a few inches.

"Senor DeMarcos wants to look at a plan, tonight."

"What plan," said Carlos Diego.

"That's all I was instructed to say. Senor DeMarcos will be waiting for him there in his office."

"But he has had no sleep," Maria called after him, as he got into his truck.

"He said now, tonight," the visitor reiterated, as he slammed the truck door and drove away into the darkness.

"Who did he say he was," Miguel asked, as he splashed some water on his face from the basin beside the bed.

"He never said. I do not like it. I need to go with you."

158

"For what? Except for my sons, I have always gone to work alone. Besides, we have children that need you here."

"At least take Carlos Diego with you."

"No. He needs his rest. He has school tomorrow. Senor DeMarcos had already told me to take tomorrow off and rest. He probably just wants to deal with something tonight, so I will not have to go back in tomorrow."

Maria walked over and grabbed his arm.

"But you have never gone at night like this," she said, emphatically, worried. "I do not like it."

"I have never had a son in jail that needs to get out," he said, loudly, his exhaustion overriding his desire to keep the truth from Maria.

Maria was stunned. She sat down on the edge of the bed and buried her face in her hands. *She knew her husband had not told the truth about their son.* In spite of believing that he would come home, that the rebozo she had wrapped her Marco in would be used again to swaddle his baby; despite those assuring dreams that she knew had come from God, she also knew that her boy was in danger. There was something dreadfully wrong. It was more than just the fact that Marco was in a far away land in jail, the hour, a stranger, Senor DeMarcos demanding a meeting this late--all of it, terribly wrong.

"I have to know the truth," she said, getting up from the bed, and standing next to

159

Miguel.

He would not look at her, but stared blankly at the crucifix on his towel-covered dressing table as he buttoned his shirt, as though it were a mirror that would help him button faster.

"If everything looks as good as you said for Marco, why do you need to get him out?"

"I have to get my wallet," Miguel said. He was tired, and it was hard to avoid the questions. At supper, he had controlled the conversation, telling her what he wanted before going to bed. Now he felt he had to tell her more, but he could not bring himself to tell it all. Besides he did not know what Senor DeMarcos' plan was, yet.

"America is not as great a land as I once believed. I always said that I wanted to go there, take my sons there, and take you there," he said. "No more; it is not a Biblical Canaan flowing with milk and honey."

"Is Marco in danger?"

"You must trust me," Miguel said, as he walked out of the bedroom toward the front door, looking away from her still, as he left. She followed him out of the bedroom past Carlos Diego, who was still sitting in the main room of their small house, listening, watching his mother begin to cry, as she followed his father step for step to his truck.

"Maria," he said, pulling his wife close, holding her, a long embrace, as if it were the last time. With her face in his hands, he looked deeply into her eyes.

"I am so sorry," he said.

"For what? She asked, as the tears ran down her face.

He tried to say more, to tell her the truth, but he could not. The truth was too hard. Words would not come, but as he looked into her eyes, he knew they would tell her what his lips could not say. *A man's eyes are the light of the soul*, and Miguel knew that his soul was in turmoil, and its reflections would show through his eyes a bruised and beaten young man, kept in a place that was dark and damp and smelled of raw sewage, of shackles that were too tight on their little boy's red and swollen wrists and ankles. Too long a look and she would also see what all of this had done to her husband, for he had become a hardened man; not just the outer part, created by a hard life in the sun-drenched fields, but the inner man, crusted and calloused through and through. The type of deep inundation that makes a man bitter to his core, making him forget that there is goodness in the world, causing him to think and do things that before he would not have contemplated--something, anything, even if it destroys that hardened soul and weary body in order to effect it. She could see, now, that the realities brought to bear by the cruelty done to Marco had created in him a hardened, resolute perspective, and that Miguel was determined with or without DeMarcos' help, to do what was necessary to

161

save their son. And that was why he had to go, tonight.

While his eyes told of pain, hers still spoke of love, just as they did long ago on a full moon night like tonight. Shining on her beautiful hair as it lay on her shoulders, and as he looked into her eyes, he remembered how she looked on similar moonlit nights as a girl of sixteen; how the revealing light from that moon, shining so brightly on innocent youth could make a young Miguel imagine the moon was placed there just for him, at that moment, just to see the most beautiful girl in all of Mexico.

Just as the current realities of life had hardened him, these same realities had also affected his Maria: wrinkles on her face, the gray streaks in her hair. *He didn't remember seeing them, even before he left to see Marco.*

She was still beautiful, but weathered, and the young boy's view of his innocent sweetheart and her surroundings was no longer the same. The full moon was not there for them, and the light that once helped to display beauty was now a shining reminder of age, of the pain that accompanies life—their life. He knew, as he looked into those now older, beautiful eyes to say goodbye, that she would see in his eyes the hurt, the pain, and the cruel injustice that he so wanted to spare her. *That's why he told her he was sorry.*

The gentle breeze of innocence that Miguel and Maria had felt as young lovers was gone, and in its place an evil wind of destruction neither one had ever known before was blowing freely across their world, and their son was trapped in that wind.

"Miguel, our life has been good. You have been the best husband and father that a family could ask for," she said as tears rolled to the ground. "You never once let us down."

Her unprepared but intense words, spoken in past tense had come so fast and emphatically that they were shocking to both of them. They rang hard, as a bell would toll for an ending, as though the good in their life was over and there was nothing left but goodbye.

Wiping a tear from her cheek, he held her close once more and whispered, "Goodbye, my love." He kissed her then got into his truck and drove away.

Maria stood as she had been doing for over nineteen years watching him leave. For years, whenever Miguel left for work he had always driven away into the light at the beginning of a new day, and with that light there was always hope, but not tonight. She did not know about these plans he had, or what this meeting was about and she did not understand why a meeting was necessary-- tonight. But she watched as the only man she had ever loved drove away into the night and for the first time that she could remember, she felt alone and hopeless and afraid as his truck disappeared into the darkness.

TWELVE

"Senor DeMarcos is expecting me," Miguel said, as he handed his identification to the guard at the entrance gate of The Factory. It was 10:15 p.m. He had never arrived here this late.

The guard motioned to another man inside to open the gate. "Senor Begal is expecting you," he said, as he handed Miguel his company card back.

"Senor Begal is here too?

"Si, everybody's in the office."

As Miguel put his identification back in his pocket, he said. "You are new. How long have you worked here?"

"Not very long," the guard said, as he stepped back inside his cubicle and slid the door closed.

Miguel proceeded to the office building located at the back corner of the compound and parked his truck next to Senor DeMarcos' Mercedes. The new guard was troubling to him, a stranger, possibly American.

All the buildings, including the office area appeared deserted. No trucks were being loaded or tow-motors running inside any of the buildings.

Usually two shifts were always working.

The hall was dark leading from the outer

office. At the end of the hall, to the right, a dim light could be seen coming from under the door of Senor DeMarcos' office.

That is odd, Miguel thought. *No guard at his office door.*

No one, just an empty hall with portraits of two dead men and a sense of foreboding permeating the very air Miguel was breathing.

"I'm just tired," Miguel said out loud, as he walked toward Senor DeMarcos' office door, his words attempting to dispel the paranoia.

Miguel's three knocks, while tentative, reverberated more loudly than during the daytime. There was an unusual deadly silence. During the day work sounds of a front office with its ringing phones and the answering of them and machinery outside the factory and the people that make the sounds would have filled the void.

After what seemed to Miguel to be an extremely long wait, a voice from inside the office said, "Come in Miguel."

Was that Senor DeMarcos?

Miguel opened the door and stepped inside.

~~~~~

It was just before midnight; the call had come from Ken Begal at the factory: "Phillip get up here immediately," he had said. No discussion, no explanation. "Don't ask questions, I am on a cell phone." Then, he hung up.

The Factory grounds looked normal. *I guess no shifts are running tonight,* Phillip thought, as he drove through the gate and parked beside an old truck in front of the main office. He recognized Ken's vehicle and Tony's vehicle. *But whose old truck is that?* Ken was standing just outside the entrance to the building at the top of the stairs.

"What is wrong," said Phillip, as Ken walked down the steps to meet him.

"It's Tony," Ken said, placing his hands on Phillip's shoulders in somewhat of a comforting gesture. "He's been shot. He's dead."

"Where is he," Phillip demanded, as he swiftly walked up the steps. "Phillip, I don't know if you need to see this. I'm just his friend and it was not easy for me."

Phillip pushed Ken aside and ran up the stairs into the building, continuing to run until he got just inside Tony's office door.

The initial gathering of details was difficult, for the only light in the office was a single floor lamp in the right corner of the room.

His brother was sitting in his office chair, his white shirt and tie saturated with blood. His head was leaned back and his eyes and mouth open; his empty hands hung to his side. The desk was neat, normal, except for a gun lying in front of him. On the floor, lying face down was a man in blue jeans and a jacket with a gun in his right hand, and a stream of blood pouring from underneath his body to each side.

Phillip walked first over to his brother and touched his face. *Funny*, he thought, *he didn't remember ever doing that before-- touching his brother's face.* Their age difference had made it difficult for closeness. They had grown up so distant, so far apart. Tony, with his *Brooks Brothers* suits, hand stitched shoes and love of books and business and fortune was always comfortable in an office setting. Phillip, on the other hand, was the hunter and adventurer, feeling more at home in L.L.Bean attire, out on a cold, mountain's edge with a high powered rifle at sunrise waiting for the deer to gather for their morning drink.

Clinically, Phillip leaned his brother forward. *No exit wound.* He opened his coat. With his knowledge of weaponry, Phillip knew the caliber weapon that had killed his brother was small, a 0.22, maybe a 0.32 caliber. *A shot, straight into the heart*, he thought.

"You are now with God, my brother," Phillip said, softly, now with a flood of emotion, as he reached with his left hand pulling his brother's eyelids closed and with his right forming the sign of the cross.

The solemnity of the moment quickly changed as Phillip turned and made his way around the desk and stood over the man lying dead in the floor. Turning him over, Phillip stepped back, looking, studying.

"He works here. I recognize that."

"Miguel Esgivas," Ken said, "his son is the one in jail in Alabama.

Staring at the body, Phillip's tone was one of disbelief as he spoke. "My brother was good to him, to his family. Why would he do this?"

Ken shook his head as he answered. "I guess he got upset, blamed Tony for his son's troubles. He just got back yesterday from seeing his son," Ken said, as he walked over beside Phillip and stared with him at Miguel's body. "Just went crazy, I guess." Ken's voice became softer and even more solemn as he continued. "Nothing anybody could have predicted. I'm sure it took Tony by surprise."

"Why was Tony here at night . . . without a guard?" Phillip asked.

"Who knows? Maybe he told Miguel to come back tonight. I don't know, but thank God, at least this murderer got what was coming to him," Ken said, continuing to look at Miguel's dead body.

"I am going to destroy his family. His mother will regret giving birth to him," Phillip said, angrily, as he continued staring at Miguel's body.

"No," Ken said, "More killing would just bring us more trouble. Los Zetas does enough of that," There are too many killings in Northern Mexico, and too many investigations. This one has an explanation: This man's son is in jail and mistakenly, he blamed your brother."

"So we do nothing?"

"Your brother has done something. He has taken care it. There is no need for us to bring trouble to this organization. Your brother wouldn't want that."

Phillip walked over to the sofa and sat down, surveying once again the dimly lit, ghastly scene of dead brother, killer, office and blood.

"What now?" he asked, as he continued viewing the scene.

"We call the authorities and let them handle it."

"No. I mean, what do *I* do now? I am not ready to run this business. You know that."

"Don't worry, Phillip," Ken said, walking over to where Phillip was sitting. "I know every facet of this operation. I have been by your brother's side since he took over and I will be by yours," Ken said, placing his hand on Phillip's shoulder.

"Alright, so we call authorities?" Phillip said.

"Yes. I'll call them. This is nothing more than a normal homicide in a legitimate business by a deranged employee--that's all. There are no shifts running and the only employee that needs questioning is lying here in the floor," Ken said, as he picked up the phone and dialed some numbers.

"This is Ken Begal. I need to report a murder at The Factory."

THIRTEEN

Arriving by plane in Bogota, Columbia, Ken Begal could see nothing below but mountains: endless rows of emerald peaks, the tallest in the distance, white-capped. The closer view from the helicopter he took from the airport, was of rolling hills that looked like color slides of green and blue that changed in intensity as the helicopter ascended and descended with the topography.

Reddish-brown, swollen creeks and smaller blue-silver rivers coursed their way downhill to rock-bed, river valleys. At their conclusion, the jungle was so dense that rifts of dark shadows shaded the natural colors, causing the creeks and rivers and greenery of the trees to abruptly disappear into a darkened shadowed abyss.

Without warning and in sharp contrast to the unspoiled vistas a fully modern city of over a million people emerged. This phoenix of red brick and concrete rising from the depths of a jungle was cast in between two steep peaks to the north. To the east the city made its way down the side of green mountains toward the south and west.

The helicopter ride south from the Bogota airport was pleasant enough, the slower pace allowing Ken Begal to assess the varied areas of mountains, jungle, and town.

From the center of town to the north was the more aristocratic area: wide landscaped streets, with elegant and graceful mansions, blocks and avenues embellished with cathedrals and museums that gave way to office buildings, restaurants, and upscale apartment complexes.

To the south and west, the city takes on a different look: three-bedroom houses, stacked in suburban rows, with their cookie cutter, look-alike roofs, patios and fenced yards, narrow streets and occasional traffic lights. The electrical wires and poles looking like strings and sticks stretched between children's doll houses that finally gave way to the parking lots of neighborhood shopping malls with nearby schools and play grounds.

The sky-view vista of normalcy soon became supplanted by the poorer side of humanity, where masses of people resembling scurrying ants moved between row after row of side-by-side, different sized shacks. The larger ones made of bamboo and thatched roofs, while the smaller ones were constructed of an eclectic, hodgepodge of cardboard, tin, or plastic. Stacked garbage was everywhere with what appeared to be raw sewage in undefined, sporadic spaces, some of it running to a drainage ditch near a creek at the edge of the jungle; some of it standing still, a framing of smaller areas of an almost-liquid, murky and dirty. Surprisingly the pools of the liquid substance glistened, the shimmering glare promoted by the combination of sunlight and campfire-smoke, which added some primitive mysticism to an otherwise unpleasant and dissatisfying view. In spite of the 100 mile per hour average speed of the helicopter, this uninviting panorama of poverty seemed to continue unabated for miles until abruptly and thankfully being swallowed up by jungle.

So much had happened in such a short length of time, Ken thought, as his helicopter climbed higher in response to the steep terrain.

He had replayed the scene a hundred times in his mind, looking for errors that might come back to haunt him: "Come in Miguel," Ken could hear himself say all over again, as he stood in the dimly lit office of Tony DeMarcos. Miguel stepped inside. Only a small lamp in the right corner was lighting the room; enough light to see that Tony DeMarcos was seated behind his desk with his back turned toward the door. But not enough light to see that he was already dead.

The door slammed behind Miguel as he entered. It was startlingly loud.

"I came to talk to Senor DeMarcos," Miguel said, his eyes looking first behind him to the gunman who had slammed the door, then to an unmoving DeMarcos, then to Begal who stood at the right of the desk.

"We need to know what Marco told you," Begal said.

"What he told me? I do not understand."

"Did he talk to you about the cowboy?"

"Cowboy? I do not know what you are talking about."

Miguel appeared frustrated and angry with the questioning. "Senor DeMarcos," Miguel said.

"Don't go any further," the man with the gun said, as Miguel attempted to step closer to the desk.

"Did Marco talk about the cowboy?" Begal asked again.

"No. Only that he made him go on the trip."

Miguel looked again to Senor DeMarcos.

"Did he say anything about trying to make a deal with the Americans? Anything about the sheriff? This is important, If we are to help you and Marco, we must know these things."

"No, nothing."

"Did he say if he had talked about his work here?"

Miguel looked again to the unmoving DeMarcos, as he answered, as though his answers were directed to him. "Marco would never talk about this place. He gave his word. That is why he does not deserve to rot in that gringo jail. Senor? Senor DeMarcos?"

Begal could still imagine the amused look that must have been on his own face, as he walked over to Antonio DeMarcos' chair and turned it around to face Miguel.

174

"I am afraid he can't talk to you," Begal said, now standing behind the chair, with a bloody, dead DeMarcos, his head tilted slightly to one side, his eyes and mouth open, now facing Miguel.

"You see, you murdered him tonight. That's why you came here--to kill him," Begal said matter-of-factly. You just couldn't get over the fact that he caused your son to get arrested."

As Begal was talking, the gunman, on Miguel's left, moved behind the desk just to the right of Begal and DeMarcos.

"You will burn in hell. You caused my son to face death . . ."

"Oh, he'll die alright," Begal said, not allowing him to finish his statement. "All for a good cause, I assure you. As for hell, maybe there isn't one. You can let me know if you see any flames. They need to be able to recognize his face," Begal said to the gunman.

Miguel stood motionless, as though resigned to his fate, as three shots were fired into his stomach and chest.

~~~~~

Ken Begal was now in control of one of the largest drug cartels in Mexico, and with this trip he would finalize a partnership between the Antonio DeMarcos Cartel and the Medellin-Cali cartel of Columbia.

~~~~~

In the distance, just twenty miles southeast of Bogota, in a picturesque valley was Roberto Ochoa's fifteen hundred acre ranch, complete with lavish amenities: a ten bedroom home and several smaller houses for servants and guests, an Olympic sized pool, one tennis court and driving range, herds of Angus and Hereford cattle with air-conditioned barns, six spring-fed lakes stocked with fish from all over the world, as well as a heliport.

As the helicopter landed, Begal could see Roberto Ochoa, dressed in a white suit, holding a white hat, standing beside his jeep with two of his men.

"Welcome to Columbia," Ochoa said, shaking Begal's hand, as one of the men attempted to take Begal's bag and attaché—with Begal refusing.

The jeep headed away from the pad, into the jungle. "Do you feel like seeing some things before we eat?"

"Fine," Begal said.

"Take us to the Lab," Ochoa told the driver.

"Let me tell you a story," said Ochoa, as his driver headed down a bumpy dirt road, thick jungle on each side. "Just to show you how what we do helps our people, that it is not just us making money: There was a little boy. I do not remember his name. His father had died and this 13 year-old boy was left alone with his mother. Forced to drop out of school to find work in nearby Armenia, Quindío, he washed cars and cleaned floors. This job did not last long and very soon he took another job as a guide at a small hotel. At the new job, very often parties for clients were held. It was at one of these parties he met Carmelita Perez, a 23 year-old associate of mine. She persuaded him to move near here. He would stay in a house all day to learn to ingest grapes covered with baby food."

The jeep stopped, and Ochoa and his men got out and walked down a hidden, steep, rock-filled incline.

"You see," Ochoa said, continuing, "he had to get used to the texture and shape of heroin capsules," Ochoa said, as they followed the driver who was clearing brush with a machete. "He was paid $19,000.00 for one trip, enough to buy a brand new house for his mother."

The walking path turned up hill through even more dense vegetation, but with a clearer, well traveled path underneath.

Below, to the left, periodic glimpses of a deep drop-off could be seen in between the thick brush. They were walking along a trail on a cliff's edge of one of the very large mountains in Columbia. In the distance, beyond the valley below, the lush, dark green foliage was interrupted by a single, cascading waterfall spilling out of creviced rock. The smell of the rain-freshened flowers felt as if it were being sprayed in the air. All of this combined naturally and wonderfully with sounds of the jungle, so loud that listening to Ochoa's story was difficult.

Ochoa's men began removing pre-cut trees along a ledge at the side of a mountain, the last of the brush uncovering a locked door.

"With our help," Ochoa continued, as his men unlocked the steel door, "the poorest of the poor can enjoy a better life." He opened the metal door and stepped down, flipping a light switch encased in the wall. A single row of loosely hanging bulbs came on, revealing a very narrow, short tunnel, just wide enough to walk single file and tall enough to accommodate someone of average height. The path was concrete-smooth, while the walls appeared to be chiseled out by hand.

After walking through the tunnel a few seconds, a huge cave was revealed where at least twenty workers under extremely bright lights, were busy performing the tasks of processing coca paste.

Motioning for a man in a white lab jacket to come over, Ochoa stopped next to a row of tables.

"Ken I want you to meet Alfero Diego. He is in charge of this plant. Alfero, this is Ken Begal, my new partner from Mexico. Alfero has a Master's Degree in Chemistry from your Miami University. I want you to show Ken what we do here. Impress him a little bit,"

Ochoa said with a slight chuckle.

"It would be my pleasure," Alfero said, his hands in his lab jacket as though he were giving a lecture at a university. Alfero looked like any other plant manager on any given day in the United States. He wore a white shirt, silk tie and Dockers underneath his white coat.

"This facility is one of our laboratories set up close to the growing fields. Here we reduce the leaves down to a cocaine paste. The initial purpose is to make shipment more economical."

"You see, in leaf form, cocaine is bulky. It could take up to five hundred kilos of leaves, the growth of an acre and a half of land to make a single kilo of cocaine hydrochloride, which is the white powder our customers use," he said, as he moved down the line of tables filled with varying treatments of product, as workers stepped aside making way for the tour.

Pointing as he lectured to the opposite end of the cave, to a garage door covered opening on the side of the mountain that housed the cave, he said. "The leaves are brought in there on that side of the mountain, by pack animal, burro or llama, and placed in a vat, where a several-stage process begins. Sulfuric acid or kerosene is used to treat the leaves, then more lime, to begin the separation of the cocaine from the thirteen other alkaloids in the plant."

"You aren't worried about being

betrayed by some of your people who bring the leaves up?" Ken asked, his question directed toward Ochoa.

At first Ochoa appeared taken aback by the question posed in front of his worker, then responded. "The more people you have involved in an operation, the greater that risk becomes, certainly, but these people make one hundred to five hundred times what they could make producing coffee. Even if the money was not that good, it would not be worth it for them to betray us, for every member of their family would die before the next day's sunset," Ochoa said, motioning for Alfero to continue.

"Well, after the alkaloids are separated from the cocaine, the leaves will have then been reduced sufficiently so that the product can be easily transported to finishing laboratories. There, more baths are given in solutions of kerosene and sulfuric acid, potassium permanganate, and ammonium hydroxide. Then successive soakings and dryings produce a type of cocaine called 'base.'"

"You can see why I hired a chemist," said Ochoa, as Alfero and Begal smiled in response.

"This base is very potent," Alfero continued, "but it lacks the versatility of the finished product."

Stopping to put on surgical gloves, Alfero stepped over to a table with heat lamps hanging from the cave ceiling and picked up a handful of paste: a grayish muck, resembling joint compound used in drywall construction.

"250 kilos of leaves boil down to about 2.5 kilos of paste. But as I said, this lacks versatility. It can't dissolve in water so our customers cannot shoot it up, and it will not absorb into the membranes, so it is no good to snort."

Ochoa smiled, obviously pleased with his employee's presentation, and said, "To create the cocaine that Columbia is famous for requires one more operation."

"Yes," Alfero said, "the base is dissolved in ether, seventeen liters to the kilo, combined with acetone and hydrochloric acid, finally it is allowed to sit out and dry into a white, crystalline substance."

"The end result," Ochoa said, interrupting again, "is cocaine hydrochloride; the finest Colombia has to offer, light, fragile and flaky, like new-fallen snow."

Begal slowly clapped his hands together. "Very impressive,"

"Come," Ochoa said, "I'll show you what I call home, as we head back to the house."

Ochoa drove Begal around his ranch, showing him his lakes teaming with fish, the petting zoo, which included a variety of monkeys, a baby elephant and a giraffe, and of course the paved landing strip for his Cessna plane parked next to the helipad.

"My chef prepares the best

chateaubriand in the world, the beef from my cattle, so tender you can cut it with a fork," he said, as they walked from the stables housing his Arabian stallions, to the back of the house.

The meal was served in a banquet styled room, with flooring of red mosaic tile and colorfully finished concrete walls creating a cool ambience for the oak, Spanish styled furniture covered in natural-tanned cowhide.

"It was unfortunate," Ochoa said, as he and Begal sat down with a glass of brandy, "that DeMarcos felt the way he did. But fortunate for you."

Raising his glass, Ochoa said, "I want to congratulate you on your successful method of handling it. I hear everything went smoothly."

"Yes, Phillip is content to let me run the operation. To the other cartels, he is the man in charge."

"A necessity, I am sure, particularly since you are an American. The worker that took the blame for DeMarcos' death, tell me about his son."

"He is in a jail in the United States, in Alabama, charged with murder. He shouldn't last long."

"I know all that, but you know how courts are in the United States. O. J. was charged with murder, too, and up until his thug routine in Las Vegas, he was playing golf in Florida."

"Well, he has a court appointed lawyer, who I don't think would come up to the level of the *dream team*," Ken said.

"I understand. But you understand it would be somewhat awkward if this boy was to return, and even more awkward and dangerous for us both if he makes a deal and they find out details about your operation."

"I don't know how much this kid really knows . . ."

Ochoa stood, his glass in hand, the look on his face making it obvious that he was upset at his guest's complacent attitude. "And what if he gets out and decides to avenge his father's murderer. That puts you in a most vulnerable position, and by extension, I would be as well.

Realizing that Ochoa wasn't going to take no for an answer, Begal relented. "Yes, you're right. I agree he must be dealt with. I'll take care of it."

"Good." Ochoa said, satisfied, retaking his seat, motioning to the servant standing against the wall to pour more brandy. "What about DeMarcos' wife? I understand they were about to leave Mexico?"

"She's already gone. She and the children flew out by chartered plane the night DeMarcos was killed. They had already bought a house in Miami and had transferred twenty million dollars."

"I hope you do not think of me as being invasive on your end of our partnership, but I do worry about details," Ochoa said, as he leaned back in his chair.

"Neither of us wants to end up like my

good friend Pablo, or your good friend Antonio. So," he said as he stood, "we will begin the flights next week. I'll need your men to give us the coordinates of the dry lake beds where our planes are to land. We'll start with planes and switch up next month and try our new submarine with your gatekeepers at the ports."

"I want to thank you for your hospitality," Begal said, as he also stood and the two men exchanged their concluding pleasantries, including promises of plans to meet again soon.

"If there is nothing else," Begal said, "I'll head back to the airport. My flight leaves in three hours."

Ochoa walked his guest out to the awaiting ride. "And of course you will notify me as soon as this problem is eliminated, won't you?"

"Yes," Begal said. "I will."

FOURTEEN

In the Cleburne County jail, every prisoner is regarded as equal--no rights or privileges unless the sheriff gives them some standing above the others. The meals are the same: oatmeal for breakfast, fried bologna sandwiches for lunch, and grits and canned field peas and a biscuit for supper. There is one unusual treat in that on every other Saturday, fried chicken, gravy and biscuits are served.

Status among the inmates can be elevated, albeit slightly, in one of two ways: his ability (generally because of money sent from home) to purchase cigarettes, candy bars, or soft drinks from the sheriff's machines downstairs, which automatically makes an inmate popular and powerful.

Or he can become a trustee.

Charged with duties and a certain amount of work around the jail, being a trustee comes with a level of freedom unavailable to the other inmates. He gets to breathe a measure of fresh air every day, step out the back door, smoke a cigarette or take a chew of tobacco in between prescribed chores of cooking, scrubbing and cleaning. Instead of one bologna sandwich, he could have two, maybe three if he so desires.

Joe Frank had recently been named a trustee, in charge of the kitchen.

"Georgia steak, dats what we calls it,"

Joe Frank said, wiping perspiration from his face with his left forearm, in an attempt to keep it from splattering on the griddle, as he flipped and monitored twenty pieces of frying bologna.

Joe Frank liked being a trustee. He cooked and cleaned and carried garbage out, and personally served the food to the other inmates.

"Yessah," he said, standing at the griddle looking out the back window of the bottom floor of the jail, as he patted the meat with his spatula, "My daddy would go to da wholesale house in Anniston. He'd buy it in ten pound boxes. Mama would fry it up and stack it on da table a clear foot high."

"Did it come from Georgia?" Marco asked, as he splashed the mop and water over the concrete floor.

"Georgia. Naw, dats jus' what we calls it. I don't know why. Days jus' a lotta mystries in dis here life. Baloney bein' called Georgia steak jus' one ofem."

In spite of the seriousness of Marco's charge, the sheriff had allowed Marco out of his cell to help Joe Frank with his cooking and cleaning duties. Certainly there was a steel-wire fence topped with barbed wire, but the electronic ten foot wide steel-wire gate stayed open more than closed. And most candidates for trustee not only were generally charged with lesser crimes, but most were residents of the jail at least six months before being considered for the status elevation, and Marco had been there less than four. This privilege given to Marco was even more unusual, in light of the fact that his trial was to begin in less than one week for the crime of Capital Murder.

"Where he gonna go?" Joe Frank had argued to the sheriff on Marco's behalf, when the sheriff had asked him if he thought Marco would make a good helper and if he thought he would run. *"I'll make him work,"* Joe Frank had said. *"Iffin he runs off, He ain't gotta soul to he'p 'im. No sir, he ain't gonna run, cause he can't."*

"Joe," Marco said, stepping closer to the preacher so he could whisper.

"I need to ask you something while we are away from Dale."

Joe Frank looked back to the right and behind to check for deputies and continued working on the sandwiches, his back to Marco as he talked.

"O.K., but make it quick an' quiet."

"My lawyer tells me the evidence is against me, that when we go to trial next week, they will convict me and then sentence me to death, or put me in an Alabama prison for the rest of my life."

"I know," Joe Frank said, looking quickly back again to his right toward the break room and front office.

"You know I did not kill this man. This is wrong," said Marco, as he stopped mopping, his voice somewhat louder than before.

"I know, but there's nothin' I can do, Marco." Joe Frank began spreading mayonnaise and mustard over pieces of bread, looking again over his shoulder to make sure they were alone. "Keep moppin'," Joe Frank said, as he looked back through the glass paneled door of the break room, and the sheriff's office, beyond.

"You can help me get out," Marco said, as he dipped and slung water across the floor, vigorously pushing the mop.

"Marco, I'm a man ah God. I preach da word. Look I know I made my mistakes, but I gots to follow da book. I'm sposed to respect authority. How can I do that and help you git from here?"

"How can you not? You think God means for me to die or never see my family again? If there was justice here, I would not ask. You said your brother, the blacksmith, could make a key."

Joe Frank smiled and said, "Yea, he could alright enough. Facdabinnis looky here."

Laying the butter knife down, Joe Frank reached inside the waistband of his orange uniform, just as the door opened from the direction of the break room.

"Joe Frank?"

"Yessah," said a startled Joe Frank, as he looked toward the now open break room door to find Sheriff Sykes looking at both he and Marco. Joe Frank stood still for a moment, and then picked the butter knife up, continuing to

188

spread mayonnaise. Marco, equally startled, continued mopping.

"Get that food up the stairs to the other inmates and have that Mexican take the garbage out."

"Yessah, sheriff. But I needs Marco to help me take da trays up first."

The sheriff appeared to be suspiciously, studying the faces of his trustee and helper, his eyes wondering back and forth between the two.

"Well get on with it. Get the goddamn food up there and get the goddamn garbage out. No point in niggers and Mexicans moving so slow," he said, as he took a draw from his cigarette and closed the door behind him, still watching them through the glass for a moment before walking back toward the front office.

Joe Frank picked up the tray of bologna.

"Grab dat bread, Marco." With that, both Joe Frank and Marco climbed the stairs, making the three trips, up and down, necessary to serve lunch to their fellow inmates.

That night it rained. The thunder and lightning was incessant, and while other inmates entertained themselves by counting the number of lightning strikes and thunder claps, and betting cigarettes or money on the number that occurred in five minute intervals, Marco stared out through the bars of the window into the night, his mind far away.

189

Leaving this place was the only thought on his mind.

The surprise of the sheriff standing in the break room doorway had so startled the preacher and Marco that nothing more had been said on the subject of escape. They had not been alone since, and now there was more than Dale to worry about. A new guy now occupied the upper bunk above Dale. His arrival late that evening was accompanied with more ceremony than was given most new inmates.

"This is Mr. Davis Humphries," the sheriff said, as he opened the cell door and introduced their new cellmate. About six feet tall with long brown hair, beginning to gray on the sides, he was an unpretentious sort, about forty years old, a poker face to be sure with no outward expressions of his thoughts. His weathered lines, dark and entrenched, deepened as he smiled, and his rotting teeth, combined with his slight build, provoked thoughts of possible methamphetamine use.

"No need to get too acquainted with everybody. The preacher here is getting out day after tomorrow. The man he beat up decided to drop the charges and his church is paying up his child support."

"This low life, motioning toward Dale, is gonna plead in the morning. The Judge will probably give him probation and get him out of my hair; and, this here is our killer from Mexico--likes to kill state troopers. He'll be around a little while till they send him south and put a needle in his arm."

"You boys behave now," the Sheriff said, as he locked the cell back and made his way down the steps.

"Oh," he said, turning around and taking some paper from his pocket. "This letter came registered from Mexico, from your Mama," the sheriff said, as he pitched the already opened letter through the bars in the direction of Marco's bunk.

"Sorry about your Daddy," the sheriff said in a surprisingly sincere tone, as he turned and walked down the steps.

Marco jumped down from his bunk. The letter was addressed and written in his mother's hand.

Dear Marco,

I know you have more on you than you can bear right now, but I know you would want to know. Your father is dead. He was in Senor DeMarcos' office at the factory. Someone shot him. Someone also killed Senor DeMarcos. They say that your father went there to kill him because of your trouble and that they killed each other.

I do not want to say any more in this letter.

We buried him at Saint Sebastiens.
Father John did the service. I placed a flower on his grave for you. When you come home, we will all go there together.

Marco, when you get out, you will have to find us. Grandmamma will know. Senor Begal has told us to get out.

"Murderers," he told us, "are not allowed on factory property."

I know Papa told you of my dream. Believe it. Believe in its power. I pray every day for your safe return and I know our tears of grief will soon turn to tears of joy.

Your father loved you, and we love you.
Mama

Marco stared at the letter for quite a long time, reading it over and over, as though there was more to glean from the few, shocking words on the page. He thought of home, but it wasn't the same. His papa was gone and it was difficult to think about home with him gone. He had walked side by side with that man in those fields of corn and cotton since he was a toddler; working, eating, sweating, bathing the dust off at the end of the day, always talking to Marco of a better life.

A murderer? Papa was not a murderer. He was a good man. He did not deserve to die. Not like that.

To picture his Mama sitting down to supper without him, with an empty chair slid up to the table was hard. Now there were two empty chairs.

I have to get out of here, he thought, as he folded the letter and laid it on his chest and looked up from the pages to the face of the man who had become his friend.

"What I hate," Marco said to Joe Frank, "is that the last time he saw me I was in this orange suit and chains. I should have been home."

"Marco," Joe Frank said, as he looked away from Marco's anguished face, at the other cell mates who were surprisingly quiet.

"It's O.K. to cry. Ain't nobody here gwoin to thank nothin' of it."

"There is nothing inside me to cry with," Marco said, now looking out the window and lifting the letter up for Joe Frank to read.

"I understands," Joe Frank said, as he opened the small folded pages and began reading, tilting the letter toward the only source of light—a dome light, attached to the power-pole at the top of the hill, near the courthouse. The reflections of raindrops on the paper made the words appear heavier and thicker in between the flashes of lightning, which served to accentuate words like *dead, killed* and *buried*. Finishing, Joe Frank folded the letter and placed it back into Marco's hand, who stared unmoving, out the window, into the stormy nothingness of the night.

"You been through quite an ordeal. Dis place done hardened everything you needs dat makes up tears."

Why did God send da rain an' da lightnin' wi' da bad news, he thought.

"Dear God," Joe Frank began to softly pray, his left hand now also placed on Marco's

193

head, "we got ourselves a sitcheation here. I know you knows all about it. We jus' mere mortals, jus' pieces a little clay you done put together and breathed life into. Yore thinkin' an' yore ways is so much bigger than ours and we knows dat God, but we in need tonight of a little mercy, a little help, a little touch for my friend Marco."

Finishing his prayer, Joe Frank stood by Marco's bunk for the better part of an hour. The anguish he felt was as great as or greater than Marco's, he was sure. *Even if I helped him git from dis place, how would he get home? I ain't nevah been to Mexico.*

Soon Marco was asleep. Retiring to his own bunk, Joe Frank lay on his back, his hands behind his head, his eyes wide open, listening to the rain.

"Dear God what chu want from me with Marco? I don't know what chu want me to do?" He said out loud, as the rain, and the thunder and the lightning filled the night.

The new man, Davis Humphries and Dale had stayed politely and remarkably quiet, apparently content to fall asleep. All talk of lightning and rain and thunder ceased as Marco had digested the somber news, and as Joe Frank prayed his consoling prayer.

Because of this, there had been no time to get acquainted with Mr. Humphries. All that

194

was known of him was what the sheriff had said, as well as the fact that he appeared to have some sense of tact as was evidenced by his silence, as Marco had learned the news of his father.

Either in answer to the preacher's prayer, or because of the steady downpour of rain, or both, Marco, without shedding a tear had managed to fall asleep and had stayed soundly asleep until he heard his name called: a voice, his mother's, he wasn't sure--Marco! Marco!

Startled at hearing her voice, he awoke just in time to see the glistening of a knife in the dim light coming toward his face. Marco grabbed hold of the hand brandishing the knife just as the cold steel made contact with his neck. There was no time to contemplate reality versus a dream, for the reality to Marco was that the shining steel of a knife was touching his neck. It was cold and razor sharp; the hand holding it was strong and determined. For a brief moment, as lightning lit up the room, he saw the man trying to kill him, then Marco's vision was snuffed out. A pillow was pressed upon his face by a hand equally as strong as the one wielding the knife.

He pushed and struggled against the knife and now the pillow. This was no dream. He could not scream and the only sound in the room seemed to be the hard drops of rain falling on the tin roof, as the pillow was unmoving, and the knife was held steady. The

195

killer was pressing hard, and the knife was digging deeper into his neck. Marco knew that he would not hold him off much longer.

Then, just as quickly as the attack had started, it stopped. The knife pressing against his neck fell beside his face. The hand holding the knife and the hand pressing the pillow against his face both fell limp and lifeless against his chest and face.

Marco, still holding one hand of his attacker took the pillow and slung it from his face. There stood Joe Frank. *The preacher?*

Marco pulled himself up and slid against the back part of his bunk, away from a bundle of flesh pressing against his chest and body. His eyes slowly adjusted to the limited light of the room as he moved against the wall and the weight on him was removed. It was the preacher alright, pulling the lifeless body of the newcomer, Davis Humphries off of Marco. Quietly, Joe Frank laid the body down on the floor, next to Marco's bunk.

"Marco, you alright?" he said in an urgent whisper, as thunder and lightning and rain continued. "Did he hurt you?"

Taking inventory of possible injuries, and still viewing the shocking scene, Marco finally answered, "No. I am not hurt. What? Why?"

"He was plannin' on slittin' yore throat, so God help me, I had to break his neck. Shhhh. Don't wake Dale up," Joe Frank said, looking over at Dale who was curled up, asleep in his bunk, his back to the outside.

The scene accentuated by a flash of lighting, claps of thunder and hard rainfall, Marco watched as Joe Frank reached down in his sock and pulled out a black-colored, metal object. Turning his back toward Marco, he stood at the cell door for about three seconds, before quickly and quietly swinging the cell door open.

"Hurry, he'p me. We gots to hurry. He'p me get 'im outside," he said, as he picked up most of Davis Humphries' body, while Marco helped with the legs.

"Wait," Joe Frank said, motioning toward Marco's bunk.

"Get da knife. Pick it up wi yore shirt. Wipe it off. Polish it."

Marco retrieved the knife and did as he was told.

"Now stick it in his pants. O.K. let's get 'im out," Joe Frank said, the rain continuing to mercifully fall, it's steady, rhythmic, pulsing, noise which had earlier aided the would be murderer, was now masking the noise of these two men who were attempting to cover up their imposition of justice.

"Alright," the preacher said as he stopped about halfway down the castle-like, concrete steps.

"What we gwoin to do is hit his head against a step, so it looks like he jus' tripped an' broke his sorry neck."

"Alright, take one hand undah his neck

and the other on top of his head and we gwoin to bash it. Now we gots to do it hard and together."

Feeling unsettled by the entire enterprise, Marco said, "I don't know . . ."

"I do know," said the preacher, not giving him time to finish. "And you can do it, it ain't gonna hurt him. He's done dead. Cummon; One...Two...Three. . ."

With Marco on one side and Joe Frank on the other, each with a portion of Davis Humphries head in their hands, they first aimed toward the desired spot, with a trial run (trial bash) of the head, and then with all the strength both men could engage, crashed the head of the newcomer from Texas into the edge of a descending concrete step just short of the next cell.

"Dear God," Joe Frank began a whispering prayer as he remained kneeling down beside Humphries' body, "Don't consider dis here sitcheation to be murder, cause dis no-account sinner was about to kill my friend Marco dat you done put in my care. And I has to believe dat if dis here preacher had been out dare in da fields when Cain was 'bout to slew Abel, I believes you'd a wanted me to break his neck too. Amen."

Standing up from the prayer, then kneeling back down, he said. "Oh, an' God I thanks you from da bottom of my heart for my brother's smithin abilities and talents."

Joe Frank shook his head back and forth

198

and laughed, quietly, as he got back up.

"He shorenuff know how to make a good key, dat brothah a mine."

Bringing his focus from God back to Marco, he said, "Cummon," and started back up the steps with Marco close behind.

"How. . ." Marco said stopping the preacher before reaching the cell and motioning to his neck.

"How'd I break his neck?"

"Aw it ain't dat hard. I use ta ketch chickens for ole man Robison. He had chicken houses on County Road eleven next to da twin lakes," Joe Frank said, as both he and Marco made their way back up the winding stairs to their cell. "He liked to use an axe, but not me. I breaks dare necks. You holds firm at da bottom, den gives it a good jerk at da top. Jus' a little harder for a man---but not much."

Reaching the top of the stairs, Joe Frank slowly peered around the corner into the cell.

"Dale's still out," Joe Frank whispered back to Marco.

"Cummon," he said as both men slipped inside the door. Carefully and quietly, while lightning and thunder controlled the night and rain peppered down on the tin roof, Joe Frank fastened and re-locked the cell door, took the two steps past Marco and climbed up onto Marco's bunk.

Taking the key that he had just thanked the Almighty for, Joe Frank climbed on Marco's bunk to the window and slung it past

199

the jail fence, directly below, onto the hill, where it disappeared into the weeds, not far below the vantage point where Marco's father had sat a few days ago watching the jail.

Dale was still asleep and it was still raining. "Thank you Jesus," Joe Frank said, as he climbed back into his bunk and Marco hoisted himself into his.

Joe Frank breathed a long sigh of relief, as he lay on his back, his hands again behind his head, staring at the ceiling.

"Marco," Joe Frank said. "You don't know nothin'. We slept' da whole time. Been a rainin'. Couldn't hear nothin'," he said, as the combination of the rain pelting on the tin roof and occasional claps of thunder continued to fill the night with its consistent mixture of sounds. Turning on his left side toward Marco, and peering in the darkness, more intently as the lightning struck again, he said, "You hear what I said?"

"Si, yes." Marco said, raising up slightly and looking for a moment at Joe Frank before lying back down.

"Well, goodnight den," the preacher said, then rolled over on his back. "Nothin' been happening here but jus' a lot a rain," he said in a sanguine tone, yawning, settling down for sleep, talking to himself in a grateful mumble, as though indeed nothing had been happening on this stormy night in this Alabama jail but thunder, rattling rain and sleep.

"Dear Lawd, you gots to be in dis; I sure don't see no other way of this happenin' quite like dis if you ain't." He lay there for several more minutes contemplating all that had just transpired, as the storm continued.

"Just as hard to go to sleep now as it is after a good service you been in. Lawd," he said, as he looked back over at Marco, who lay still and silent.

"Lawd, what else you what me ta do for dis boy?"

Thunder clapped and lighting filled the room again as Joe Frank closed his eyes and waited for sleep.

FIFTEEN

Davis Humphries' body was found at 5:30 a.m. the next morning. Deputy Watkins, who had climbed the rounding steps to get Joe Frank to start breakfast, discovered the body face-down between cells one and two. A search of all the cells and questioning of Humphries' three cell mates produced nothing of significance. One by one they were taken from the cell to the sheriff's office, and one by one the same answer was recited to the Chief Deputy:

"It had rained. Slept through the rain. Didn't see anything, didn't hear anything."

Not finding anything on Humphries, Syke's deputies hastily searched clothing and cavity-searched every orifice of every prisoner's body for some type of hidden key or tool that could have been used to accomplish Humphries' escape from the cell.

As the inmates were carried back to their cell, the sheriff could be heard in an adjacent room responding to one deputy's suggestion that maybe the Sheriff had forgotten to lock the door.

"I locked the goddamn door," the sheriff said, incensed at the suggestion, and emphasizing that point with a stern, metallic-ringing kick of a filing cabinet.

The coroner's preliminary conclusion

was that the man had fallen in the dark, while trying to escape and had broken his neck, still leaving the sheriff and deputies wondering how he had gotten out of that cell in the first place.

"There is no sign of foul play. We will do an autopsy, of course," the coroner had said, as he stood on the steps looking down at the dead body, as the emergency team positioned it on the gurney for removal. "But, he did break his neck."

Upset, the sheriff said, "Any fool can tell that and any fool can see he hit his head. Did he have anything at all on his body?" The sheriff asked.

"Just this knife," the coroner had said, holding up a bagged up kitchen carving knife and handing it to the Sheriff.

"He was lucky and unlucky at the same time," the coroner said as he took one more picture of the head.

"What do you mean?" Sheriff Sykes asked.

"Well, he was lucky enough to have a storm to cover up any noise he made trying to escape..."

"Yeah," the sheriff nodded. "It was a real frog strangler last night."

"Yep, but then after using that knife, maybe to somehow get that door open and closed. . . "

"He didn't open that door with that knife," said the sheriff.

"Well, he got out, and he was either unlucky or clumsy enough to fall and break his neck."

"I never heard of anything like it," Sykes said, as he turned and walked up the stairs to the cell Humphries had been placed in the night before. The sheriff stood outside the cell looking at Joe Frank, Marco and Dale, who were quietly lying in their bunks, seemingly unaware of his presence.

Holding the cell keys in his hand, he vigorously shook the door that had to have been miraculously opened the night before, the keys to the cell making a horribly loud clanging noise, against the doors, arousing all the men in the cell, who looked up in wonderment at the angry and perplexed sheriff.

Opening the cell door, leaving the keys in the lock, and the cell door open, he walked over to Joe Frank's bunk.

"Well preacher," the sheriff said, smiling, chuckling a half-hearted chuckle as he began. "Don't think I believe you or this Mexican."

Joe Frank, his hands behind his head, continued staring at the ceiling, unconcerned.

"Dats da truth. Yessah, jus' da rain. Didn't hear a peep out of dat man. Jus' da rain. He never said a word da whole night, dats da truth," Joe Frank said, matter-of-factly, as he lay on his back, his hands calmly in place on his stomach, looking at the ceiling.

204

Syke's normally confident, arrogant attitude was displaced by an unchanging expression of disturbed disbelief that hung on his face like a cheap mask.

He looked first to Dale Carter, then to Marco. Both lay with their backs toward the sheriff as he turned to leave. He locked the cell door, pulling, shaking it again. After looking up and down the door, he turned and walked down the steps slowly, the jingling of the keys the only sound.

SIXTEEN

"Stand up, Mr. Marco Esgivas. Put your hands through the door," the deputy said, as he placed a set of handcuffs on Marco. "Alright, turn around with your hands against the bunk," he said, as he opened the door and began fastening leg-irons and the connecting chain between them and the cuffs.

"They're going be so glad to see you up in that courthouse. Everybody around has been waiting for your case to get tried. They just hate that we don't have hangings anymore," the deputy said, as he slowly allowed the prisoner to walk ahead of him, first down the circular stairs in the jail, then around the building to the south side of the jail yard. They progressed through the gate, and began the climb up the concrete steps on the hill between the jail and the courthouse.

Due to the crowd, today's five minute walk was taking longer than usual, and more deputies than usual. Most of the time, a single, armed deputy would easily have transported a half dozen chained prisoners, but today four deputies were being used for the transporting of one: one on each side--two clearing the way through the crowd of over one hundred people, most of them gathered around the north side (jail side)of the courthouse.

Those who had gotten to the courthouse by 7:45, gathering at both front and rear entrances, had been disappointed to learn that only potential jurors, numbering about sixty, would initially be allowed inside. The spectators would have to wait until all the venire were seated and accounted for.

At 8:30, as they watched the deputies bring Marco up the hill from the jail, many of the impatient, would-be trial attendees were still standing outside in their jackets and rain gear, prepared for the rain that the March wind gusts were bringing in. Jeering and screaming death wishes, some held placards with pictures of the state trooper and his family, along with statements written on poster board predicting and promoting the death of Marco.

TV crews, cameras and microphones were waived, then pushed to the side by the deputies, as Marco, dressed in a white shirt, tie, slacks and newly shined black patent leather shoes, inched his way toward the courthouse.

William Davis was quietly waiting, seemingly unnoticed by the crowd at the steps of the courthouse back door.

"Mr. Davis, Mr. Davis," said a reporter, as attention turned toward the steps on the realization that Marco's attorney was there. Davis ignored the reporter's and opened the door for his client and the deputies.

"Good Morning, Marco," Davis said, as

he followed him in.

The morning was filled with statements and questions by the prosecution and the defense, jury selection and instructions from Judge Munroe. Death qualifying questions were asked of the venire, making sure that each prospective juror could and would follow the law; and, particularly making sure that none of them had any qualms about considering the death penalty as punishment should Marco be convicted.

A conclusion could be drawn that Heflin, Alabama did not have a fire marshal, or that enforcement of a fire code was not a priority, for the courthouse was packed well beyond any normally perceived fire-code ordinance limits. Every seat on the one hundred year old wooden benches was filled; the walls, both side and back were lined with standing people: males and females who, due to the crowded conditions, fanned themselves with books and papers, stirring stale air and listening intently to recitations of the evidence in this case:

"The defendant was found on the side of the road, on I-20, near exit 199, in Cleburne County, Alabama. In his hand was the murder weapon that killed 34 year old Jerry Spencer, a man that for years had laid his life on the line for the people of this state, protecting us from people like the defendant."

"Through the testimony of a representative from the forensic lab in Montgomery, we will present evidence that the

208

gun found in Marco Esgivas hand was the murder weapon; that shots fired from that weapon entered the body of this law enforcement officer and that this was the cause of his death. It seems obvious that the trooper realized Marco was an illegal alien and that--"

"Your Honor I object. There is no such evidence that he can possibly present. The prosecutor is trying to create a motive that doesn't exist."

"This is opening statement. The jury can sort out for themselves what the truth is," said Judge Munroe, as William Davis sat back down.

"The truth is," District Attorney Jonathan Hudgins continued, "this man sitting at this table, next to Mr. Davis is a foreigner, not one reason to be here except to help bring drugs into the country. . ."

"Objection, your Honor. I move for a mistrial. . ."

Judge Munroe was a man who was annoyed at any interruption of one of his trials. This one had not gotten started well and Davis had interrupted it twice with objections. Attempting to restrain the beginnings of a scowl, he sat looking at neither attorney for the moment, but instead looked down, directly in front of him, as though there were some fairy sitting atop the judge's bench that he could direct his frustrations to; then after several seconds of whatever self control regimen he was into, he glanced briefly at both men before begrudgingly telling them both to approach the bench.

Davis and the District Attorney walked to the left of the Judge's bench, near the court reporter, on the opposite side of the jury.

"Your Honor," Davis said, "The District Attorney has prejudiced this jury against my client, and unless the District Attorney has been withholding evidence from me that I have requested, there is no evidence of any drug buying or selling or involvement that he can present and..."

"Judge, what else could the boy be doing up here. This is part of the State's theory."

"Do you have any evidence that you intend to present of involvement with drugs," asked Judge Munroe.

"No sir, but it is our theory..."

"Well, let's stay on track with what the evidence is."

"Judge," Davis said, I would like a ruling on my objection and I still am asking for a mistrial."

"Alright. Both of you step back. Ladies and gentlemen, as I have told you, the opening statement is the opportunity for each side in the case to let you know what to expect to see, as for as the evidence is concerned in this case. And, as I will tell you when I charge you at the conclusion of this case, what they say at this time in this trial is not evidence."

"Alright," he said as he turned his chair toward the attorneys, "you may continue Mr.

Hudgins."

"Your Honor," Davis said, "You did not rule on my objection, or my motion."

"Overruled. Your motion for a mistrial is denied," Judge Munroe said tersely. "The jury can sort out what the actual evidence is in this case and give it due consideration. Continue on Mr. Hudgins," the judge said, as he wrote something down on the legal pad in front of him.

"Yes, Your Honor. Ladies and gentlemen, the facts are this man is a foreigner and that he had no legitimate reason to be in Cleburne County, Alabama and that he killed Jerry Spencer. We would ask that, at the conclusion of this trial, you find him guilty as charged of capital murder. Thank you."

With that, the prosecutor, who except for his visit to the Judge's bench had stood at the same five foot distance in front of the jury box during his opening, now turned and took his seat next to his assistant and the investigating officer.

"Mr. Davis," Judge Munroe said.

"Ladies and gentlemen," Davis said, as he stood and walked slowly around to the front of the defense table and stopped, taking out his pocket watch from his vest pocket, appearing more interested in winding it than in giving an opening statement.

"If you were to vote right now on whether or not Marco is guilty or innocent; if all you got to hear was what Mr. Hudgins just said, it still isn't enough to convict him."

"I will admit," he said, placing the pocket watch back in his vest pocket, "that Mr. Hudgins makes him sound guilty, and if I were you I'd be leaning toward guilty right now," turning as if to walk back to his seat then turning back to the jury, and almost as an afterthought said, "if . . . that's all you got to hear. But, you see, that's the reason we have a trial. That's the reason each side is allowed to present evidence and witnesses, and to cross-examine those witnesses and to object when necessary. Cause, you see, you haven't heard it all. In fact, you haven't seen one piece of evidence yet, and if you find him guilty or innocent, it will be based on evidence that is admitted by this court, or from proper testimony that comes from this stand, not what the District Attorney says that makes him sound guilty."

Davis, having now walked back toward the jurors, stood in front of the witness box, his left hand on the front of the box and his right hand thumb sharing the vest pocket holding the end of the gold watch chain.

"Not theories or conjecture, but fact. Something one of your five collective senses can appreciate," he said, still striking the same pose as though ready for a forbidden picture inside the courtroom.

"When I objected a moment ago, I said that the prosecution was trying to create a motive. Is a motive important? Sure it is, and what you will see as you listen to this case is that they don't have one; not one reason why eighteen year old Marco would want to kill Jerry Spencer. And they need one, for you will realize as you listen to this evidence, that this crime scene is contrived. Certainly, Jerry Spencer died that day. You will see and hear evidence of that. Yes there was a murder, and Marco was found *unconscious* with the murder weapon in his hand, and I guess you noticed," Davis said, as he moved toward the witness box seat and sat down, now closer to the jurors, "that the prosecution failed to mention that Marco was unconscious. Is that important? It is, and even now I know you are wondering why this young eighteen year old boy who had never been away from home; never been in trouble, never been arrested, and with no criminal record, finds himself unconscious on an interstate a thousand miles from his mother and daddy, a gun in his hand, allegedly used to kill someone, yet unfired by Marco's hand."

Davis stopped for a moment as though contemplating what he would say next.

"*Whoa, Mr. Davis. Are you saying there is going to be evidence that Marco didn't fire the murder weapon?* That's right. It was in his hand," Davis said, lifting his left hand into the air, "yet the evidence will show they could find no powder residue on either of his hands."

He was now holding up both hands for the juror's perusal. "This, you will learn,

213

indicates he did not fire that weapon. Somebody shot Jerry Spencer and somebody knocked Marco unconscious and somebody placed the gun that killed Jerry Spencer in Marco's hand."

Getting up from the witness chair, Davis took off the glasses that had been sitting on the end of his nose, wiped them with a handkerchief and said, "Too many holes ladies and gentlemen, too many unanswered questions, too many facts that will show that Marco shot no one, and after you hear all that evidence, I believe you will find this young boy not guilty."

Davis walked back to the defense table and sat down next to his client.

"Anything else, Mr. Hudgins?"

"No Sir, Your Honor."

"Call your first witness, Mr. Hudgins," Judge Munroe said, looking up from his writing pad and laptop computer to view the crowd lining the courtroom walls, and packing the benches. The aisle in the middle of the courthouse separating the two rows of benches was kept clear, and there was another area of space, a ten foot distance between the benches and the bar that separated the court personnel: attorneys, jurors, judge, and four deputies, two on each side of the courtroom near the exits.

"The state calls Lamar Morrison," the prosecutor said.

The deputy standing nearest the double doors to Judge Munroe's left opened them up, calling out the name of the witness, and then held the swinging door open.

Lamar Morrison was an investigator with the Alabama Bureau of Investigation. Not given to being a commanding presence, the short, overweight detective with his extremely paunchy stomach, burst through the opened right side of the double doors into the crowded courtroom. As he walked in, he promoted an air of self ordained importance, his shining bald head held in an almost backward-tilted manner which elevated his nose and prevented his ample double chin from taking prominence. His suit was light blue polyester with a matching polyester tie, both local products made just outside town at Sewell Manufacturing on Highway 46. In spite of the fact that the buttoned coat hid the tie that was tied too short, it did not adequately cover the exposed, rotund belly.

Turning toward the judge's bench he headed through the bar that separates the public from the court officials. Without looking at the jurors, he passed them, stepped up to the witness box and just as he had obviously had practice doing before, stood with his body squarely toward the judge, his back to the jury and raised his right hand ready to be sworn.

Whispers of *Who is he* and *What does he do,* ceased, as the judge raised his right hand as well and turned in his chair to face the witness.

"Do you solemnly swear or affirm that

you will tell the whole truth and nothing but the truth?"

"I do."

"Be seated please."

"Please state your name, sir and your occupation," said the district attorney.

"Lamar Morrison and I am employed with the State of Alabama as an investigator with the Alabama Bureau of Investigation."

"Tell us about your training."

"Your Honor," Davis said, "we will stipulate as to Mr. Morrison's adequate training for his job."

"Alright," Judge Munroe said, "continue Mr. Hudgins."

"In your capacity as an investigator did you work a homocide in November of last year on I-20 near Exit 199?

"Yes, sir."

"Please tell the ladies and gentlemen of the jury what you saw."

"Well, when I arrived, the Sheriff and two of his deputies were already there and the coroner had just arrived and was taking pictures. Trooper Spencer was lying face down in a pool of blood, at the edge of the interstate, on the east bound side."

"I show you some photographs that have been marked as State's exhibit numbers 1 through 10, and ask you if you can identify these?"

"Yes, sir. I took those pictures at the crime scene."

"I move to admit them Your Honor."

"No objection," said Davis, briefly rising, then seating himself again.

"They'll be admitted," said Judge Munroe.

"Where was the defendant?"

"He was also face down. He appeared to be unconscious."

"Did he have anything in his hand?"

"No, but I did recover a 0.38 caliber Smith and Wesson revolver from the Sheriff. I checked the cylinder and two shots had been fired."

"Is that the picture of the Defendant in exhibit number 3?"

"Yes sir, that's him."

"Did the sheriff tell you where he got the gun?"

Both the Judge and the District Attorney turned toward the defense table expecting an objection from Davis on hearsay grounds, but nothing. Davis to their surprise looked unalarmed.

"Yes sir. He got the gun from the defendant's hand."

"I show you what has been marked as State's exhibit number 11, and ask you if you can identify it."

Taking the tagged gun from the prosecutor and briefly looking at it then handing it back, he said, "Yes, sir. That's the gun I recovered at the crime scene."

"Thank you. Any fingerprints?"

217

"Objection," Davis said. "This officer can testify to what he saw, but he has not been qualified as a fingerprint or as a ballistics expert."

"Sustained."

"Alright, I'll pass the witness."

"Mr. Davis," said the judge.

"Mr. Morrison, how is it you were able to arrive so quickly to the crime scene?"

"What do you mean?"

"You got to the crime scene at about the same time as the sheriff and deputies. Marco was still unconscious."

"Well, I got a direct call from the sheriff as he was going to the crime scene, and I was already in Heflin."

"Really, the sheriff called you directly?"

"Yes."

"When you arrived, tell me the number of vehicles that were there."

Officer Morrison's quandary at having to count vehicles appeared to be overtaxing his brain. In what could be described as an attempt at equalizing the blood-flow to the brain, he stretched his head upward, grimacing as he did, then to the side. As there was no answer yet, he tried another maneuver, that of tilting his head backward, as though he were seeking help from the Almighty or possibly just looking for the answer to the question on the courthouse, celetex ceiling. With his head still affixed so, and his eyes still toward the sky he said, "Seems like there was just three."

"Name them please."

"Well, the trooper's car, the sheriff's car and the deputy's car."

"I thought there were two deputies."

"I guess they rode together, or with the sheriff."

"You said three cars. No other vehicle?"

"Oh, I'm sorry there was a seventeen foot truck, sort of like a moving truck-- unmarked; the wrecker had already got it."

"To your knowledge, had anyone disturbed anything at the scene?"

"No, they were waiting on me and the coroner and the lab guys. Except..."

"Except what?"

"The Sheriff had removed a gun from the defendant's hand."

"They removed a gun and the truck allegedly driven by my client was already moved?"

"Yea, that's right."

"Do you know if the truck was dusted for prints?"

"Your Honor, Mr. Davis objected a moment ago when I asked about prints. I'm afraid I'll have to object now."

"Your Honor the District Attorney asked specifically about specific prints. Unlike the District Attorney, I am not asking for an opinion on whose prints were found or if any were found. I am simply asking if this witness knows if anyone from his office dusted for prints."

"Overruled. You may answer."

"Yes, sir, Mr. Thomas from the lab dusted for prints.

"Thank You. Were Officer Spencer's emergency lights active when you arrived?"

"No."

"Did you check the tape back at the State Trooper's Headquarters in Jacksonville of Officer Spencer's call as he stopped his vehicle on the Interstate?"

"Yes, I did, but there was no record of him making a stop around that time near Exit 199."

"Hm." Davis said, his right hand raised to his chin. "Did you check his equipment in the patrol car to see if his radio was functioning properly?"

"Ah, no I didn't"

"Isn't it protocol for a trooper to call in a stop as it is being made?"

"Yes sir it is."

"Do you have an explanation as to why Trooper Spencer did not place the required call when he supposedly made this stop?"

"No sir, I don't."

Davis picked up one of the photographs from the area in front of the court reporter and handed it to the witness. "Exhibit #3 is the picture you have identified as being that of Marco lying face down. One hand appears to be underneath his body and the other hand is outstretched. Could you tell the jury which hand is outstretched?"

Investigator Morrison frowned as he studied the picture being held in front of him. It was fairly obvious that Davis' questions were causing Morrison's brain some discomfort.

"The left," he finally said, seemingly proud of himself as he recited the answer; so proud that he decided to repeat it. "It was the left hand."

"That is the hand where the gun was found according to the Sheriff and the deputy, wasn't it?"

"Yes, sir, as I said they had already kicked the gun away from the defendant's hand, but yes, that's the hand the gun was in."

"Thank You. Did you or any other investigator see any sign of a struggle?"

"No, sir."

"Thank you, that's all I have, Your Honor.

"Mr. Hudgins, any more questions?"

"No, Your Honor."

Lamar Morrison carefully stepped down from the witness chair and again without looking at the jury proceeded to reinstate his nose in the same upward position, as he walked from the courtroom.

"Call your next witness."

The State calls Sheriff Sykes.

Unenthusiastically, Marco had been watching the goings on in the courtroom. He barely noticed the crowds of people, and found it difficult to concentrate. His thoughts were a constant interruption of scattered black and white snapshots of the scenes of the last six months: *the ride here with Ray Tarpley; the arrest and murder charge; Mama's letter, papa killed; the attempt on his own life and the killing of Davis Humphries, the last time he saw his mama, his papa.*

"Yes, sir," the sheriff said in answer to Hudgin's question, "I arrived there and found Trooper Spencer dead, shot twice, looked like one in the back and one in the front. That Mexican boy was lying face down with a 0.38 revolver in his hand. I removed it and waited on the ABI to get there."

"Thank you, sheriff. No further questions."

Judge Munroe turned toward Davis.

"Sheriff, did you see any sign of a struggle, either by what you saw by viewing Marco's unconscious body or the body of Trooper Spencer?"

"No."

"Thank You. Your Honor, I don't have any more questions at this time, but would reserve the right to recall this witness."

"Alright, you may step down sheriff. Ladies and gentlemen, due to jury selection taking most of the day, we got off to a late start and Mr. Hudgins' next witness has to come from Montgomery and won't be available till in the morning. I am going to release you for the day, and I remind you not to discuss this case with anyone. Alright, I'll see you in the morning," said Judge Munroe rising to stand with the jury.

"I appreciate all your work," Marco told William Davis, both of them respectfully standing looking toward the jurors as they filed out of the courtroom, "but, no matter how much you do, you know it won't be enough."

Had he given up? Davis did not quite know how to take Marco's words.

Three of the four deputies who had escorted Marco that morning were standing beside the table ready to go back to the jail, apparently only three needed for the return.

"Mr. Davis," one of the deputies said, "we got to put the cuffs on and walk him down unless you need him."

"Marco, do you need to talk to me," Davis said placing his hand on Marco's shoulder.

"No."

"Get some rest then. I will see you in the morning. I'll be at the jail before court," Davis said, as the deputies attached the handcuffs and ankle bracelets and proceeded with the slow motion walking out of the courtroom.

An attorney's success shouldn't be measured till there is a conclusion, Davis thought, *but today was a good start.*

He quickly packed away his notes and books and followed Marco and the deputies down the stairs, arriving at the bottom just in time to see among the crowd of people a very large black man, well dressed in a navy colored suit.

With the crowd, Davis had not noticed him earlier. He watched as the deputies stopped their slow walk, and allowed this man to talk briefly to them and to Marco. What remained of the crowd of interested people seemed to be of the quiet variety; the more vocal sign-toters apparently satisfied that the beginnings of justice in this matter had finally arrived. The dozen or so remaining onlookers watched with interest, as did Marco's lawyer, as the black man was allowed to stop the processional.

"Hello preacher," he heard someone say. "You got all your troubles straightened out?"

"I believe I has," Davis heard the man respond, "time now for me to help those in need."

Davis stood at the bottom of the stairs, watching as the deputies, Marco and the man he later learned was Joe Frank, continued the slow walk out the double doors, through the courthouse parking lot and down the concrete steps leading to the Cleburne County jail. He could hear what sounded like preaching, as they walked, and was puzzled that a preacher would choose to ply his trade while they were walking his client to the jail.

SEVENTEEN

William Davis always got up early, especially early when trying a case. On the second day of State of Alabama v. Marco Esgivas, Davis was up before sunrise, perfecting the questions he intended to ask the pathologist, Dr. Thomas, while drinking his morning coffee, black and strong, sweetened with a touch of Irish whiskey.

Technical questions, boring to most and bordering on gore to many, the upcoming medical presentation would be an unpleasant and necessary part of the prosecution's case, and could be just as important for certain aspects of the case for the defense.

He could already see where this trial was headed, and he now believed there would be ample argument for reasonable doubt.

I'd love to tell Marco of my assessment, he thought, as he tied his tie and glanced out the window to check for clouds. *Good, a sunny day*. With three children in college and one in law school, the house was quiet. *No wonder my hair is trying to turn white*, he thought.

Yes, he would love to tell Marco that if ever a trial had begun as he had hoped, this was it; that based on the state's first witness, reasonable doubt was a guarantee. But he couldn't, for his desire to avoid giving false hope to any client was too great.

The prosecution's case on the surface appeared strong: a dead officer who had stopped the defendant for an unknown reason; a vehicle registered to a company in Mexico, which would make someone think it very well could have been a drug run, and the murder weapon in the hand of the defendant--an illegal alien.

Those facts would certainly be enough for many juries to find a defendant guilty. But, there were holes in the prosecution's case: Marco was unconscious. Why? It was only one factor, but Spencer's body was five feet away with no sign of a struggle, and the murder weapon had not been fired by either of Marco's hands. And what the jury would learn later in the week was that Marco was right handed and the gun was found in his left. Except for a smudge, the gun did not have any fingerprints on it, suggesting the gun had been wiped clean of prints. *Of course, admittedly a gun is difficult to get a fingerprint from.* The truck had also been wiped clean of prints–even Marco's prints could not be found in the truck. Who drove it there? And, why did the Sheriff have it taken away before forensics arrived?

At 7:15 a.m. Davis pulled up to the gate entrance to the jail. Even though a visit to his client was unnecessary, he wanted to see Marco before they brought him up. Since Marco had been told very little about strategy, he wanted to give him some idea of what he had in mind, now that the trial had started.

It's about time, Davis thought, as the ten foot tall aluminum gate finally slid open. *They are usually a little more prompt this early in the morning.* Several deputies and the sheriff were looking out the side window, of the front office, very much like little children might stare out as company is coming up the driveway.

Unusual, this many folks here so early in the morning, Davis thought, as he pulled in and parked beside the Sheriff's car. He had heard, as had the whole county, about the recent escape attempt and accidental death of one of Syke's prisoners, Mr. Davis Humphries.

Maybe more deputies are here for beefed-up security, Davis thought, as he walked inside the small room crowded with sheriff and deputies, comprising the entrance to the jail.

"Good morning, gentlemen," he said, as the throng of deputies seemed to stop talking and stare as one unit at the defense attorney. "Everybody's out mighty early this morning. What's the matter, your women kick you out of bed?"

"We ain't in a cheerful mood, counselor, and I ought to lock your ass up at least for 72 hours till we sort this out," the Sheriff said, his harsh, loud tone an obvious suggestion of a problem.

"Sort what out?" Davis said, looking at the other deputies hoping to gain some insight into why the sheriff was shouting.

227

"When's the last time you saw your client?"

"Why? You writing a book?"

"By God," the sheriff said, his anger appearing to multiply. "Give me one more smart-ass answer and I'll lock you up for sure," he said, even louder than before, as he came around the counter and moved closer to Davis, his deputies wide-eyed with wonder.

"Well I don't intend on being questioned or answering *any* of your questions," said Davis, who was becoming slightly angered (and louder) himself.

"Where is my client?"

"Your client ain't here," the sheriff said, in a voice best described as restrained.

"Where is he?"

"He's gone like a goddamn Mexican Houdini, and I ain't answering any more of *your* goddamn questions either. I've got a prisoner to find." the sheriff shouted, as he and his deputies walked briskly out the door, climbed into their respective cars and sped out the opened gate leaving a very surprised attorney and jailer staring at each other.

"Jerry," Davis said, "tell me what's happened here."

"Mr. Davis, it's the damndest thing you ever saw in your life. I went up a little before 6:00 a.m., like every morning to get one of the trustees to start breakfast. Just so happens that the new cook is in the same cell as your client. Sun barely was coming up so it's still pretty dark, when I open it up to let Benny out and look over at the top bunk on the right where your client sleeps-- it's empty!"

"Was the cell locked?"

"Sure it was locked, just like Humphries."

"What do you mean?"

"Well the cell was locked like it was with Humphries--when he fell and broke his neck."

"I thought Humphries was trying to escape. He was in a locked cell?"

"The cell was locked, but somehow Humphries got out. Broke his neck on the steps."

"Any other prisoners escape besides Marco?"

"Nope. Everybody's here but your guy."

~~~~~~

The news had already spread. It was now after 8:00 a.m. Davis, deciding to leave his car parked at the jail, hurried up the hill to the courthouse, his mind a torrent of thought: *continuances, motions. Dismissal? The judge was going to love this.*

~~~~~~

"No," Judge Munroe said, "why should I dismiss this case and give your client the benefit after he has escaped."

"First of all," Davis said, "his not being

here violates his constitutional rights, particularly when, as we speak, there is no evidence that he has necessarily escaped."

"Your client is gone, Mr. Davis, how is that not escape?"

"That is certainly what the jury will think. This is a small county. They will know it and be prejudiced against my client because of it. What if he were forcibly removed from his cell," Davis said, calmly stating his argument as he began to walk from the table toward the judge's bench.

"Please Mr. Davis," the judge said incredulously.

"There is no evidence that he left through any other way, except through a locked door that was still locked when the jailer found him missing. With no disrespect to the sheriff, as much as I am sure he wants this to look like an escape. . ."

"Judge," Hudgins said, "there is no point in Mr. Davis trying to smear the reputation of the sheriff. . . "

"I am not interested one way or the other in someone's reputation. The facts are that my client is missing, and the cell door was locked. It also could look like someone with a key removed my client from that cell and did not put him back. With that a possibility, you cannot go forward with a trial, and even if the facts were not as they are and it looked like a clear cut case of escape, he has a constitutional right to be in this courtroom to assist with the defense of his case. Besides, there is no prejudice to the state, but my client will be irreparably harmed and prejudiced by having a trial in absentia, and I don't think there is any precedent for a capital murder trial in absentia."

"Your Honor," District Attorney Hudgins began, "We want a conviction. We want this murderer off the streets, but we want it to stick. As far as we are concerned we will try him on escape charges in addition to capital murder as soon as we find him. The state would ask that you continue this for a few days and give us time to find him."

"Jo, I can't keep these jurors hanging like that. We either go forward or I declare a mistrial and send the jury home."

The room was silent, the judge, the lawyers, and the law enforcement officers were all in a state of bewilderment. Nothing like this had ever happened before.

"Bailiff, bring the jury in."

Davis barely heard the judge explain to the jury that they would be dismissed, free to go.

"The defendant is missing," Judge Munroe said, "the circumstances are not known. I am afraid I will have to declare a mistrial. We will find him and unfortunately have to start over when we do."

Davis was drained. He watched as the jury filed out of the courtroom, their heads turning almost collectively as a group toward the defense table; *certain,* Davis thought that *they probably want to compare the look of the empty chair against yesterday's memory of Marco in the chair.*

Davis' thoughts were running wild as the last of the jurors made their way out the door, leaving a befuddled look on the faces of courthouse personnel, with most of them, the judge, the clerk and prosecutor looking at Davis.

The tape he had of the sheriff. Maybe he needed to expose what he knew. No, the connections he had discovered between the Sheriff and Texas and Mexico needed to be kept quiet till trial. That surprise was going to be effective—if I get to use it, he thought, as he packed his bags and headed back to the office.

EIGHTEEN

"What do you mean he is missing?" a very upset Ken Begal said, sitting at the desk previously occupied by Tony DeMarcos, his morning coffee being interrupted by Sheriff Sykes call.

"What kind of jail are you running up there? The man we sent to take care of this gets his neck broken in your jail, and now a kid that can barely tie his shoes has escaped!"

Begal listened intently for only a moment before continuing.

"All I can tell you sheriff is that I have partners, now, who don't have my pleasant disposition. They expect problems to be taken care of and I suggest you find this problem and take care of it if you have to follow him to Mexico to do it," Begal said, as he ended the call by slamming down the phone. *One takeover of the DeMarcos Cartel was certainly enough*, Begal thought, as he looked up from the phone to address his new employee.

Sandy Bowman, a tall, slender thirty-one year old man from New York had been sitting in the corner of Ken's office. New, he had only been in Mexico for a few weeks, and had a varied history that included work as a body guard and private detective. Proficient with firearms, this had already been put to use with the killing of Miguel and Tony DeMarcos. Unfamiliar with Mexico, and with much of what went on in this particular organization, he came highly recommended from a corporate acquaintance of Begal's back east, and Begal hired him right after his release from prison at Riker's Island. His unfamiliarity and lack of association with Mexicans and Columbians was attractive to Begal, who was uninterested in hiring anyone who had networked their way through related cartel businesses.

"Has the Esgivas family moved out of their house, yet?" Begal asked Bowman.

"Yes, sir," Bowman said, "but I can find them if you need me to."

It would have been much easier to watch for this kid if the family were still in that house, Begal thought, regretting his decision of forcing the family to vacate their home.

"Find them," Begal said, "Take one of the men from the dock with you, one of those that I just hired." Begal had made it a point to replace as many men as possible that might have allegiance to Phillip. "I want to know where they have moved to and beginning tomorrow, I want a man watching their old home to see if Marco Esgivas comes back there."

"And if he makes it home . . .?" Sandy asked.

"Let's just say he's of no value to me in

234

his present condition."

"Yes sir," Bowman said, buttoning his suit jacket and turning to leave the office.

NINETEEN

The escape of a man accused of capital murder from a small town jail in Alabama is, as one would expect, an unsettling event not only for the townspeople, but for the county's citizens as a whole.

The imaginings run wild, as thoughts of a killer roaming freely in their midst are heightened by false sightings with porch lights flicking on with the barking of a dog, and anywhere people stopped to talk, all across the county, the discussion was about the killer and the lack of preparedness by the sheriff and his deputies.

"Every jail has had escapes, before," Sykes had shouted to news reporters who had pummeled him with questions, crowding his car door, as he exited his running vehicle in the courthouse parking lot the day after Marco's disappearance.

Syke's deputies were sent with pictures to every store and church in the county. Pastors were asked to remind their congregations of how dangerous this young man was; his *kid next door picture* looking out of place under the captioned words 'escaped killer, extremely dangerous' which was placed on the church bulletin boards next to the announcements of upcoming Bible schools, weenie roasts and bazaars.

Opinions of where this young man was and how he escaped were plentiful and varied: "He ain't nowhere round. I betcha he hopped on the train as it went by; probably went to Atlanta and got on another one back toward Mexico."

"Somebody had to help him," the pastor of First Methodist of Heflin told one of his deacons, as they stared at his picture on the bulletin board of the church at the end of Sunday Morning service.

"You don't get out of a jail without a little help and you sure don't make a clean break like he did without help."

"They've been saying we need a new jail. Them ole locks just don't work that good. The kid got him a piece a metal and picked the lock and walked out the front door," said a patron of the Trickum Valley Trading Post on Highway 46 near Ranburne, in Cleburne County.

"That's how he did it," someone responded, "but he's still around. They're looking everywhere, between here and Mexico, and if he tries to use the roads, they'll catch him."

~~~~~

The old Howle and Turner store building sits on Highway 9, five miles or so south of Heflin, on the banks of the Tallapoosa River, in southeastern Cleburne County. A testament to a once thriving area, the original

1880's era block and brick structures, consisting of three large buildings had once provided this rural farm community with the necessaries of farm living: corn grinding, bolts of cloth from Atlanta and New Orleans, overalls and sewing needles, farm implements, tobacco, seeds, elixirs, and nostrums and remedies for every known malady of the day.

Today's store, while selling some groceries, seed, hardware and plumbing supplies, barely occupied a third of the original space. Two of the original three buildings remained boarded up and empty, one of those housing the old mill.

From the turn of the 20th century and on into the late 1940's, the brick and concrete structure sitting along the western edge of and parallel to the river, was the place where the county's citizens brought their corn to be ground into meal. From as far away as Ranburne and Fruithurst to the north and even Oxford in neighboring Calhoun County to the west, they came, at least once a month. As the corn was ground, the man of the house would talk with Mr. Howle about farming, cotton prices, or politics, while the lady of the house shopped in the adjacent store.

In the recent past, the main store building and the adjacent buildings had been used for storage, with wooden crates, old store fixtures and burlap sacks stacked head high in a corner of the building on the river side of the back building. And, according to Jimmy Hugh

Erwin, Joe Frank's brother, of no importance, for nobody had been in that building for at least ten years.

"I should know, I been workin' there as a second job since before daddy died in 1979 and we both grew up there, playin' around Uncle R.C. on Saturdays. They paid him a dollar an hour to load feed for folks," he had said to Joe Frank, the day before Marco vacated the Cleburne County jail, *"and that warehouse is the perfect place for him to hide."*

Marco opened his eyes and quickly sat up. *It was Thursday.* The river side of the back of the building, the east side, and the three non-boarded up windows on that side had the beginnings of morning light filtering through the hardened dust that lined the panes.

Damp and cold with the river mist and sustained by a loaf of bread, cans of pork and beans and Vienna sausages, Marco had existed in this place for three nights in a row. Piles of burlap bags filled with old ground-up corn or wheat, he wasn't sure which, combined adequately with the two quilts provided by Jimmy for a tolerable mattress and pillow.

Laying one of the quilts across his shoulders, Marco removed one of the surrounding boxed crates he had positioned around him and slid down the pile of burlap sacks to the concrete floor.

Still dressed in his orange jail uniform, he squatted down next to the milling

239

apparatus, a combination of wheels, gears and cylinders, and sat down next to the huge wheel, his legs hanging down through the two foot wide opening in the concrete floor to the river about ten feet below. He watched the paddle wheel turn its steady counterclockwise turn. The bouncing sounds of the rushing river were loud on the hard surfaces of concrete and brick; a total, inundating sound leaving no room for hearing anything else.

It was cold and except for two pieces of bread, Marco was out of food. He knew someone would be coming to get him, but he didn't know who or when. The wheel turned. Daydreaming was easy.

"Marco," said a muffled voice from behind. Marco calmly turned around. It was Jimmy, Joe Frank's brother.

"Hope I didn't give you a fright?"

"No. What am I going to do if you *were* a deputy, jump in the river *and* get shot?"

"Yea. Ain't no use in gettin' wet *and* gettin' shot. Sides, they might not wait for you to jump. Might jus' shootcha in da back," Jimmy said with a big grin on his face.

"I can certainly tell who your brother is," Marco said, smiling.

"Heah, I got some more clothes and a biscuit. I guessed at the size" he said, handing Marco blue jeans, shirt, tennis shoes and a jacket, along with a sack containing a ham and biscuit.

"Gimme that orange jumpsuit, I'll get

shed of it."

"What are we going to do," Marco asked, as he ate his breakfast and proceeded to switch out the clothes.

"I'll pull round to the side. You gonna hop in the trunk. Joe Frank's gonna meet us the other side a Birmingham. Sheriff's boys been watching him purty regular. Got to be a little sneaky to get this done. They figure he's got something to do with you getting' out. They just ain't figured out about me makin' a key yet," Jimmy said, that consistent big smile stretching to a huge grin across his face at the last statement.

"How will I get out without someone seeing me?" Marco asked.

Jimmy was looking next to the milling apparatus, at the gap in the floor where Marco was sitting with his feet hanging down.

"This should work," he said.

Marco watched as Jimmy took out a small rope from his coat jacket, tied an end to a piece of metal protruding from the concrete floor and threw it down the space toward the river.

"Right there. You gwoin to climb down," he said pointing toward the end of the building, "walk along the edge to the other side where I'll be waitin'."

Hoping to manufacture in himself the same air of confidence that Jimmy had for his plan, Marco squatted down, pulled on the rope to test it and while holding the rope, leaned

241

over the edge to follow with his own eyes the path just described.

Indeed there was a small ledge, maybe one foot wide next to the river wall of the building which was also adjacent to the dam and the wheel. Marco assumed this pre-designed opening in the floor, approximately two feet by ten feet, was probably put there to make repairs on the mill grinding wheel or the paddle wheel or the dam.

The rope Jimmy had brought wasn't quite long enough, stopping about halfway down, making Marco's drop to a foot wide ledge more precarious, considering the fact that the dam and the paddle wheel were all equally close enough to aid the river in drowning him.

Ahyieyie, he thought, as Jimmy went back to the car with his orange, jail clothes and the garbage Marco had created. Marco laid over on his back for a moment of contemplation, listening to the water, splashing over the dam, flapping against the turning paddle wheel, reminding himself that swinging on a rope down to the one-foot ledge below was a piece of cake compared with getting that key from Joe Frank to get out of the jail: Joe Frank had walked up to him at the bottom floor of the courthouse on Monday afternoon. He had asked the guards to let him speak and pray with me just for a moment and how, not waiting for an answer, he began preaching as though one of his fire and brimstone sermons was about to break out.

"Thus saith the lord," he began. The deputies, amused at the beginnings of perceived entertainment, stopped walking. Everyone on the first floor of the courthouse seemed to stop to take in the show, their comments and opinions of the proceedings of the day suspended, as they listened to what the preacher was saying.

"You need deliverance, and you needs it tonightah. Jus' like Joshua with his hands in the air an' da sun straight up, when dat clock hands is straight in da air at midnight, right den it's gonna happen," he said, the deputies grinning and shaking their heads as they looked at each other.

"Fust you gots to find the sose of yore salvation. Its at da bottom of da hill, you here what I say, at da bottom is yore salvation!"

"He's facing the death sentence preacher, I think he's at the bottom right now, don't you Harry?" Deputy Barnett said, laughing.

"O.k. preacher, I think he's got it. Move aside we got to get him to the jail."

"At da bottom Marco. Look for yore salvation-on yore knees, at da bottom," the preacher concluded watching after Marco and the deputies as they walked past him to the jail-side exit of the courthouse.

Marco hadn't known Joe Frank very long, but he had known him long enough to know that this preacher wasn't just giving a mini-sermon. He was trying to tell him something, and there was intensity in his voice when he said the words '*at da bottom.*'

Trudging forward, one deputy on each side and one in the lead, Marco looked at the bottom of the two steps leading to the parking lot from the back door.

Nothing there, he thought as he stepped to the pavement and made his way to the long row of concrete steps that lead to the back gate of the jail.

"Wait a minute," one of the deputies said. Marco looked up, afraid that they too had understood the preacher's message, "let's take off the ankle bracelets so we can walk faster down these steps, I'm hungry."

"Fine with me. If he runs we'll have target practice," Deputy Jacobs said, as he took his key out and began taking off the ankle bracelets.

"O.K. let's go kid, before that preacher follows us and tries to take an offering up," the other deputy said.

Marco walked forward, faster now. He had counted the steps. There were eleven. At the bottom was a conglomeration of broken concrete and grass.

Eleven, ten, ninth step. Marco could see the grass and the broken concrete at the bottom, but nothing else. Surprisingly the deputies were not holding each arm, as they had been at the courthouse when people were looking on.

Eight, seven, sixth step. There was something dark at the bottom, almost hidden in the protruding grass, two inches long maybe; he was still unable to make it out with the almost setting sun.

Five, four, third step. The lead deputy was unlocking the back gate, and the other deputies were talking to each other; nothing Marco was paying attention to, for he was completely focused on the object, now just three or four feet ahead.

Second step. Marco fell forward, his chest landing just beyond the first step, his face buried in the grass just to the right of the landing, his bound hands scooping up the dark metal key that Joe Frank had left 'at da bottom.'

"You stupid tonk, can't you walk?" Deputy Barnes said, as both deputies pulled him up from the ground.

"Wipe that grass off of him. The sheriff'll think we been throwing you to the ground."

"I am sorry," Marco said, the key clutched and hidden in his right hand.

Walking on through the opened back gate, the lead deputy said," If you boys can't keep a prisoner walking, we'll have to get some new deputies."

"We can't help it we got a clumsy prisoner," Barnett said.

"Wonder he didn't trip when he killed that trooper," the other deputy chimed, as they opened the back door of the jail and Marco walked in, the key now hidden in his mouth.

"Probably why he was unconscious—fell down after he shot him," the other deputy said.

Joe Frank was right, Marco thought, as he sat in his bunk that night, the key safely tucked away in his sock.

My salvation was 'at da bottom on my knees', and when the clock was straight up at midnight, true deliverance came for Marco.

Using the key, he opened the cell door, slipped outside and re-locked it; making his way down the steps of the fortress-like jail, barely hearing the sounds of snoring men, as he passed the other cell doors.

Marco walked out the back door and after sliding under the fence on the back side, he looked up to see a car on the side street flashing its lights on and off. Behind the wheel of the car was a smiling Joe Frank. No inmates. No deputies. Nobody had seen him leave.

Everybody's gone to a lot of trouble, Marco thought, still laying on his back, next to the wheel, his mind now concentrating on the river below and the business at hand. *I don't need to slip and drown and mess everything up.*

Jimmy was gone, waiting outside; the quilts and empty cans collected, and the door already boarded back up. Taking one more look at what had been his home for three days and taking one more test pull on the rope, he climbed down the rope as far as he could go, hung there for a moment, before letting go and landing on the ledge.

With the spray from the river dam, hitting him in the face, he then made his way along the wall to the side of the building where Jimmy was waiting, standing beside the open trunk of his brown, four door 1973 Chevrolet Caprice.

"In ya go," Jimmy said, his hand on the trunk lid ready to slam it shut.

Marco quickly jumped inside, the trunk closing behind him. Jimmy had arranged the quilts creating a somewhat softer area to lie on, one quilt as a pallet, and one as a pillow.

I certainly won't miss this place, Marco thought as Jimmy's car pulled into the main road.

Alabama, to Marco, was not country folks, cotton fields and kindness. His experience had exposed him to a different side: to him, Cleburne County, Alabama, was a place where the devil ruled; where evil and evil doers were allowed to run rampant. Evil men were in charge here, and the evil wind his priest had talked about blew unabated across the land.

There were some good people here, Marco thought, his eyes growing heavier in the almost absolute darkness of the closed trunk. He had rested for three days, but he was still tired, and the hum of the engine was peaceful. He meant to ask Jimmy how long it would take to get to Birmingham. He meant to thank him.

247

It was good to have friends, he thought, as his eyes closed and the consistent hum of the engine caused his thoughts to drift. Soon he was asleep.

~~~~~~

The entrance to the Alabama Adventure Theme Park near Fairfield, just west of Birmingham on I-20 was gated shut. This smaller version of Six Flags in neighboring Atlanta, with its prominent, silver roller coaster, the tallest of the seven major attractions, would not be open for business till early summer, another month away. Surrounded by woods, the park was isolated. Its one acre parking lot, a wide empty expanse of two year old asphalt and painted yellow lines, stopped abruptly at the edge of the woods with no buildings in sight.

Joe Frank got out of his 1994 Ford Explorer to stretch his legs and look around. He knew Sykes suspected he was responsible for Marco's escape. His deputies stopped him outside Heflin as he was leaving this morning, and for no apparent reason, a trooper pulled him over near the Pell City exit east of Birmingham, explaining, as he looked inside the vehicle, that he had stopped him by mistake.

Good luck I spose, Joe Frank thought, as he stooped down to pick up a penny from the asphalt. The only kind of luck he truly believed in was the *God* factor.

Either God is on yore side or he ain't, he would often recite in his sermons. *But,* he would always add, *it don't hurt any to keep a rabbit's foot tucked in yore pocket jus' in case. God ain't got nothin' 'gainst a good rabbit's foot, or a lucky penny,* he thought, as he watched his brother's brown Chevrolet coming toward him from a distance, thankfully with no cars following.

"Hey brothah," Joe Frank said to Jimmy, as he got out of the car and stretched his arms.

"Any trouble?"

"Naw, What about you?"

"Well day been watchin, alright. Stopped me twice. Searched it," Joe Frank said, pointing to his Explorer, "but when day saw my tackle box and rods and reels, day jus' wanted to know where I was gwoin fishing. I told them anywhere I could find some wadah with fish in it," he said, the signature grin across his face.

"How's our boy doin'?"

"I guess O.K.," Jimmy said, as he unlocked the trunk and helped a squinting Marco climb out. Shielding his eyes as he adjusted to the light, Marco surveyed his surroundings.

"Where are we?"

"Jus' west of Birmingham," Jimmy said, as he took hold of Marco's right hand and helped him out of the trunk.

249

"Yep, got us a little mo travelin' to do fore we get to Texas. I'd love to stay and visit brothah, but I guess we needs to get goin'," Joe Frank said.

"Jus' get in da front Marco. I ain't got a good way to hide you on dis ride. If day stop us, day ain't a lot to be done except talk."

"I'd let you take mine," Jimmy said pointing to his old Chevrolet, its paint flecking and the left bumper slanting toward the ground on the driver's side, about to fall off. "But I ain't sure you'd make it all the way to Texas and back."

"Awe, we'll be fine, brothah. God done brought us dis far," Joe Frank said, as he and Marco got into the Explorer. "Sudie made us some biscuits. I got my rod and reel to catch fish, and I brought six gas cans full of gas, sose we don't have to stop where somebody might see us. We gwoin to take da back roads for a while till we gets through most a Mississippi. Da county done stopped me outside Heflin and a trooper stopped me fore I got to Birmingham, so we ain't out of da woods yet," Joe Frank said, as he cranked the Ford and pulled away.

"You take care, brothah. I'll see you when you get back," Jimmy called after them, as he watched them leave the parking lot.

Neither Marco nor Joe Frank spoke for several miles. Marco had gotten used to being alone over the last several days, and was content to look out the window, enjoying the pine trees, squirrels and occasional rabbits that darted out into the road leaving their safe haven to risk the crossing to the other side.

It was good to see something untouched by man. It must be getting close to Easter. Too many of them, he thought, as he watched another rabbit dart across the road.

The building on the river where Joe Frank and Jimmy had hidden him was a wonderful halfway house, a healing transition from the jail. But it was still imprisonment, still cinder block and concrete and nowhere to go.

Whether I make it home or not, it was good to be out of that jail and it would be even better when they get far away from Alabama, with my friend, Marco thought.

"I better stop and look at dis map again," Joe Frank said, pulling off to the side of the road and spreading his map across the steering wheel.

So far, they had stayed on two lane roads; some asphalt and some a mixture of hardened mud and creek gravel like the one they were on now.

"Dis road ain't on da map," he said partly speaking to himself and partly speaking to Marco.

"It's a new map too, got it fresh dis mornin' at da stoh," he said, tapping the map for emphasis. "We'll be alright. It ought to connect wih dis here road dat keeps us headin' west," he said, tapping again on the map as he

251

talked.

"Have you ever been this way before?"

"Naw, I ain't nevah been out of Alabama cept to go to Georgia every now and then, Atlanta, Douglasville," Joe Frank said, as he started the Explorer and pulled on to the road.

"Iffin I was to get out in normal times, I'd stay on da interstate and drive real smooth," he said, as he swerved to miss a huge pothole. "But," he said, turning over toward Marco with that wide grin, "dis ain't normal times."

"Da thang is, if we gets stopped we got to not say no mo dan is necessary. Let me talk. Day liable to catch yore accent."

"I want you to know," Marco said, still looking more at the outside than at Joe Frank, "that I am very sorry for putting you and your family in this situation."

"Well it wadant you. God been puttin' his chil'rens in sicheations since he made dis ole world; puts us dare to help other chil'rens in dare sitcheations. I can't blame you for dis no mo dan I could blame Eve for Adam eating dat apple." Joe Frank stopped talking, his mind traveling down some road of reflection.

Laughing out loud he said, "I heard some say dat Eve is da one started all dis sinnin', but I always remindsem dat it takes two to do a tango, and jus' cause a woman offers it up, don't mean ya got to *taker* up on it," he said, his eyes straight ahead on the road, the grin gone, and his mood changed to a more solemn one. Uhm, uhm. I tell you, I know what ole Adam was gwoin thru, and when dat temptation stares right atcha in da face, ooh Lawd, it's hard to walk away."

Obvious that Joe Frank's parallels with Adam and Eve had taken his mind on some private journey, Marco left him to his thoughts, looking out the window at the farms and woods, as they drove, waiting several minutes before speaking again.

"Why did you change your mind?"

"About what?"

"Getting me out. You told me you could not, that you were a man of God."

"I'm still a man a God, Marco, and dats why I had to help."

"Is it because Humphries tried to kill me?"

"Partly. I knew dat fellow was gonna try an' kill fore it happened.

"How could you know that?"

"Well, it was fixin to be my last day. Sheriff knew I wadant no criminal, so day sort of gave me da run ah da jail and I was in da back part, back dare next to Sheriff Syke's office. I heard him talkin to some fella bout yore daddy; something bout how you was gwoin to get killed just like yore daddy; how you wand't gwoin to make it to trial, that some boys in Mexico wanted you dead and dat Humphries better do it right or he would have to take yore place."

Marco had appeared almost

uninterested in what Joe Frank was saying, continually watching the wildlife along the road as the story was told. But on hearing the word *Daddy*, his appearance of complacency was gone, replaced by a look of bewilderment, as he turned to look and listen to Joe Frank. And, as Joe Frank filled in some gaps in Marco's puzzled story of existence in Alabama, his mind was inundated with a flood of facts and half-facts; of past and present scenes of Mexico, The Factory and, of course, Alabama.

"You mean the sheriff was connected with The Factory? With Papa's death?"

Joe Frank saw the anguished look; the same look he had seen at the jail on his young friend's face on learning of his father's death. He knew before he started down this road about his father that this would possibly be even more painful to Marco than just the news of his father's death. Someone dying is one thing. But to know that the man in Alabama that beat you and locked you in a cell was a part of the treachery of not only having your father killed, but also of trying to kill you, is a lot for a young man to digest. The look of torment on Marco's face told Joe Frank that his young friend was having difficulty processing what he had just told him and all that had happened to him.

Joe Frank waited, giving Marco time to think it through.

"So Sheriff Sykes was involved with Mexico, with Humphries, Papa's death,"

Marco said. His statement, almost a repeat of a moment ago, but obvious to Joe Frank that Marco's stunned and tormented mind needed to say it again, a way to process the treachery.

"Well," Joe Frank said, as he swerved to miss a turtle crossing the road. "He involved enough to try and kill you and he knew something bout yore daddy and the killin'. I know dat much."

"Why? Why would they want to kill Papa?"

"I don't know, Joe Frank continued, "but den I saw da guy dat was gwoin to kill you." I watched him through a crack in da door, talkin' to da sheriff like day was buds. Da sheriff said, 'I'll get you out soon as you done, he told him; said, 'he'd tell da coroner you pulled a knife on da new guy, Humphries, and how day gwoin to say you got dat knife from da kitchen while he'pin me.' I figured dat must been why day let you out to help me in da kitchen," Joe Frank said.

Avoiding another pothole in the road, Joe Frank glanced again toward Marco to assess his reaction, his emotional condition. He had seen enough crazy people to know that you couldn't always tell about the mental part, sometimes not until they snapped. He knew Marco was tough; that he could take the physical pain. He had seen him almost kill Dale Carter, and he knew the sheriff and his men had roughed him up. But he worried about the mental part. Being arrested in a

255

foreign country, charged with murder, an attempted murder on his life; and, not to mention the beating they gave him when he got there, and his papa dying; all of it was enough to put a balanced and strong tempered man over the edge, much less a boy.

"I knew tellin you all dis, 'bout da sheriff and all was gwoin to be upsetting. But you had to. . ."

"What is it?" Marco said.

"Looky yonder. We got us a little problem."

Up ahead, several hundred feet away, were two Mississippi State Patrol cars, one on each side of the two lane road, their emergency lights on; two troopers standing on each side of the road.

"We jus' gwoin to stay calm now," Joe Frank said, as he slowed to a stop in front of the trooper and rolled his window down.

A young slender man in his early twenties, this trooper stood with both hands propped up on each side of his leather utility belt. His flat trooper-styled hat completely covering his head and forehead, giving the impression that the hat was too big, since it touched the top of his aviator, mirrored-styled sunglasses, making eye contact and any possible indication of his intentions--through the eyes at least, impossible.

"Afternoon," the young man said, as his partner looked on from Marco's side of the road.

256

"Evenin', officer."

"I need to see your license and registration," the officer said, as his partner began walking around the vehicle and looking through the glass at the backside of the hatch.

"Yessah," Joe Frank said, as he reached into his wallet and handed them out the window."

The officer looked at the license and registration, holding them as he talked. "Alabama? Long way from home ain'tcha?"

"Yessah. Y'all lookin' for some bad guys today?" Joe Frank asked.

"Sort of," the officer replied. "Who's that you got with you?"

"Jus' my nephew," Joe Frank said matter-of- factly.

The officer looked again at the license, then at Joe Frank and over again at Marco, who was looking out the passenger side window at the other trooper, who had now walked to the front side of the Ford Explorer.

The trooper pulled his sunglasses down, letting them sit on the edge of his nose. "He's just a little lighter skinned than you are to be your nephew. Ain't he?" The trooper said with a disbelieving tone.

Leaning out the window to whisper, Joe Frank said, "Yea, my sister, she high yella. She like to mix-breed thangs." Joe Frank's eyebrows arched upward after he said it, a you-know-what-I-mean look on his face. "You know how some of dese young folks are. No

257

offense, but when I was young we didn't mix-breed like some young folks do now a days. You jus' didn't see none ah dis salt and pepper stuff."

"I know exactly what you mean," the trooper said, seemingly jubilant that he had someone, even if it was a black man from Alabama that agreed with his racial sentiments. "If we don't watch it we'll have a nation full of gray people and look where our country'll be then."

"I'm tellin' you," Joe Frank said, nodding his approval.

"Y'all going fishin'?" The trooper said as he looked behind Joe Frank at the easy to see fishing gear in the back of the Explorer. Where you heading?"

"I got a brothah lives over near the Big Black. We gwoin dare to wet a hook or two and see if da catfish are bitin'."

"Really? Where does he live?"

Marco was intrigued at how well Joe Frank was handling this conversation; extremely curious to hear the answer Joe Frank would come up with about where his brother lived.

"Near Brownsville, near da petrified forest."

"What's his name?"

Joe Frank didn't answer quickly as before and for a tense moment Marco was afraid the ride in the Explorer was coming to an end.

"Now I know you boys got something better to do than talk with dis ole colored preacher out of Alabama 'bout his relatives, 'specially since I got several moh hours to drive and I doubts anybody gonna have me any supper fixed if I don't get dare in time to catch it. . ."

"O.k., o.k. Sorry, somebody robbed a bank over in Philadelphia and we got a call they were heading north toward Louisville," the officer said, as he handed Joe Frank his license back.

"Well I'm heading southwest tordge the Big Black," Joe Frank said, as he put his license back in his wallet and put the Explorer in gear.

"Hope you fellas' catch dem bad boys," Joe Frank said as he pulled ahead, past the trooper cars, looking initially straight ahead, and then checking his rear-view mirror to make sure they weren't following.

"Whew," Joe Frank said, "I about thought day had our number, Marco."

"Do you really have a brother here in Mississippi?"

"Shore does, a brothah in Christ. Used ta be a deacon in my church. Lives near Brownsville, near da Big Black River. We ain't gwoin to see him though. We gwoin to find us a good fishin' spot either on the Big Black or on the Mississippi and camp for da night, den head on to San Anton."

TWENTY

Maria Esgivas stood inside the main office building of The Factory, in the hallway, just outside the private office of Ken Begal. She stared at the pictures of the DeMarcos men her husband had admired. They looked like good men. She knew nothing about them, except the stories her husband had told about the elder DeMarcos: how, he and Senor DeMarcos would walk the fields, discussing things such as better irrigation and harvesting methods for the corn. He always made sure Miguel got paid, even when the harvest was bad.

As for the dark side of the business, Miguel never talked about it.

That was another world, another time, when life was still good, she thought. Now there was very little money left. Most everything she and Miguel had saved had gone into the house that had been purchased by Senor DeMarcos, the mortgage owed to The Factory, the house now taken from them.

Just as well, she thought, *I couldn't continue the payments*. Upon being given the eviction notice, she and the children had moved in with her mother, a four-room house, already crowded with six people living there.

In spite of her misgivings about this place, she had agreed to Senor Begal's request that she come and see him, assuring her through his hand-delivered letter that what he had to say would be very helpful to her family. She assumed and hoped that Miguel was probably owed another paycheck, which she needed desperately.

"Senor Begal will see you now, senora," a man announced as he held the door open for her to come in.

I am out of place here. Sewing, children, her husband, cooking, these were the things she was familiar with, she thought, as she timidly walked through the open door.

She had never met Ken Begal, the American friend of Antonio DeMarcos, and Miguel had said very little about him; his only comment being that he was not as good a man as Senor DeMarcos.

"Mrs. Esgivas, thank you for coming," Ken Begal said, as he rounded the desk and stood greeting the widow in the same area where her husband had been killed, his hand outstretched with a used car salesman smile on his face; businesslike, he wore a light gray, shark-skin suit that shined.

I have no choice but to be here and to listen to what he as to say, she thought, as she shook Ken Begal's hand.

"Please, sit down. May I get you anthing?"

"No. Gracias," she said as she sat down in one of the two office chairs directly in front of his desk.

Her brief survey of the office showed

that it was filled with what appeared to be new furniture: tufted, black leather chairs and a matching sofa with accented beads whose new leather smell competed with the unmistakable smell of new, thick-napped burgundy colored carpet.

Two men, dressed in expensive dark-colored suits, sat on a black, leather sofa to her right, against the wall. Both of them stared ahead in silence. *Why are they here*? She thought.

Maria was unnerved by their presence, particularly after she recognized that one of them was the American that had brought the message summoning Miguel to this office the night that he was killed.

"Would you like something to drink? Some coffee, perhaps?"

"No, gracias," Maria said, as she sat looking down at her hands that were folded in her lap.

"Let me get straight to the point. I want to first extend to you my condolences. "I don't know what happened to Miguel," Ken said, as he paced in front of his desk, his hands raised in a questioning manner. "Perhaps he went crazy because of your son, I don't know. What I do know is that he worked for the DeMarcos family for a very long time."

A man who spoke words without meaning to him, she thought, as she looked up from her hands to study Begal's face. Maybe it was the fact that her husband had died

262

somewhere in this room, perhaps, or that this man thought her husband was a killer. Whatever the reason, she did not like him. His face had the appearance of sincerity that his voice lacked.

My face probably is not indicating my true feelings either for I despise being here, she thought. And the more Ken Begal talked, the more disdain she was developing for him.

"I have decided as the Chief Executive Officer of this company to do what I consider the proper thing. I have here a check for $1,000.00. It isn't much, but I am sure it will help you in your transition."

"Gracias," Maria said as she took the check from him.

"I am very grateful for this," she said, as she rose to her feet, assuming that her business here was concluded.

"One more thing, please," Begal said, as he motioned for her to re-take her seat.

Maria reluctantly sat back down.

What else could there possibly be, she thought. She was in no mood to listen to more about her husband being a killer.

"For what I am doing, you cannot assume that neither this company nor I have anything but disdain for what your husband did. But I believe there were factors beyond his control that impacted what happened. Because of that, I have decided to let you move back to the home where you and your family were living, that is if you still want to live there."

"It is—was--our home. But I do not know if we can continue paying for it," Maria said, thinking how truly generous this was under the circumstances, and yet suspicious of the gesture.

"I knew that would be a problem, so I have taken the liberty of making your payments for the next year . . . to give you time to get on your feet," he said. "Here is a receipt showing that all mortgage payments on your property have been paid in full for one full year. You won't have to worry about a place to live anymore."

This time Maria could not disguise her feelings. *Miguel must have been wrong about this man,* she thought, and in exuberant fashion she began thanking him.

"This is extremely generous and unexpected. I don't know what to say."

"Your husband earned this for you," Begal said, "for your family. It is only right. I am afraid with the murder of Senor DeMarcos, as a company, we may have overreacted."

"Gracias. When can we move back in?"

"Today, right now. It is your home."

Maria walked toward the door clutching the check and the receipt, glancing only for a moment at the other two men, who seemed unmoved by Ken Begal's gesture or her exuberance, their stoic faces and their silence blending well with the dark colored sofa.

"By the way, tell Marco when he gets home, he still has a job here if he wants it."

264

"Gracias, we all pray that he will come home soon," Maria said as she opened the door to leave and stepped into the hallway.

"You should see him soon, sooner than you know," Begal said, smiling.

Quick turns and reactions were not the norm of Maria Esgivas. She was a woman of calculation and study, but not necessarily when it came to her children. Her downward gaze, much like the rest of her bashful ways were particular to her gender for centuries, taught by her peers, sanctioned and re-enforced by generations of male domination.

But with the statement about her son, she quickly turned and came back inside the office. In a fashion inconsistent with her character, she stared deeply into the eyes of the man she had just met in an effort perhaps to find truth.

"You didn't know. How could you know," Begal said in a laughing, almost mocking tone, his steely gaze searching not for truth but for weakness; his satisfaction with himself and with the shock on Maria's face, apparent. He allowed her to look in his eyes, because there was truth in the fact that Marco was probably on his way home.

"That's right; it appears your son is coming home."

"What do you mean?" she asked in an excited, not quite believing tone as she moved at first toward the bearer of the good news, then stopped, as she realized how this made her look, particularly to the two men staring at the scene from the couch.

"Your son escaped from the American jail."

Maria dropped the documents she was holding to the newly carpeted floor, her mouth emitting a slight whimper, as unexpected air swiftly passed from and into her lungs across unprepared vocal chords.

She was stunned by the words. Everything she had dreamed was flashing in front of her eyes: *A little boy lost in the darkness unable to get home; the rebozo,* her words to Miguel assuring him that their boy would be coming home--the very home that had just been given back to her. *But escape?* She did not think he would have to escape to get home. *I do not care, she thought. My boy is coming home.*

"Here, let me help you," Begal said, as he picked the documents up and handed them back to Maria.

"Please, sit down again, if you like."

"No. Gracias. I want to stand. When did he . . . escape?"

"Monday night, I am told. Walked right out of the jail, somehow. He saved us the trouble of getting him out. You see, we already were working on a plan with some of our agents in the states to get him out of that horrible place," Begal said in as sincere a tone as he could generate to this grieving wife and mother.

266

Unable to differentiate lies from truth, all Maria could do was listen and ask simple, to the point, questions.

"Do you know where he is?"

"No, but it wouldn't surprise me if he were on his way home right now."

Maria knew she needed to leave. It was all she could do to refrain from bursting into tears and she did not intend for these strangers to watch her cry.

"You might see him as early as this weekend," Begal said.

"He is alright then? He will be able to get here without a problem?" Maria stood in the doorway ready to leave but wanted reassurance.

"Certainly. You have nothing to worry about. He's a smart boy. He'll get here without trouble. He escaped from an American jail, so getting here should be easy," Begal said, as he stood by the door, preparing to close it behind her.

"Gracias," he could hear her say as she passed by the door.

"Mrs. Esgivas," Begal said, leaning over to her, in a quieter, confidential manner, "as soon as you see him, would you tell him I want to talk to him . . . about his job here?"

"Si," Maria said before turning to walk down the hall, this time with the DeMarcos portraits unnoticed.

Begal stood by the door, as he listened to her tiny feet picking up the pace, the further she got down the hallway. He stood in the doorway, smiling.

"I had no idea you were so nice, boss," one of the men sitting on the sofa said, his effrontery not appreciated by Begal.

"Not that I need to explain everything to you," Begal said, his smile now gone as he looked at his brazen employee sitting beside Bowman, "but putting that family back in that house makes it easier for you boys to see when he comes home. Anybody who has the brains and the balls to break out of an American jail, and then makes it all the way to Mexico--if he does, deserves a proper welcome," Begal said, as he sat down behind his desk.

Maria smiled and clutched the two pieces of paper she held in her hand even tighter, as she climbed into Miguel's truck. A neighbor's husband had driven her here. He didn't ask what the papers were that she held in her hands as they drove and she didn't offer explanations.

Sitting on her passenger's side in silence, she cried those tears of joy that had been restrained in front of the strangers she did not trust, her head turned away from the driver. She would tell no one, not even her family, not yet. Marco was coming home, and she was sure that in spite of her letter telling him to check with grandmamma about where they were staying, he *would* come home first. And she would be there waiting.

TWENTY ONE

"*Come over here and cast your line Marco. You will not catch a fish like that,*" said Miguel.

"*Why, Papa?*" said Marco.

"*Your shadow. The fish will not bite with your shadow over the water. You must get lower so they will not see you. If you see the fish, they can see you.*"

"*The birds are loud, Papa. They sing songs to each other. Won't that scare the fish?*"

"*No. That is a good sign. They are happy because there are so many fish in the water.*"

"*How long is it?*"

"*The river? I do not know, but it runs all the way to Falcon Lake that borders on the United States, in Texas. That is a fine place, the United States. They have everything a man can dream of having. Everything you would ever want is waiting there. You and I will go there someday, stay in a fine hotel and sleep on a mattress so soft it feels like you are floating on air.*

"*No,*" Marco said, his face, the face of a child, upset.

Looking into the air, Miguel was happily envisioning this fantasized trip.

"*We'll wear fine clothes and eat in a fine*

restaurant. I'll have a steak this thick--"

"No, you cannot go there. They will lock you up. You do not know what you are saying. You will not get to come home," Marco said, tears filling his eyes and anger racing in his voice as the chirping of the water birds and the squawks of the gulls became louder.

"That is crazy," Miguel said, as he re-cast his fishing line a little further out. "What makes you say such crazy things? You are just eight years old. You've never been to the United States."

"I know what I am talking about and I will not go," Marco said, as he threw his pole in the water. Doing so disturbed a flock of gulls, which immediately climbed into the air, frightened, joined by an egret, which was at rest near the edge; their choruses of squawks, chirps and cries sounding like a flapping free-for-all of agitated fowl excitement.

Upset at being disturbed, they all flew to the other side of the river, their loud singing echoing in the distant hills making the dozens of birds sound like hundreds, easily drowning out the screams of a little boy in answer to a father's imaginings.

"No," Marco said, his hands covering his ears to dampen the bird's singing. "No. I don't want to hear it. No. No. . ."

"Marco, Marco," Joe Frank said, shaking him gently.

"Wake up Marco. You jus' havin' a bad

dream, dats all."

Marco opened his eyes. The gulls were still singing and croaking their songs along with the chirping of different types of birds; all of them sounding as though they were right outside the tent that Joe Frank and Marco had slept in the night before. The river's lapping was a consistently pleasant sound and in the distance a small, motor-powered boat could be heard, its steady hum against the lapping river water was a pleasant backdrop to the singing of the birds.

Looking around, Marco sat up, realizing where he was.

"I'm sorry. I was dreaming about papa."

As he rose up his head touched the top of Joe Frank's homemade tent.

"Little tight in here. Sudie didn't quite make it big enough. But it's alright."

"How'dja sleep?"

"Good, a few dreams."

"Yea, I heard some of it."

"Looky here," Joe Frank said, as he held up a wire basket full of fish.

"It's a shame we ain't got some way a freezin' dis," he said as Marco exited the tent, wiping the sleep from his eyes.

"Dis Big Black's alright. Be a fine place to live if a fella didn't have a place," Joe Frank said, as he began cleaning the fish.

Marco walked to the edge of the water, watching a small boat in the distance.

"I hope you like fish for breakfast." Joe

Frank said, as he pulled away a piece of meat from the bone and threw into the skillet.

"If I said no, would you go and get me something else," Marco asked with a grin.

"Nope. Like I used to tell my chil'rens. Dis is what da Lawd's provided and if you hungry you'll eat. Here, I done cooked dese," he said, pointing to an aluminum foil covered plate sitting on a rock. Marco uncovered it to find five or six fried catfish fillets.

"Don't worry, this looks good," Marco said, as he picked up one of the fillets and began eating.

"Mind if I see if I can catch one?" Marco asked as he picked up the rod and reel.

"Go ahead catch us some moh. We'll have dem and da last I cleaned for supper."

"I doubt that I am as good as you are," he said, reeling in the line and recasting. "You amaze me," Marco said, as he watched the float bobbing in the gently moving river water, holding the rod in one hand, while eating fish with the other.

"How's dat?"

"You seem to know a lot about a lot of things."

"Well, when you deals with people and dare troubles you learn a lot."

Marco's float sank below the surface and popped back up again. Cramming the last of the fillet in his mouth, Marco watched intently to see if the float stayed under, then watched it pop back to the surface.

"You gettin' a nibble," Joe Frank said, as he scooped up the last of the frying fish, moved the skillet off the fire and watched intently the bobbing of Marco's float.

"Joe." Marco said, as both he and Joe Frank waited on more movement from the float.

"Yessah?"

"You ever killed anybody, before that guy at the jail?"

"Why you ask dat?"

"You seemed experienced...at killing, the way you broke that man's neck at the jail."

"Like I said dem chickens. . ."

"No," Marco said, turning to look pointedly at Joe Frank.

"You didn't learn that from chickens."

Joe Frank leaned back against a big pine tree and chewed on a piece of fish as he watched a flock of birds fly over head.

"You know," Joe Frank began, still looking at the last of the flock of birds and searching the sky for more, "God gave us dominion over certain thangs in dis world: birds, animals, land. To a certain extent he gives us authawty over other people. It's a gift he entrusts you with. Now I say dis right up front," his speech now less sanguine and more intense.

"God don't like killin'. He made dat clear when Cain gotta hold of Abel and he kicked Cain's butt out of da garden. See Abel was doin' good in dah sight of God. He didn't need killin'. He didn't need to be bothered by somebody dats evil like his brothah. Some folks, dats all day about is evil, and God didn't put us here to be run over by dem," he said, his voice growing still louder, not quite to the preaching level, but close.

"Now if these kind of folks will leave ya alone and not be messin' withya, then lettum live; Live and let live. But if day won't," he said, as his voice built up to a crescendo, "well den some folks jus' need killin'."

Marco pulled at his line, moving it gently to the left and reeling in slowly, as it began to bob up and down.

"You've killed before haven't you?" Marco looked toward Joe Frank as he asked the question and continued looking as he waited for the answer. Suddenly there was a giant tug on his line. The float had disappeared. Responding to it, he pulled hard.

"I've got one. It's big."

"Careful. Don't break da line. Easy now, dats right. Reel him in slow; work with him."

"Yea, dat's a biggun alright, at least ten pounds."

"Hee, hee, you doin good," Joe Frank said, as he stood to his feet, chewing the last of his fish and watching Marco work his catch closer to the edge.

"Lawd Marco, looks like you done got a turtle."

"What will we have to do, cut the line?"

"We may have to cut da line, but if it's a

turtle, we gettin' it fust," Joe Frank said, excitement building in his voice.

"You ever ate turtle fore?"

"No," Marco replied, straining to keep it in play, his rod bent in the air.

"Hold whatcha got," Joe Frank said, as rain began peppering down and a thunder burst sounded overhead.

"I can't pull any more. It's going to break."

Without hesitation, Joe Frank jumped from the bank into the cold muddy river. It was about knee deep with a small current. Wading out further, the water up to his hips, he grabbed hold of the line and bent down to have a look at Marco's catch.

"It's turtle alright. Niceun too,"

"Just keep da line tight. Dat's right, keep it tight."

Without further warning, Joe Frank reached into the water and picked the turtle up and slung it onto the bank.

"Keep it tight. Keep yore line tight," he said, as he walked swiftly out of the water and climbed the bank.

"Don't let the line loose. Keep it tight," he said, as he pulled out his knife and proceeded to cut off the turtle's head, slinging it to the side.

"Good bait for later," he said, as Marco watched in amazement.

Joe Frank, having completed the head cutting portion of the turtle-catching ritual, picked up the turtle, and in a triumphant gesture held it high in the air while turning in a circle.

"At least twenty pounds, moh like thuhty," he chanted in song-like manner, as he turned in a circle, dancing and chanting with the headless turtle held over his head. Marco, tired from the battle, laid down on the bank, laughing at seeing his friend acting in such a way—over a turtle!

"Um, um, shore gwoin to be some good eatin' tonight," he continued in the chanting mode, as he headed toward the tent, the turtle still vaulted over his head, the rain coming down harder.

"Let's get in out of da rain a minute. I'll clean it when it quits," he said.

Taking a nail from his pocket, he hammered it into the tree with a rock and wrapped fishing line around the turtle's shell and feet then wrapped the other end of the line around the nail.

"Dare now. Dat'l keep da varments off till we get ready to clean and cook. Come on, let's get some wood bundled up fore it rains good," Joe Frank said. As the wind picked up, it thundered in the distance and rain pelts became harder.

Marco helped gather several bundles of wood, putting some in the Explorer and some in the tent to prevent it from getting wet. While it rained, he and Joe Frank got into the homemade tent and lay on their quilts.

Surprisingly neither of them talked.

The rain, the thunder; all the sounds were similar to that night in the jail, Marco thought.

Within an hour the rain had ended and Joe Frank crawled out of the tent and got a fire started. The fire was a welcome treat, for the rain had put a chill in the air, and although the weather had been unseasonably warm, it was still the very early part of spring.

Marco gathered more wood as Joe Frank de-shelled and skinned the turtle. The day was spent fishing and gathering wood, and talking. Marco didn't ask about killing any more that day and Joe Frank did not bring it up. The day had been cloudy with spurts of rain and sometimes thunder. As the sun was setting, the rain and clouds were all gone, leaving the air colder for the night. Marco worked on the fire, building it to a nice warm level as Joe Frank began fixing supper.

"We gwoin to have it two ways," Joe Frank said, "skewered over da fire and fried in da skillet. Take dem tators out of da Explorer and wrapem up good in da aluminum foil and layem on da rocks next to da fire."

"What did you say this place is called?" Marco asked, as he sat down by the fire.

"The fish camp. Dis river's da Big Black. It's muddy, but not near as muddy as the Mississippi," he said, as he placed some turtle meat on a skewer.

"I thought you had never been out of

Alabama," Marco said.

"Oh, I ain't, but I's had plenty of folks tells me about it. You can see da fish in dis river, but day say da Mississippi is so muddy you can't see yore foot when you steps in it ankle deep. Now dats muddy. Listen to da sounds," Joe Frank said, as he handed a skewer of turtle to Marco.

The nighttime noises on the Big Black River were just beginning: an amazing orchestra of wondrous and intense sounds that can lull you to sleep or keep you wide awake with their intricate arrangements. The birds, so loud and prominent in the morning with their choruses of songs and chirps were quiet tonight, resting up it seemed, for tomorrow's morning performance, and except for one occasional squawking bird who roamed from one side of the river to the other, as though looking for some lost relation, bird-participation in tonight's musical was non-existent for the moment.

The tree frogs, while not being a part of the morning's rendering were the evenings' featured instruments. Their incessant grunts echoed back and forth, taking center stage and drowning out the crickets and katydids and other lesser-volume insects, as well as the occasionally heard comforting laps and splashes of the river.

While far from melodious, the tree frogs were heavy-weight participants, filling the night with a steady tempo of bass-grunting

278

sound, perfect as a loud and sometimes competing backdrop for sleep or conversation.

"Theys something nice bout the sounds of a rivah," Joe Frank said, as he placed some more wood on the fire, and then picked up a skewer of turtle, working on it intently, smacking his lips in between bites. The river sounds were so robust that the crackling of the pine knots just placed on the fire could barely be heard.

"Do you camp out much," Marco asked.

"Naw. Did when I was younger. Used to go coon huntin' a lot at night like dis. Had an ole coon-dog, a blue-tick hound dat could tree any coon God made."

"What was his name?"

"Stiffler. I loved dat dog. Never did know what went with him either. Just got up one day and he was gone."

"Joe, you ever kill anybody else?"

Joe Frank sighed heavily. It had appeared to Marco, just before the turtle catching, that Joe Frank was about to tell Marco some things about his past, but the turtle had interrupted.

"Why you want to know da answer to something like dat?"

"Tomorrow, the next day, or the maybe the next, I will be in Mexico. You will be back in Alabama. We will never see each other again and I want to know you as well as I can before we say goodbye. I believe you did, and I want to know."

279

"You done heard me preach. I got you outtah dat jail. You done seen me fish! Ain't dat enough? Cause it pains me to think on it."

With a huge sigh, and with the river sounds of the night, and the crackling fire providing a comforting, steady background, Joe Frank began to tell another of his stories:

"When I was sixteen, my Mama would work for a white man name of Cantrell. I never did like dat man. Tried to get Mama to not work for him, but we needed da money. Daddy had got hurt workin' at da Cordage in Anniston--on a rope windin' machine. Couldn't work much anymore, hurt his hand purty bad. Da money day give him for da hurt hand didn't last a month, so all of us had to work. Daddy preached, but dat didn't pay nothin', not back den."

Marco threw another stick on the fire, and moved closer to Joe Frank.

"I went to pick Mama up one day and her hair was mussed up and her dress was tore and you could tell she was mighty upset. She wouldn't tell me nothin'. I tried again to get her to quit workin' for him. Said she couldn't. 'We'd starve if she quit,' she said. Next day I went to his farm, he was out baling hay, an ole Massey-Ferguson square baler and a John Deere tractor. I tole him dat I was upset at da way my Mama looked and I wanted to know what happened. He tole me dat he paid my mama to be dare and he'd do what he wanted with her and tole me to get off his farm. I left."

280

"Da next week, on a Friday, after she put in her hours at Sewell's, I carried her over to Mr. Cantrell's to clean his house, once a week like usual, except dis time, after droppin' her off, I parked da car at da edge of da woods, sneaked over to da house and I watched out and listened. Mama was puttin' up clothes in one of da bedrooms. I was watchin' through da window, hidin' in some bushes as dusky dark was settin' in. He came in, tole her to take off her clothes. She tole him she couldn't, dat she was a married woman, and she begged him to please not do dis to her. He slapped her cross da face. By time I got in da doh, he was on top jerkin her dress up and his pants down. I tell ya Marco, I wonder sometimes if maybe I should have give him a chance to pull his pants up. But I didn't. Mama was screamin' so, I jus' grabbed his neck tween my two hands, jus' like I did dat man at da jail and I broke his sorry neck."

Joe Frank stopped, his hands held out in the fashion of how he had grasped the man's head. The pause giving the listener the chance to grasp and absorb what had just been said, while the river's night sounds very adequately filled the void with the rhythmic background provided by the frogs, crickets and other rattling wildlife and insects, but now joined by a variety of birds.

Unlike the morning participants who sang without backup, the nighttime fowls with their squawks and screeches provided complimentary counterpoints and solo movements to the steady rhythm led by the frogs. All these sounds, including the incessant lapping and splashing of the muddy river on the grassy bank, were the perfect soothing sounds needed to provoke the digging up of memories, even if unpleasant. Joe Frank stared into the fire as he talked. The hurt of what Marco had forced him to delve into, obvious, and Marco wondered if he should have pressed him.

"If I had went to da sheriff, don't know how it would of come out, black boy killin' a white pillar of da community and all. So, I throwed him over my shoulder, took him out past da barn and cranked up dat John Deere tractor dat was still connected to dat Massey-Ferguson square-bale hay baler. I turned on da baler, got it goin and fed him into da baler head first, his pants still hangin' round his ankles. Didn't take too long fore dat baler got all clogged up with body parts and clothes and such. Probably stripped da gears out. Mazin' thang was dat baler kept tryin' to bale. Dem Massey-Ferguson's was built good. I left da tractor runnin' and da baler tryin' to run, went back to his house and got Mama. We went home. Day found him da next day. Body stuffed down tween da spokes dat picks up da hay, head first, his lilly-white ass stuck up in da air. Coroner said it was an accident, dat he fell in dat baler tryin to clean it out. Funny thang is day never did figure out why he had his pants down."

For at least another hour, both Joe Frank and Marco sat in silence, except for nature's symphony, which continued at full volume, while the two traveler's backs leaned against two very big pine trees, not far from the water's edge.

Aged pine knotted logs and sticks of poplar heaped in criss-cross stacks on the fire in front of them caused popping, crackling and hissing, as the gasses escaped from the wood. The half moon's light was plenty to create a visual glimmering on the water, as the wind picked up, pushing the river harder against the banks, and the two travelers rested with the story and the night and the sounds.

"Let's go to sleep my friend," Marco said, placing his hand on Joe Frank's shoulder, as they both crawled into the tent.

"Ain't never tole dat to a livin' soul, not e'm to Jimmy," Joe Frank said, as he secured the opening to the tent for the night.

"I am glad you told me. You had to save your Mama, just like you had to save me."

Joe Frank shook his head, as he lay down to sleep.

That night they both slept well.

TWENTY TWO

Joe Frank and Marco started out early the next morning heading south toward I-10. From there it would be an easy ride to San Antonio. From San Antonio, Marco would take the bus into Laredo, then find a ride or walk the rest of the way home. As they neared the ramp for I-10 west, Joe Frank asked Marco to drive.

It looked as though they might just make it, and there was plenty of time to think about home and the future. Even with his father gone, the future still looked good. He still had the rest of his family, and Adidra, of course. He would find a job. They would get married and start a family. Life would be good again. It was going to be good to be home—if he could survive. Marco knew that the reason for wanting him dead, and whoever it was that wanted it was probably still there. It had to dealt with.

I might talk to Father John at the Catholic School to see if he could help me get into a college. But that might be difficult if they check criminal records world-wide.

Anyway, I will talk to him. When he hears this story, I expect he will tell me that God intervened. I'm sure he would say that God used Joe Frank, like he uses other mortals to do his bidding. I can hear him now.

"You were just a tragic hero in a Greek Tragedy. Although I cannot remember if Odysseus lost his father, Marco thought, as he checked his speed and the heat gauge. *No Cyclops, but there had been some Homer-type characters and events: Ray Tarpley, the Sheriff, the murderer in the jail. My escape! And the women in the strip club had made for great comparisons to the sirens. And, of course, the story's real hero, Joe Frank.*

"Where we at Marco," Joe Frank said, lifting the ball cap from over his eyes as he sat up, interrupting Marco's driving daydream.

"Almost to San Antonio."

"Since you behind da wheel you got ta keep check on dat heat hand."

"Yes sir, I've been keeping my eye on the gauge and the speed ever since we started on I-10.

"Dis country lookin' different from home," Joe Frank leaned over to check the gauge for himself.

Marco grinned. "Hey, have a little faith."

"I got faith, but sometimes reassurance can increase da faith."

"Joe, have you ever heard of a Greek writer called Homer?"

"Seem like I remember something bout him from school. He was a King wadant he?"

"No, a Greek poet, a writer. He wrote about Odysseus, King of Ithaca. Odysseus was forced to fight in the Trojan War, leave his family. It takes him ten years to get back home."

"Well, one thang about it, I know you been away from home a while but me and da good Lawd gwoin to get you dare, hopefully before ten years.

"At least since we got away from Alabama, the adventures have been a little more tame and fun."

"Oh yea," Joe Frank said, now remembering parts of the story. "He da one dat got captured by dat one eyed monstah and dem naked women sittin' on da rocks wooin' him and his men in?"

"Yes, the sirens, and the one eyed giant was Cyclops."

"Uhm uhm. Women dat gets da devil in them can jus' suck a man right in till he crashes on da rocks," Joe Frank said, as he stared straight ahead appearing to now have his own daydreaming, metaphoric visuals of rocks and siren-like temptations.

"I suppose," Marco said.

"Sometimes a man needs to be tied up like ole what's his name," said Joe Frank, clearly stirred by thoughts of Marco's historical comparative.

"Odysseus."

"Yea Odysseus. Uhm, uhm. Life jus ain't changed much," Joe Frank said, as he lifted up the cap, sighed and looked out the window. "Ole devil will work overtime to bring a good man down."

"At least," Marco said, "we won't have

problems from a Mythological God like Neptune making our journey difficult. When Odysseus returned home he found his wife Penelope being forced to marry another man."

"I'll say dis, if anybody was trying to hunt us, da trail we cut was a zigzag deal," Joe Frank said, staring at the map, again, and changing the subject. "We left I-20 fore we got to da Mississippi line and headed northwest; in da middle of Mississippi we headed southwest across Louisiana, den fore we got to Texas turned southwest to I-10 and now we right at San Antonio."

"Does that map of yours tell you how to get to the bus station? I know you are ready to head back home, and there might be a bus leaving this afternoon, if we can get there in time."

"Naw, it don't. And it's getting late in da day. Better pull up at dis service station and I'll find out. Park at da back, don't want nobody to see us."

"When you get back, you need to drive," Marco said, as he stopped and handed Joe Frank the keys.

"Yea, I better. Be dark in a little bit. If somebody was to bump us from behind in dis city, you wouldn't need to be drivin'. But I'm glad you drove some--I needed da rest. Be right back," Joe Frank said, as he closed the Explorer door.

It was quiet, a fenced yard in behind the service station, and a limited line of sight, so

Marco decided to get out and stretch his legs.

It had been a long drive since the fish camp. He walked past a row of dumpsters, directly behind the station. Behind them and parallel to the building was a wooden fence, tall, with an open, gated entrance to some apartments, with green shrubs lining the fence on the other side.

Making sure no one was looking, he stepped into the waist-high bushes, next to the fence, unzipped his pants and began relieving himself on the bottom of the fence.

Loud voices and some scuffling could be heard from behind the fence. Marco would like to have seen what that was about, but finishing his business, he headed back to the Explorer. A muffled scream from the other side of the fence changed his mind.

Running to the end of the row of shrubs and seeing a wooden baseball bat in the grass, he picked it up as he went through the wooden gate.

Inside, ten feet or so away, a man lay on the ground. He was bound and gagged, his left ear bleeding—an earring forcibly removed; an opened switch blade thrust in his face, held by a heavily tattooed, non-muscular, young man who stood over him, apparently ready to inflict further damage.

The muffled scream came from the girl held by two others, her hands were also bound, her mouth sealed with duct tape, her face pushed in a downward direction, forced to watch the events taking place on the ground.

"Hey, Slash," said one of the men holding the girl, who was wiggling and still attempting to scream. "We got company."

"Get him Slash," the other man said. Equally decorated in tattoos, he grinned, showing his darkened teeth, as Slash, having already turned from the one on the ground began walking toward Marco. Do *I talk, use the bat, or run.* Fortunately for Marco, he didn't have to decide.

"Well Marco, seems like I can't take you nowhere without you getting yoreself in some kind a fix. Here, let me have dat bat. I used a do a little ball playin'." Joe Frank took the bat and did a small practice swing, the swishing sound making an impression on the would be attacker.

Slash stopped in his tracks.

"Now fellas, here's da way it's gwoin to be. *You* are gwoin to lay down dat knife, and *you*," pointing to the one holding the girl," are gwoin to let dat girl go; and *you* gwoin to take yore other buddy and skedaddle."

"You try that and Stick'll hurt her," Slash said, looking back at his comrades who indeed had a firm grip on the girl.

"Well, I realize Stick could do dat, but dis one thangs for sure. Slash? Is dat what I heard him call you? Well, Slash, while Stick is doing dat to her, yore brain gwoin to be pourin' on da ground getting it real soupy. Now Mister Stick over dare he may hurt dat

289

girl, he may even kill dat girl, but fore *he* can get dat done and run, I'll done be finished openin' yore skull, cause I'm closer to you. Then six steps over yonder, I'll be crackin' his head open and getting *dat* part a da yard soupy," Joe Frank said, as he took a step toward Slash, the bat lifted to a threatening, swinging position.

"Let's get out a here Slash," said the third one of the bunch, looking very unconfident of he and his friend's position.

"Well that boy's got some sense," Joe Frank said to Slash. "Maybe when yore gone, they'll call him Slash number two in yore honor. But it don't have to be today."

Slash looked around at the scene, but more pointedly, he appeared to be sizing up the resolve of the very large black man, swinging a child's bat.

"O.K., old man, sometimes it's better to re-deploy and wait for another day," Slash said.

"Well now who ever said you wadant smart," Joe Frank said, as he slapped the bat in his hand.

"Guys, let's go. We'll get Snake later," Slash said, turning to head toward the gate past Joe Frank.

"Ah ah, dat way," Joe Frank said pointing the bat toward the apartments, and leave da knife."

"Come on guys," Slash said, as he flipped the knife to the ground, which landed inches from the face of the bound man. All of them ran toward the apartments and were soon out of sight.

Marco ran to the man on the ground, and took the tape off. Using the knife, he cut the plastic cords binding the man, then began to cut the cords holding the girl.

"You guys saved my life and my girl's. Thanks," the man said, as he rubbed his wrists. "My name is John T. My friends call me Snake. This is my girl, Katrina."

"Come on, we better get gone. Day might come back with some help," Joe Frank said.

"You got a ride?" Snake asked.

"Dis way," Joe Frank said, as they headed out of the shrubs, through the gate and climbed into the Explorer.

"Jus' slide dat fishing gear to da side," Joe Frank said, as he cranked the Explorer and pulled out into the street.

"You know dis city?"

"Like the back of my hand. Where you boys want to go?"

"Bus station," Joe Frank said, as he stopped for a red light.

"What did y'all say your name was?"

"I'm Joe Frank and dis here's. . . Mark,"

"No it ain't," Snake said,

"No it ain't what?"

"Well, I'm sure your name is Joe Frank, but the pictures they got hanging up all over town--*including at the bus station*, don't have the name Mark, they got the name Marco

291

Esgivas under it: killed a State Trooper in Alabama, the poster says, and that he escaped from an Alabama jail. Says that they suspect he," pointing to Marco, "may be in the company of a colored man," pointing at Joe Frank, "named Joe Frank. And, there's a $5,000.00 reward for information leading to his arrest," pointing again at Marco.

Back in Alabama at the Tallapoosa River, in his orange jail uniform, as the cold wind had blown in from that river, and Marco slept in spite of the cold on those bags of old molded corn or grain, he hadn't dared to believe. Home was just too far. But with each state, with each mile and with every breath of free air breathed, as he and Joe Frank made their way here, Marco had begun to believe that God was truly on their side. And as they drove across the Texas state line, so strong was his belief that he could almost see home-- everyone, except for his Papa of course, running out the door, waving, crying: "welcome home brother; welcome home son. *I knew you would come home.*" He had imagined his Mama and Adidra squeezed in between brothers and sisters hugging and attempting to kiss away months of hurt and loneliness.

But, as Joe Frank pulled off the street and into a Wal-Mart parking lot, the realities of the words of this stranger sitting in the back seat of this Ford Explorer made those visions seem more like dreams of a fool.

292

"Well," Joe Frank said, staring straight ahead, the tone of his voice sounding weary and defeated. "I'm sure anybody can use $5,000.00."

He turned the engine off and waited, bracing, as though he expected Texas Rangers to drop from the sky any moment.

"Yea, anybody can use $5,000.00, but I'm not going to turn you in. First," Snake said, as he leaned back, placing his left arm on the back of the seat over the shoulders of Katrina. "Y'all just saved my life. And second, I ain't got nothing for cops. Hell, they probably wouldn't pay the reward money to me anyway if I was to turn you in. Besides, I've got my own gang and in six months I'll be taking in more money than I know how to spend."

"The Vipers," Katrina smiled and said with pride, "that's the name of our gang."

"I assume y'all are heading to Mexico. So, let's quit talking about people turning people in, and let's see what my boys can do to help you make it all the way."

"If the authorities are actively looking for us here, we will need a new ride," Marco said.

"And one with Texas plates," Snake said.

"Do you know Donnie Ray Tarpley?" Marco asked.

"I know who he is, over on 410, the southern bypass, Cowboys. Why? Is he a friend of yours?"

"No, but I need information from him

before I go home and considering some of the circumstances he has put me in, I think giving me the use of one of his cars is the least he can do."

"Marco, you know dat man ain't gwoin to talk ta you. Sides, he'd jus' turn us in or shoot us," Joe Frank said, puzzled at what Marco was saying.

"I'm a cop-killer, remember," Marco said, a half serious look on his face, holding up the knife just confiscated from Slash.

"Well, I know everybody's got their own ways, and I never like to interfere with another man's method of interrogation, but if you like, I could use my lie detector and get the information you need out of him," Snake said.

"Well, dat would be a big waste. Cause what I done know about dis cowboy is dat lying comes purty easy, so yore machine telling us he's lying ain't really much help," Joe Frank said.

"My lie detector is different from the ones the cops use. It won't tell me if he's lying, it will make him tell the truth. Snake said, as he dialed a number on his cell phone. "Turn down this street, then look for 410-west."

Joe Frank reluctantly started the Explorer, as he listened to Snake's call.

"Yo, man. Listen. Check this out. The 'bloods' just tried to do me. No man, I'm O.K. But check this out, the guys that saved me are in some trouble. I need you and as many of our boys as you can get over to Cowboys car lot on

410 and keep the owner, Tarpley, from leaving till we get there. Oh, and bring Marvin," Snake said, as Joe Frank, satisfied that this was the best he and Marco could do at the moment, pulled out of the parking lot onto the street heading toward Cowboy's car lot.

~~~~~

It was half past five o'clock. Except for used cars, decorated with red and yellow ribbon, the parking lot of Cowboy's Used Car Lot appeared empty. Inside, a late arriving potential customer (presumably arriving without a car), neatly dressed, her purse in the floor beside her, was sitting in front of Ray Tarpley's desk silently looking at payment options. An impatient Tarpley sat behind his desk, his gold tooth shining with his salesman's smile, ready to close the deal.

"Can I help you boys," Tarpley said, as three men came in the door. a motley crew of desperates and undesirables, attired with bomber jackets, t-shirts, slitted jeans and tennis shoes accentuated by Mohawk haircuts, piercings, and tattoos of reptiles and animal life. All of them had their hands in their jacket pockets, except the one holding a gray-colored very large shoe box.

"That's O.K.," said the man holding the box. "We'll wait till she gets done." Two of the men sat down beside her, and immediately began looking over her shoulder. The man holding the box sat down in front of the adjacent desk. Looking up from the payment schedules and looking extremely uncomfortable, the young woman stood up, laid the payment schedule on the desk and walked out the door without saying a word.

"What can I do to get you to take this tonight," Ray Tarpley called after her, as he stood up and watched her walk through the door.

"Well, you boys gonna have to buy somethin'. Looks like y'all scared her off. My name's Ray Tarpley. What can I do for you?"

While Tarpley was talking, two of the men had walked around his desk and were standing next to him, one on each side.

"Hey, look fellas, what is this? I don't keep cash here, it's mostly credit sales. See, I can show you. . ." Tarpley said, as he reached down to open the middle drawer of his desk.

"Get his hands out of that drawer. Put him over here," said the man holding the box, motioning to the chair just vacated by the lady.

"Pete, see what you can find in that desk."

"R.D., check out back and make sure nobody else is around."

"Ooh, you was gonna be real bad with this," Pete said, mockingly, laughing, as he pulled a pistol from the middle desk drawer, held it in the air, took the clip out, then re-inserted it.

"Here's the keys," Pete said, as he

shoved the pistol in his front pants.

"Nobody back there," R.D. said, as he walked back through the door, after checking in the back. "The back door goes to a garage."

"Lock the doors, R.D. and keep an eye out front." Pete pitched him the keys.

"Pete, make sure Mr. Cowboy here ain't got another weapon on him."

Walking past Tarpley as he was being searched, the man with the shoe box--Duke, made his way in between the two desks and sat down behind the one adjacent to Tarpley's, the shoe box carefully placed on top of the desk. Duke turned on the computer and began scanning through the hard drive.

"Well just make yourself at home," Tarpley said, as Pete continued his search.

"Looks like you make some nice home movies. That looks like a nice camera over there," referring to the Sony video camera sitting on a tripod in the corner.

"Let's see what this batch is here. Hey Pete, R.D., look at this," Duke said, as he clicked, uploaded and viewed several different files on the computer. "Mr. Cowboy's the star of his own porn movies. He records with that camera and then downloads to his computer. Now ain't you a naughty boy. I wonder if she's legal," Pete said. "You know I'm all for a man having sex, but having a girl that's under age is just not right. We might have to be good citizens and turn you in. I think I'll download this to a disc for safe keeping," said Duke, as

297

he took a disc out of the middle desk drawer and put in the machine. "I really love that close-up shot. I can see your face and hers real well."

"Here they are," R.D. said, as he unlocked the door upon seeing Snake get out of the Explorer.

Disturbed by the prospect of more people joining these men, Tarpley who was trying to see past Pete, said, "Who is this? Who's coming in? Look, I got some important friends and they ain't gonna appreciate me bein' treated like dis. . ."

"Sit down, Mr. Cowboy. Tie him up," said Duke. Tarpley jumped from the chair but stopped as Pete pointed the gun pulled from the front side of his pants pocket directly at the cowboy.

R.D. pulled a roll of duct tape from his pocket, as both he and Pete began securing Tarpley's hands and feet together--the hands from behind, then the duct tape wrapped around his chest, arms and back of the chair, preventing movement of the upper body.

"You want everything?" Pete asked.

"Yea, everything."

With that, Pete also covered Tarpley's eyes, wrapping the tape fully around his head then placing a strip across his mouth. Finally, he wrapped the feet around the legs of the chair, making cowboy and chair into one unit.

"What's up? Snake said, as he walked in, tapping Tarpley on the back of the head and walking to each of his men, performing a slapping hand shake and half hug to the chest. "I see y'all got the package all wrapped and ready. Did he give you much trouble?"

"Naw, not much. He's a real talented fellow, makes some nice porn movies. Looks like some of the co-stars are under-age. I downloaded a copy. We might use it to collect some money. How about you? I hear you got into it with the Bloods."

"Yea, we'll have to tend to that."

Duke turned Snake's head to the side as he looked at the coagulated blood and tissue paper at the bottom of his left ear. "Looks like they tried to take your ear off. Better put something on that."

"Yea, I will, soon as this business is done. My new friends out there saved my life. I owe them."

Looking down at the desk, Snake saw the gray-colored shoe box and said," Ah, you brought my baby."

"Yea, lie Detector's ready to go."

Katrina was smoking a cigarette, walking around looking at the different cars for sale, Snake having ordered her to stay outside as a lookout.

Marco could see the worry on Joe Frank's face as they stood just outside Tarpley's office. Through the glass door they could see Tarpley being tied to a chair, his men taking over the office. Marco knew that up until the last thirty minutes, everything had gone according to Joe Frank's plan: the escape, avoiding the law, driving across four states without incident—and now only a few hundred miles from the border.

In Joe Frank's mind, everything was wrong, and Marco knew that his friend could not conceive of any reason why we should be here, the very place where his four month long nightmare had started.

"Joe, I have to have some answers from this man," Marco said.

"I don't understand how you expect to get him to talk and I don't understand what he's got to say dats worth the risk."

"With Snake and his men, hopefully I can get the answers I need--answers that may help me and my family stay alive.

"Dis ain't safe," Joe Frank said, "and you need to get on home, away from here."

"My home is still a very long way from here, and the people that killed Papa and tried to kill me will be waiting."

"But he ain't gonna help you--"

"Somebody wanted me dead. I have to know who and why, or when I get home, whoever was behind trying to kill me in Alabama will probably be successful in Mexico."

"And how you expect to get answers in here?" Joe Frank asked, as he looked again through the glass into the office.

"Remember, in the eyes of Snake and his

men, I am a killer. *They* respect that and I will use that fact to find out what I need to know before I can go home. Then I can make things right."

"I didn't get you out of that jail for vengeance, and your killer reputation ain't gwoin to mean nothin' to dis cowboy. He knows you ain't no killer."

"Joe, you talked about situations that are placed on us in this life. I have to use this one the best way I know how, or everything you have done for me will have been in vain."

Unsatisfied and unsure of Marco's intentions, he stared for a moment at his friend, before finally nodding. "O.K. I understand, I guess."

"Maybe you should wait outside with Katrina, if you are uncomfortable with this," Marco said, his hand on the door, ready to walk in.

"Naw," Joe Frank said, taking a big gulp of air, but without his usual smile. "God done put me here to get you back and I'm stayin'. Chil'rens of Israel had dat red sea pop up in dare way, and day went on. Ain't no reason to be fainthearted now. Let's go,"

Marco started to open the door.

"Wait," Joe Frank said. "If you gwoin to be da man in charge, I needs to open the door for you."

Joe Frank pushed the door open and held it for Marco.

"Come in," Snake said.

I hope Mama is praying about now, Marco thought, as he walked in, grim faced.

"Guys, this is Mr. Marco Esgivas and Joe Frank Erwin," Snake said.

Ray Tarpley's taped head raised from its downward-tilted position, and he began pulling against the tape as he heard the introductions.

"You're the cop-killer from Alabama," Pete said, in a solemn, reverent tone, as though he were now in the presence of greatness.

"Escaped without firing a shot, I heard," said Duke, as all of them, Snake, R.D., Pete and Duke nodded in approval.

"Gentlemen, I am pleased to meet you," Marco said, without emotion, as he walked closer, acknowledging each of the five men there, looking each in the face, before stepping closer to Tarpley's desk, and stopping just in front of Tarpley.

Joe Frank walked nervously passed the men to their right, his concerns about all of this heightened, as he passed Tarpley attached to a wooden chair with duct tape wrapped from head to toe, and his misgivings still not ameliorated as he got a closer view of Snake's men. He stood against the glass-curtained wall, as far away from those in the room as possible, as though the distance would separate him from what he was afraid was about to happen.

"Does this work?" Marco asked, looking

at the stand-mounted video camera.

"Yea, it works great. Duke says Mr. Cowboy's got all kinds of home movies stored on his hard drive."

"Good. Set it up. I want to record what we do here," Marco said.

Snake, with a concerned look gave the nod to Duke.

"Joe Frank, close those blinds," Marco said, calmly as he walked around the desk.

"Yessah," Joe Frank said, as he did as he was told.

"Duke, do you have enough light?"

"Yea, I'm good," Duke said, as he adjusted the camera.

"What angle do you want? Do you want somebody to be able to see that he's tied up?"

"That's fine. I just want you to record me and him. Nobody else," Marco said.

"OK. We ready," Duke said.

Snake leaned over to whisper to Marco. "You sure you want to tape this?"

Ignoring Snake, Marco turned, walked over to the front door and looked outside—just Katrina, no one else there.

"Take the tape off his eyes," Marco said, as he sat down behind Tarpley's desk, the order given to no one in particular but with Pete responding, who began peeling the top row of tape off with seeming enjoyment.

"Funny how that tape pulls hair and all when it comes off," Pete said, grinning as he peeled the sticky tape from head and hair, as

303

Tarpley began muffled cries that lasted through the peeling process.

"Sorry about that," Pete said, his sarcastic tone totally lacking in sincerity, as he took the tape that was now lined with strands of Tarpley's hair, wadded it into a ball and pitched it in the floor.

For the first time in over four months, Marco looked into the eyes of the man who had caused him so much pain.

Difficult to really see a man without seeing his eyes. Impossible to know his thoughts.

The blinking for which Tarpley was well known began and was continual. *Blinky*, Marco remembered, was the name one of the girls had called Tarpley in the strip club in Birmingham.

"Nobody's face but me and this Cowboy. Alright turn it on," Marco said.

"I trust you remember who I am."

Tarpley's head was unmoving in response.

"In just a moment I will have them take the tape off your mouth. I will ask you some questions. You will answer my questions truthfully and quickly. If you decide that lying to me or not answering is the better choice, then I will turn you over to my friends."

There was still no movement. Except for the blinks, Tarpley's dark, glassy eyes resembled shark eyes--unintimidated, unfeeling, soulless. His glassy, cold stare, an

304

exercise in illusory debate, and just like the shark gave no indication of predator or prey.

"Take the tape off his mouth," Marco said as he sat down behind Tarpley's desk, in his chair.

Pete ripped the tape from Tarpley's mouth in a fashion apparently intended to inflict more pain. "Dammit boys, rippin' out half my hair and using that goddamn tape was uncalled for," Tarpley said.

"I'm glad y'all are makin' a movie. I'll fry everybody's goddamn ass with it," Tarpley said, looking one at a time at Snake and his men before leveling his gaze on Marco. "Well, I should of given you more credit. I thought you were just a two-bit pup--wet behind the ears, now look atcha. You the big man, got boys workin' for you, the big escaped killer from Alabama. I guess I have to take a little credit. You know I told you I was gonna teach you a few things. . ."

"There are a lot of things you should take credit for. If we were in Alabama and I had the time, I would see to it that you were given the credit due, but I am not here to discuss that," Marco said, as he walked around the desk and stood directly in front of Tarpley.

"You better tread careful kid. You were a dead man once. It still can happen," Tarpley said.

"The trooper in Alabama, who killed him?"

"Now how the hell am I supposed to

305

know? You will regret this, and you are wasting my time. . ."

"That is not the answer I need. Snake," Marco said, still looking at Tarpley as he spoke. "I guess it's time to demonstrate your lie detector for us."

Snake, his back to Tarpley, began working with the gray box on the adjacent desk. Unable to see what he was doing, Tarpley, his face bordering between half-grin and half-smile, mockingly invited his captors to bring their lie detector to bare.

"Yea, strap me up. I'll show you I'm tellin the. . ."

His bravado, however, quickly changed to alarm, as the man called Snake turned around to face Tarpley holding a four to five foot long, black rat snake, the head of which, with its large jaws and steel-cold eyes was huge; it lay in the hands of its holder, its body expanding and contracting, its head coiling in a striking posture, its mouth closed, and except for the occasional tongue wiggling its way in and out of the unopened mouth, the head appeared lifeless, its cold dark eyes set in the same direction.

The scene was shocking. The serpent's body shifted slowly with its subtle movements and gyrations of its skin over its skeletal system, flexing back and forth, an effortless continual stretch, appearing to extend itself away from the one holding it and toward the terrified man taped to the chair.

"Ah, shit man! What the hell? Ahhhh," Tarpley screamed, as Snake the man and snake the reptile moved closer to him. His legs and arms fastened securely to the chair, Tarpley's instinct to run overwhelmed his bound body as he lurched backward, turning the chair and himself onto the floor, onto his left side.

"You keep that goddamn snake away from me," Tarpley said, continuing to attempt to bounce and rock his way on his left side toward the door.

"This is what is amazing. Watch this," Snake said proudly, as he walked past the turned-over chair and laid the snake on the ground, approximately a foot in front of the cowboy. Tarpley, horrified, perspiring heavily, stopped his own gyrations, apparently afraid that movement would make the snake bite.

Joe Frank, whose eyes had been as wide open as any in the room, watched as the snake stretched out to its full length across the floor, as its master reached down and picked it up by the tail. Except for the tongue, the snake was unmoving, stiff, wood like, protruding from the hand in a magical, biblical-like spectacle.

"Lawd, Jesus. Jus' like Aaron in front of da Pharaoh," Joe Frank said under his breath, as he watched, wide-eyed from the corner.

"Stand the chair up. Hold it still," Snake said to R.D. and Pete.

Snake, holding his lie detector in front of him, backed up in front of Tarpley, as his men stood him up. "Now I can stick his face close to yours without me getting in the way, and as long as I just hold the tail, why he'll stay straight as a board. Ain't that cool?" Snake said, smiling as he held the board-stiff, hissing, snake, so that its probing tongue was touching Tarpley's nose, who was paralyzed with fear.

"Ok. Ok. Please," Tarpley said, tightly moving his lips, his eyes now blinking erratically, as he spoke, his words broken and barely audible. I'll tell you what you want. Take it away, please."

Snake looked to Marco for instructions who motioned for him to back away. "Alright," Snake said, "but understand, it's going to upset Marvin that I took him away, so if he gets close enough to kiss you again, he'll probably try and eat your nose, so I suggest that you tell Mr. Esgivas what he wants to know so I don't have to get him out again."

"Now, answer my question," Marco said, calmly, still seated behind the desk, watching the snake's head being petted, as it was folded and put away into the gray box.

"Look, could you let me stand up, my feet are falling asleep," Tarpley said, sweat dripping from his forehead, his breathing heavy, his chest moving up and down as though he had been running.

"As soon as you answer my questions."

"Begal and me and the sheriff and that Trooper were in business together. . ."

"Which one of you killed the trooper?"

Hesitating for a moment as he looked

toward the snake, Tarpley then said, "I did."

"Who wanted me killed?"

Tarpley hesitated again.

"If he brings that snake back out I will not stop him until the snake has had something to eat," Marco said.

"Begal," Tarpley said, quickly.

"Why?" Marco said, visibly puzzled, "I hardly know the man."

"The Columbians, his new partners, they wanted you dead. Said you knew too much to be in a jail up here."

"And if that bothered him, why did he volunteer my name to carry the shipment to you?"

"When he sent you with me on the run, the Columbians weren't there. Besides, we just needed somebody to blame for the trooper in Alabama. Then after he took over, him and the boys from Columbia got a little worried about things you knew. That's when Begal called. He wanted somebody I could recommend that could put you down."

"So you gave him Davis Humphries for the sheriff to put in my cell?"

"Yea, what happened to him, anyway?" Tarpley asked.

Ignoring his question, Marco said, "I want to know who killed DeMarcos, and my father."

Slowing down his breathing, Tarpley looked again at Snake and the now closed gray box sitting on the adjacent desk.

"Begal," Tarpley said. "He told me that DeMarcos was turning down the Columbian's offer. He thought that was stupid--suicide. Columbians offered him the top spot if he would take care of DeMarcos."

"You know for a fact *he* killed my father?"

"I don't know if he pulled the trigger but he told me it was a sweet set up--you in jail, yore Daddy comin' back after a visit, upset with DeMarcos for puttin' you there. He said yore Daddy was the perfect one to blame for the murder of the head of a Mexican drug cartel—and it would be totally unrelated to him takin' over."

"What about DeMarcos' brother?

"That's why yore daddy was the perfect one. His younger brother would never suspect Begal, and Phillip wasn't ready to run no cartel, so he lets Begal do it.

"How did he keep the other cartels from coming after him?"

Looking again at the gray box and Snake, Tarpley said, "They think Phillip is da man."

"The Federation and all of the Cartels think Phillip is in charge. He goes to Federation meetings with Begal, acts like he runs the place. He's happy; Begal's happy, and the other Mexican cartels think a Mexican is in charge of the DeMarcos Cartel.

"You said you did not know if he pulled the trigger. Is that how my father was killed?"

"Yea, same room as DeMarcos. Made it look like DeMarcos had shot yore Daddy as yore Daddy was shootin' DeMarcos."

"How could he get away with this with DeMarcos' men?"

"Begal had new boys in place the night of the killing. People from up here."

The questions were over. Marco sat for a moment, unmoving, stunned at the answers, surprised that he had succeeded in getting them.

The gang members and Joe Frank had all remained respectfully silent. Intrigued by what they were hearing. They had watched and listened, as Tarpley seemed to have forgotten he was being recorded, more concerned about Marvin than a video recorded confession.

"Ok, can I get up now?" Tarpley asked.

"What's in the back room?" Marco asked.

"Garage. Nobody's there," Snake said.

"Take him back there," Marco said. Carry the chair. Leave him taped up for the moment.

"Hey listen here you piece a shit. I told you everything. . ."

"Tape his mouth up," Marco said.

Tarpley watched as Pete stripped off more tape.

"Ok, look I'll be. . ." Tarpley began, as Pete slapped the tape across his mouth, and he and R.D. picked the chair up and carried Tarpley to the back room.

311

I need to talk with you," Snake said, nodding to Marco, watching his men carry Tarpley out.

As the garage door was shut behind Tarpley, Snake became animated, walking back and forth, motioning toward the back where Tarpley had just been carried.

"You know you got to kill him," Snake said, pointing toward the garage. "If you leave him alive he'll contact this Begal and your Mother will only get to see your corpse--if he lets her live."

"He is going to call him in a few minutes, Marco said.

"Who is going to call who?

"Ray Tarpley is going to call Ken Begal."

"I don't understand," said Snake, a bewildered look on his face.

"Snake, bring Duke in. Tell him to download our home movie we just made. I want at least two copies on a disc, one for you, and one for me. I want it ready to send over the internet," Marco said.

"Alright," Snake said as he went to get Duke.

"Joe, go out and pick out a car that I can drive to Mexico. The keys are hanging over here," Marco said, pointing to a board with rows of keys. "Try and pick out one with plenty of gas."

As Joe Frank went out, Duke was already hooking the camera to the computer.

"Here's your discs. It's downloaded,

where do I send it to?" Duke asked.

"I'll tell you in just a minute," Marco said, as Joe Frank came back through the door.

"I gotcha one. Jus' a Chevrolet, but its got a full tank; maybe it'll make it," Joe Frank said.

"Good. Marco opened the desk drawer and pulled out some sales paperwork. "Write down the vin number and description on this bill of sale," Marco said, as he handed him the document and a pen.

"Snake, bring everybody back in."

"Be ready to send it when I tell you," Marco said to Duke, as Pete and R.D. carried Tarpley back in, everything still taped but his eyes.

"Take the tape off his mouth and hands. Leave his legs attached," Marco said, as he turned the desk phone toward Tarpley.

"Mr. Tarpley I want you to call Ken Begal for me."

"You got balls. I'll give you that," Tarpley said, laughing out loud, while he attempted to wipe off the sticky remnants of the tape from his mouth.

"Sure, I'll call him. Hand me the phone."

"Day can start diggin' a hole for you," Tarpley said, still laughing and shaking his head as he dialed the number then sat back in the chair,

"Hey, I need to speak to Ken. Tell him da cowboy," Tarpley said.

313

Marco reached over from behind the desk and took the receiver from Tarpley.

"Hey, I thought you wanted me to talk to him," Tarpley said.

Snake slapped the back of Tarpley's head. "Shut up. If he wants you to talk he'll let you know," Snake said, as he pointed to the box containing Marvin.

"Hello," someone could be heard speaking on the other end.

"Is this Ken Begal?"

"Who is this? Cowboy?"

"I had Tarpley to call you. This is Marco Esgivas."

Ken Begal was silent.

"I have something you are going to be interested in seeing," said Marco. "I need to send it to you right now."

"Marco, I'm so glad to hear from you. We have all been so worried. I saw your. . ."

"Mr. Begal. Your pleasantries and insincere concern for my safety are a waste of your time and mine. I need to send this to you."

"What do you mean? I talked with. . ."

"Do you have the internet?"

"Yes, but I don't understand," Begal said.

"Would you rather I get Cardenas' E-mail address or one of the other cartels and send this to one of them first?"

"Alright, alright, I'll give you the address, but this isn't the way to talk to a man

314

in my position," Begal said.

Marco wrote down the internet address Begal gave him and handed it to Duke.

"I am going to stay on the line while you look at what I am sending you."

"Marco, we really need to meet."

"One word of advice. Do not send someone here to kill me until you see what I am sending you." Marco laid the phone down, placed it on speaker-phone and leaned back in Tarpley's chair, his eyes closed.

"They made me say dat shit," Tarpley called out.

"Tape his mouth and his hands back up. If he gives any more trouble, tape his eyelids open and get the snake out," Marco said. Tarpley instantly quieted down.

Joe Frank came back in, handing Marco the completed bill of sale.

After approximately ten minutes, Begal was back on the phone.

"Alright, what do you want?" Begal asked, his tone louder than before, and easily heard by the entire room.

"First, I want the house belonging to my mother and father paid in full, the deed delivered and recorded by close of business tomorrow. I want his salary at the factory paid to my mother, beginning with back pay to be received when the deed is delivered."

"For how long?"

"I will let you know when to stop."

"We've already given her some of your

father's pay that was due him."

"This is not a negotiation."

"If you think just because you've got a forced confession from some piece of shit in Texas that I'm going to dance to your tune, you're crazy."

"Mr. Begal you will dance, and here is why. A copy of this video disc will be placed with a friend of mine in Texas, and in other parts of the United States and Mexico. They are being instructed that if anything happens to me or my family, a copy is to be delivered to Osiel Cardenas and Phillip DeMarcos. As head of the Federation, I don't believe Cardenas will appreciate the fact that one of the heads of a Mexican Cartel was killed without the Federation's approval, much less that it was by an American. I am certain Mr. DeMarcos' brother will be equally displeased. If they see this, you will not live long enough to be worried about the FBI or the DEA, or SEIDO, who will also receive a copy."

"How do I know you won't get mad and decide to turn the video over anyway," Begal said.

"You don't. It is in your best interest to keep me happy."

There was silence on Begal's end. Marco also remained silent, waiting for his response.

"It looks like I have underestimated you. Maybe you and I should talk about your future," Begal said.

"How you treat me and my family will

determine if you have a future," Marco said, as he hung up the phone.

"Take the tape off his mouth and hands." Pete again jerked the tape from Tarpley's mouth and unwrapped the tape from his arms.

"You think you got it all figured out. Don't cha, kid?" Tarpley said.

"Mr. Cowboy, you have a vested interest in this as well."

"And why do you think I give a rat's ass what happens to one cartel member. I deliver for anybody that'll pay."

"If I find out that my friend Joe Frank is being harassed by any of *your* compatriots between here and Alabama; or, that your sheriff-business-partner in Alabama is bothering him, then I will send the video to the authorities in the United States, including Alabama. Even if they think this was contrived, it would be enough to mess up your business. At the very minimum, it would get the sheriff charged with attempted murder or maybe the murder of Humphries, with you as an accomplice."

Tarpley looked from face to face at the people in front of him in wild-eyed disbelief.

"Well, well, well. Looks like all of us underestimated you," he said, finding it difficult to muster even a fake smile.

"Here, sign this." Marco laid the bill of sale that Joe Frank had filled out and a pen in front of Tarpley, who signed the document without reading it.

"What is it?"

"You just sold me a car," Marco said, as he put the paper in his pocket. "I do not want to be accused of theft. Empty your pockets."

Tarpley did as he was told, and Marco picked up the cash he laid on the table.

Joe Frank stood beside the light gray 1997 Chevrolet Impala, the light of the day fading, the driver's door open, waiting for Marco. A street lamp at the edge of the parking lot was beginning to shine, striving to replace the sun's light as Marco walked from Tarpley's office.

In spite of the dimly lit parking lot, Joe Frank's face was alive with that light that Marco had seen in the jail months ago. Still subtle yet powerful, it was an inner glow that again caused his countenance to shine, even in the dim light of the closing day. But there was more than just mere spiritual illumination, for etched and carved and painted in the face of this caring, Godly man was the hardship of endurance; of a miraculous journey of faith for him and for others predicated in the righteousness of cause. Marco could see that he was a man that had seen God and the enemy and through his faith in his God he had prevailed and endured. While enigmatic at first glance, on closer inspection, with that subtle illumination you could see the encounters of the journey on his face. He was singular yet plural, an expression of confusion and order, intensity and relief, of sorrow, joy and pain; a man that knew too well the inside of the jail cell, of seasons of sinning and pleasures. Yet, in the end, his journey was one of redemption gained from a higher power that saw worth in his frailties, just as Joe Frank had seen the worth of a young Mexican boy in an Alabama jail.

As Marco stood next to him, his voice broke just a bit as he spoke. "Looks like dat red sea done parted, Marco, and you almost to da other side."

It was over, almost. And the realization of the enormity of what this man had done for him was now replacing Marco's thoughts of home.

"You saved me and you taught me," Marco said, as he looked at the man that had risked everything for him.

Marco stood in Cowboy's shaded car lot with its dozen or so cars, with the setting sun hidden behind San Antonio's buildings, realizing that it was time to leave and that his time with this wonderful man was at an end.

"Even before I had met the Ray Tarpley's and Sheriff Sykes of the world," Marco said, "my view of people outside my own mestizo race was pretty poor, even poorer in regard to Americans."

Marco's soliloquy was interrupted by a bumping, struggling sound from Tarpley's office. Both men turned to watch Snake's men come out of the office, carrying Tarpley, whose body and feet were still tied to the chair, attempting to kick his way free; his struggle quite `the show.

"Days some bad apples, no mattah where you look," Joe Frank said, continuing to watch Snake's men handle Tarpley. Turning back to Marco, he said, "But, it's me dat needs to say thanks."

"Why? For making you a potential felon? For breaking me out? For causing you to kill a man. . .?"

"Dat needed killin," Joe Frank interrupted, as they were joined by Snake.

"Might even get Jesus and da Holy Ghos' to dese boys before it's over," Joe Frank said, with a hearty laugh, as Snake looked at the both of them with a questioning expression at Joe Frank's proposition.

"That's a way for you to get in touch with me, if you need me," said Snake, who handed Marco a piece of paper with phone numbers written on it. "I got a feeling you just might need me again. Nodding in Tarpley's direction, he said, "We'll keep him on ice till you've had time to get home."

Marco shook Snake's hand and all of them watched Ray Tarpley, still squirming and attempting to kick as he was being placed into the back of a Dodge Minivan.

As the van door closed on the noise, Marco turned back to Joe Frank. There was so much he wanted to say, so much he needed to say. *But, what do you say to a man that has brought you from death to life?* Whatever that is, Marco did not know it. He hugged him, the way you would hug someone you cared for that you had known for a long time; an embrace with that closest friend, knowing this was the last time you would see him.

"I wish . . . " Marco began; he wanted to say that he wished that Joe Frank could come to Mexico and meet his family, but Joe Frank answered before he could finish.

"I'll do it, but if I do, you gwoin to have to find me some church to preach in," Joe Frank said, smiling his one-of-a-kind, unforgettable smile, as Marco climbed into the Chevrolet.

Rolling the window down, he said, "Because of you, I will have a life again."

With that, Marco drove out of the car lot and pulled onto the empty street, his headlights shining as he made his way up the ramp of the southern bypass. Just as the car reached the top of the ramp, Marco looked back, one last time, before losing sight of his friend. Both of Joe Frank's hands were lifted high. In goodbye? In praise to the God that had brought all of them this far? Probably both.

~~~~~~

For the first time in quite a long time, Joe Frank felt like a man that had completed a divine mission.

Over the years, he had gotten a lot of folks to walk different aisles of different churches, recite invigorated promises, proclaim their change to a congregation of like believers and sign their name to a church role. Sometimes it stuck. Sometimes it didn't.

Sometimes the aisle-walkers were so completely changed by their experience that they walked a straighter, narrower path than even the pleading minister. Some were back walking waist deep in sin before the next service on the next Sunday, leaving the Joe Frank's of this world with an incomplete mission.

Marco Esgivas had been different. With Marco there was completeness; a finality of a mission that any preacher like Joe Frank wanted to see.

Sorta like Moses, Joe Frank thought, as he watched Marco disappear into a sea of moving vehicles, his hands raised to the sky.

I done led dat boy out of bondage, through da Red Sea and even though the Rio Grande ain't exactly the Jordan and Mexico ain't exactly the Promised Land, he's gonna cross over without me. But dat's alright, I needs to go back home. Got plenty more folks needs savin' back home.

Joe Frank had waited till Snake and his boys had left and stood alone in Cowboy's parking lot for a while, basking in the achievements that he gave his God credit for.

Complete darkness was now settling in, and the headlights of a traveling Texas world filled the horizon of the bypass, as Joe Frank pulled his Ford Explorer out of the deserted car lot onto the eastern bypass.

The people I done met on dis journey, Lawd: Marco, Snake and his men, my, my. I ought to be tired, but I'm not.

Reaching into some wrapped tin foil on the console, he retrieved a cold biscuit; in another piece of foil he found some of the fish from the Big Black. As he chewed, he watched his head lights shine across the road signs: 'Houston, Beaumont, Lake Charles.'

The ride to Alabama would be good. Life would be good.

Time was passing fast, and soon the Louisiana State Line was only five miles away. Joe Frank began to sing: *'They that wait upon the lord shall renew their strength; they shall mount up with wings as eagles. They shall run and not be weary; they shall walk and not faint. Teach me Lord. Teach me Lord to wait.'*

As he crossed over into Louisiana, he was still singing, and soon he started preaching or praising or praying, it would be hard to say which, and the deep resonant hum of the Ford Explorer engine, and the rhythmic chanting of praising, preaching and praying was suddenly interrupted by a loud outburst of irrepressible laughter that was so hard, soon his face was streaming with tears, making

323

driving difficult.

Pulling the Explorer to the side, under an overpass, his engine still running and his lights still on, he stopped. So did the laughter. Still holding his biscuit, tears and more tears flowed, till his face was awash, as his mind was deluged with the happenings of his time with this young boy from another land: the first time he saw him, preaching for him in the cell: Laughing out loud, again he said, "I know he ain't never seen dat before." The killer in the jail, and the escape, the trip here with the fishing and the campfires. "My oh my, I can't believe I tole him bout dat hay baler. But I'm glad I did." Snake and his boys, "I gots to get dem boys saved, Lawd."

Vehicles passed, horns blew and tractor-trailer trucks would rock the parked Explorer as they flew by. None of that disturbed his wonderful remembrances.

"Sins, sinnin, salvation; *A life ain't over cause of a little sinnin'*, Joe Frank said aloud. *"God can still use me."*

As he sat on a lonely interstate in Louisiana in the middle of the night, Joe Frank realized that everything that had ever happened to him in his entire life had culminated in this purposeful venture to save this young man.

"God you set it up good," Joe Frank said aloud, as un-wiped tears continued dripping from his face and the remnants of cold biscuit and fish clinging to his lips were mixed with the salty tears.

"You made it a two way deal. I always thought you put me in dis young boy's life soze I could save *him*. But it wadant jus' him, it was me too. You put *him* in *my* life and my life got saved, too."

THE END